GALAXY OF HEROES II:
War Heroes

Gus Flory

GALAXY OF HEROES II:
WAR HEROES

Copyright © 2011 by Gus Flory

All Rights Reserved

No part of this book may be reproduced in any form by photocopying or by any electronic or mechanical means, including information storage or retrieval systems, without permission in writing from the copyright owner.

This is a work of fiction. All the characters and events portrayed in this book are either products of the author's imagination or are used fictitiously.

ISBN-13: 978-1533355607
ISBN-10: 1533355606

First Published, 2011
gusflory@yahoo.com

Cover art by Seungyoun K. Chong

GALAXY OF HEROES II
War Heroes

Part I

Escalon

"Mingus. Can you hear me?"

Capt. Jace Spade looked into the face of the big woman who was strapped to a gurney in the clinic's operating room.

Mingus opened her large blue eyes. She cringed in the soft light.

"It's painful, Jace. It hurts."

Her voice was deep and husky. Dr. Viz Ebos looked down at her and passed a handheld scanner over her eyes.

Mingus closed her eyes tightly. A pained expression crossed her face.

"They're stabbing us," she said. "They're killing us, Jace."

Dr. Ebos typed on a panel with his thin fingers, fine-tuning the chemical solution that was entering Mingus' bloodstream.

Dr. Ebos wore a white lab coat. Glowing red lenses covered his eyes. He was a skinny Paltran man and by far the most talented physician on Escalon Station.

Capt. Spade placed his gloved hand on Mingus' large, meaty palm.

"It's OK, Mingus," Spade said. "They're gone now."

She opened her blue eyes and stared at the ceiling. Her pupils were badly dilated. She blinked repeatedly in the light, but kept staring upward.

Mingus was a big, muscular Megalan woman, but her frightened expression made her appear small and helpless. She looked as though she had just witnessed something awful.

Spade squeezed her huge hand.

"We were waiting for you, Jace," she said. "The ground was shaking from all the explosions. Something bad was happening outside and we were afraid."

Her dilated eyes stared up into nothingness as she recalled those last moments.

"Leonard wanted to blast off and leave you but I said no. We were arguing about you when Craaldan soldiers burst into the ship and killed Tanaka. We tried to fight them but they were so fast with their bayonets. They butchered Leonard in front of me. I ran from them. They chased me into the cockpit and I tried to fight but a Craaldan soldier stabbed me. It hurt so much."

She started to cry.

"He was killing me, Jace."

Spade ran his hand through her black hair. Her long pony tail slowly twisted and coiled in the zero gravity of space.

Her blue eyes met his. She was frightened and confused.

He wiped the tears from her cheeks with his thumb.

"Where are we?" she asked.

"We're in a medical clinic on Escalon Station," he said.

Her eyes were less dilated now and she looked about trying to get her bearings.

"Jace, I felt the blade puncture my throat. Then he stabbed me in the chest and in the belly. It was fast and awful. It was so painful. I knew right when he pulled the blade out that he had killed me. I could feel the life leaving my body. I was so mad at you because you promised you were coming back and I waited and you never came. I died mad at you."

"I'm sorry, Mingus. Things got a little crazy out there. Better late than never, right?"

A look of confusion crossed her large face. "I thought for sure I was dead. I mean, I stood at death's door and stepped through."

"You were dead for quite some time," Dr. Ebos said. "Reviving you was one of the most challenging medical procedures I have attempted as yet."

"I was really dead then?" she asked.

"Roger," Spade said. "When I returned to the Red Wrath, I found you, Leonard and Tanaka dead from bayonet wounds. I kept your bodies frozen in the storage bay hoping to find a doctor with the skills to revive you. I met Viz here and he said he would give it a shot. Escalon Station has a top-of-the-line medical clinic so that helped, too."

"It was a complex and intricate endeavor," Dr. Ebos said. "When Captain Spade showed me your corpse, I told him that reviving it was impossible, especially with the limited facilities on this station. Your cells were badly decayed and the structural damage was severe. But Captain Spade was insistent that I attempt the procedure despite my lack of confidence in a positive outcome. His hopefulness and sincerity persuaded me to give it the old college try. I began to repair your cells at the molecular level. Fortunately, your corpse was frozen almost immediately after death, and Captain Spade had the good sense to keep you on ice. It was tediously painstaking work as I individually repaired or replaced your damaged cells and rebuilt badly degraded tissues. My biggest challenge was the lack of a functioning clinic, but I was able to make do with the remnants of the medical facility here on Escalon Station. The station's supercomputer was invaluable. With a little ingenuity and after a lot of hard work I began to see progress. Eventually, I was able to restore you to normal biological functioning."

Ebos looked at his scanner. "Now that you are awake and coherent, I will go out on a limb and state that this procedure has been a success."

Spade slapped the doctor on the back and shook his hand. "Viz, I never doubted you."

"Weird," Mingus said.

Dr. Ebos scanned through data on a flat-panel display. "She has returned to the living with a clean bill of health."

"Outstanding," Spade said. He looked down at Mingus. "This guy is a miracle worker."

"This was not my first successful attempt at reviving a corpse, but it was the most challenging because of the lack of proper equipment. The learning curve was quite high, but the experience I have gained, and this new clinic we have constructed, will be valuable resources for us. We have now turned this clinic into quite the medical facility. Captain Spade, if you are ever killed, I am confident I can revive you."

"Don't worry about that, Doc," Spade said. "I ain't the dying type."

Spade and Dr. Ebos unfastened Mingus from the gurney. She floated upward in the zero gravity and pulled herself to Spade. She wrapped her huge arms around him and gave him a bear hug, squeezing him tightly.

"It's good to have you back, princess," he said while buried under her large mass.

"Jace," she whispered into his ear. "Please tell him not to call me a corpse. It's creepy."

"Roger that," he said.

Dr. Ebos left to attend to another patient. Spade and Mingus exited the clinic and pulled themselves up a transport tube, emerging onto an observation deck with large windows that looked out onto a vast flotilla of spaceships that surrounded the enormous superstructure of Escalon Station.

Spade recounted the events that had transpired since Mingus was attacked in the Red Wrath on Naos. He told her how he had met up with Genie, Sgt. Grimes and Capt. Casey, and how Grimes and Genie had disappeared into deep space. He told her about the horrific Craaldan assault on Gallos and how he and Capt. Casey had led the surviving refugees to Escalon Station.

The humans here on Escalon were the last survivors of the attack on Gallos. There were only about 5,000 of them. Spade was their leader.

He told Mingus that he and Capt. Mina Casey were a hot item and the talk of Escalon. They were in a solid, long-term relationship. Mingus looked at him skeptically when he told her that he had really fallen for Mina.

"Is Leonard alive?" Mingus asked.

"Negative," Spade answered.

"Are you going to revive him?" she asked.

"Do I have to?"

"Of course," she said. "Jeez."

"What about Tanaka?" she asked him.

Spade gazed out into space at the array of ships that surrounded Escalon Station's slowly rotating superstructure. Every manner of spacecraft was out there—large Megalan cargo ships, Paltran schooners, ramshackle Heliac warships and several other types of space vehicles cruised silently through the black void.

"The Doc tried his best but Tanaka was too brain damaged to bring back," Spade said. "A good percentage of his life functions had been mechanized or made electronic so that made things even more complicated."

Spade was silent for a long moment. "I miss that little guy," he said.

Mingus put her beefy arm around his waist.

"Where are you leading us, Captain?" she asked.

"To the Calli Sector," he said.

Executive officer

Spade pulled himself hand over hand up the large transport tube that ran through the center of Escalon Station. The tube was crowded with humans who moved past him in the weightlessness of space.

They greeted him as they passed by. He acknowledged them with a nod and a smile. Sometimes he winked and pointed his finger like a pistol at those he recognized.

Everybody recognized him.

Spade pushed himself down a hallway in the zero gravity until he arrived at a large doorway. He opened it and entered a conference room where a dozen humans sat at long desks that curved from one side of the room to the other. The desks were arranged in rows in ascending levels.

"Room, attention!" Capt. Mina Casey said.

The humans all stood from their chairs.

Capt. Spade floated to the front of the conference room. His magnetized boots hit the floor with a click. He stood in front of a large screen that displayed the station and the flotilla of ships that cruised alongside it.

"As you were," Spade said.

The humans took their seats behind their desks.

Spade looked down at Capt. Casey who was sitting off to his right and looking into a handheld display. Her short black hair was wet and slicked back as she had just emerged from the swim tank. Her black coveralls fit her body like a glove.

"We've intercepted radio transmissions from the planet Biop," Capt. Casey said. "It's not random noise, either."

"What?" Spade said. He took a seat next to Capt. Casey. "This changes things."

"Vomica has been analyzing the transmissions, which appear to be communications between small planetary airframes."

"Biop is inhabited then," Spade said. "Have we been detected?"

"Negative," said Escalon Station's intelligence officer, a skinny space drifter named Vomica Nux.

Spade looked up at the humans seated behind the desks. These were the leaders of the motley crew of refugees that now called Escalon Station home. Once a week, Spade convened a leadership meeting to get a rundown of how the voyage was progressing, and address problems as they emerged.

Escalon Station had become a refuge and sanctuary after the Craaldan attack on Gallos. The few humans that had survived the onslaught had been in a confused and desperate state. Spade had taken charge and had organized their escape from the smoldering planet. Spade's competent leadership in their time of need had earned him the trust and affection of the shell-shocked refugees. He had organized them in military fashion, assigning them to five work battalions of about a thousand humans each. He assigned a commander to each battalion, and under the leadership of these battalion commanders he was able to bring order to their chaotic retreat from Gallos.

The refugees had crammed into spaceships parked in orbit above Gallos. Then Spade led their rickety flotilla to Escalon Station—an abandoned space station that was orbiting the Largos Star, which was a red giant threatening supernova.

Upon arrival at Escalon, the refugees set to work rebuilding the station. It was large enough to accommodate them all, and with their efforts, it became habitable again.

From the Largos solar system, they collected minerals, gases and the various elements necessary to sustain life. They built huge engines and crafted them onto Escalon and blasted away from Largos.

Then they drifted for an extended period through the void with their heading set toward the planet Biop, which orbited the Cextos Star.

Biop was the last rocky planet in this sector. The sector was a long finger of stars that extended out to the galaxy's edge.

Beyond Biop was a vast expanse of space that seemingly stretched to eternity.

Intelligence files concerning Biop revealed that it was a lifeless rock that had been bombarded and sterilized by the Craaldan war machine over two millennia ago. No one was expecting life there.

Spade looked up at his five battalion commanders. The first was Lt. Col. Greg Skyles, who had a battle-scarred face and a blonde flat-top of hair. Then there was a Paltran named Tarvey Rigo, who wore glowing green lenses. Sitting next to Rigo was a giant Megalan man named Ramone Bombero, who had dark hair and large, hairy arms. A space drifter named Jober Mope was the leader of a battalion of about 800 space drifters like himself. Then there was an Escalonian woman named Doxy, who was the representative for the Escalonian people who had built this space station and occupied it before abandoning it and settling on Gallos. Spade had once had a relationship with Doxy, but that was long ago in another life. Doxy sat next to her silver cyborg companion who never left her side.

Also seated in the room was Spade's staff, which included a supply and logistics officer named Pervez Anax; an operations officer named Bruce Borneo; the intelligence officer Vomica Nux; Dr. Viz Ebos, who was in charge of the station's medical staff; and Capt. Casey, who was Spade's executive officer.

Capt. Casey looked up from her handheld display screen. "Vomica, can you give us the intel update?" she asked.

Vomica Nux pushed herself up from her chair and kicked over to the front of the conference room, landing beneath the display screen with a click of her boots. She was an incredibly thin space drifter with skinny arms and long legs. Her spiky hair was tinted purple on top before fading to green on the sides and then yellow and red where it was pulled down over her shoulders and onto each side of her chest. Her sultry green eyes looked out from behind her spiky hair that fell over her forehead. She wore a baggy white shirt and skintight black pants.

Vomica looked up at her audience. "Our radio intercepts reveal that about 250 aircraft are using an airstrip near Biop's equator," she said. "These are not spacecraft, but planetary vehicles that do not leave the atmosphere. They appear to be flying supply missions, heading off to various points around the planet to gather resources before returning to their base."

"What's the population estimate for the planet?" asked Lt. Col. Skyles.

"My estimate puts the total population at 15,000 humans, all residing in a walled base that abuts the airfield," Vomica said.

"You said humans," Capt. Spade said.

"Yes," Vomica answered. "The transmissions I have intercepted are fragmentary, but they are definitely from humans. It appears space drifters set down on Biop about 300 Earth years ago and decided to stay. However, the planet is not ideal for settlement. The Craaldan 26th Expeditionary Fleet eradicated all life there 2,500 Earth years ago. In their attack, they fractured Biop's small moon. Now every decade or so, moon debris pelts the planet with meteor showers to devastating effect, sometimes rupturing the planet's crust and setting off volcanic eruptions. Also common to the planet are radioactive dust storms that suddenly rise up and whip across large sectors of the surface."

"Sounds like paradise," Capt. Casey said.

"How do you think the humans there will react when we arrive?" Spade asked.

"Unknown," Vomica said. "I suggest we proceed with caution. Isolated human outposts are often spooked when large numbers of outsiders arrive unannounced."

"This system is our last stop before we begin a thousand-year deep space journey to the Calli Sector," Ramone Bombero said in a baritone voice.

"We can't afford not to stop here, whether they are hostile to us or not," Lt. Col. Skyles said.

"I didn't say they are hostile," Vomica said. "There are not that many of them on a planet that is Earth-like in size. It's not like there isn't plenty of room down there. Maybe they'll welcome us. Maybe not. We won't know until we make contact."

"Let's make contact then," Spade said.

Monogamy

Spade lay in bed with Capt. Casey in their spacious living quarters. He gazed out a large window that looked out into starry space. Capt. Casey slept peacefully in his arms.

He knew that a change had come over him since they left Gallos. His plan had been to fire up the Red Wrath's engines and head back to the Inner Galaxy to resume his search for his maker, Dr. Zander, who was possibly held captive in the Malafax System.

Instead, he and Capt. Casey had taken charge of the Gallos survivors and had organized their flight from the planet. The refugees had needed a leader and Spade fell into the role and had thrived in it. The role came naturally, which came as a surprise to him. These humans willingly followed him.

He had spent so many years searching the galaxy, driven by a need to find the man he had looked up to for much of his life. Now these people were looking up to him.

He ran his hand over Capt. Casey's bare shoulders and then down her back. Her skin was smooth, warm and soft. The two of them had been through so much together, so many ups and downs.

He had broken her heart once and deeply regretted it. It took some doing, but he had won back her heart.

He knew that taking responsibility for the welfare of these people was a factor in her allowing herself to get close to him again. She knew he had changed his evil ways for her.

What was odd to him was that he had never desired the responsibility of leadership, but now he was as happy as he'd ever been. The instinct that had driven him to hunt the farthest reaches of the galaxy for Dr. Zander had faded, and a new instinct was expressing itself inside him.

He needed her. The responsibilities of leadership weighed heavily on him and having her near brought comfort and security. Having her at his side meant he didn't waste his energy chasing after every female that caught his eye. His energies were now focused on her, and on those who relied on him to lead them to safety and to a new life far away from the destructive war that was raging through the galaxy.

Capt. Casey stretched and wrapped her arms around him. Her sleepy dark eyes opened and met his.

She watched him curiously for a moment. "Have you been thinking again?" she asked.

"Maybe," he said.

"Uh oh."

"I've been thinking about you and me," he said. "About how funny it is the way things work out."

"You're telling me," she said. "Who would have thunk that Captain Jace Spade would end up being the savior of humanity? A frontier pilot from Naos, of all people. And I'm his sidekick."

"We make a great team," he said.

"Right," she said. "How long do you think we'll last this time, Jace?"

"Come on, Mina," he said. "You know I don't like it when you talk that way."

"I know," she said. "But this is experience talking."

"I'm in it for the long haul this time," he said.

She looked at him skeptically. "I see the way all the girls on this station look at you. You won't be able to resist temptation forever. Don't think I'm a dummy."

"Give me a little credit, would you?"

She raised an eyebrow and then smiled. "Look, I know I'm a lucky gal to have Jace Spade for my man. But I've got to be realistic."

"You know, I took on this whole leadership thing just to impress you," he said. "I did it because I wanted you back. Now everybody wants a piece of me all the time. They want me to make decisions and take action and give them direction and purpose, and half the time I'm just winging it. But things have been working out somehow—for them, for me, for us."

"All these people would follow you to the end of the universe, Jace. They love you. You've become this larger-than-life hero to them."

"I'm a big hero, huh?"

"You sure have them fooled," she said. "Me too, sometimes."

"I was thinking, Mina," he said. "Every larger-than-life space hero has a cool space babe at his side. Now, don't get me wrong, I've been around the block a time or two, but hands down you are sexiest space babe in this galaxy."

"Who, me?" she asked.

"The super coolest. No doubt about it."

"I do have my moments," she said.

"I've fallen for you, Mina. You're the only woman I care to be with. In fact, this spaceman can't live without you."

"You need to lay off the Hormolian wine," she said.

Spade pulled her in tight and looked into her dark eyes.

"Marry me, Mina," he said.

"Now you're talking crazy."

"I'm serious."

"Like a forever commitment?" she asked.

"Roger," he said. "Always and forever. Big wedding, honeymoon, a dog, kids, the whole deal."

"Jace, marriage wasn't such a big deal when life spans were short. You knew it was going to end sooner or later. But after aging was cured, forever has a literal meaning now. These days, forever is a really long time."

"I'm crazy for you, Mina. I love you."

She propped herself up on her elbows and looked into his eyes. She cocked an eyebrow. "You're serious."

"Marry me."

She swung her leg over him and got up on top of him and looked down at him, searching his face.

Spade ran his hands over her smooth thighs and up her waist, looking up at her.

"Well?" he asked.

"Don't rush me."

She kissed him on the forehead.

The communicator by the bedside rang. It rang again, and again.

"Answer it, Jace. Someone needs you."

He hesitated for a moment, and then reached over and hit the receive button. Mingus' big face appeared on the screen.

"Whoa!" Mingus said. "Is this a phone call or the adult movie channel?"

Capt. Casey rolled off Spade, pulled the sheet over herself and smiled at Mingus.

"You're lucky that's not me, Jace," Mingus said. "Dr. Ebos would have to surgically remove the grin from your face, and you wouldn't be able to walk for a week."

"What's on your mind, Mingus?" Spade asked.

"The Doc revived Leonard," she said.

"Great news," Spade said. "How's he doing?"

"He wasn't happy to learn that you're the captain of this station; but otherwise, he's doing great. He's still a little annoyed that you got him killed, but he'll get over it."

"I'm glad he's back," Spade said.

"I've got more great news," Mingus said. "Dr. Ebos said he can bring Tanaka back. He thinks he can do it now."

"That's fantastic news!"

"I'll keep you posted," she said.

"Mingus?" Capt. Casey asked. "Can I ask you a question?"

"Sure. Go ahead."

"What was it like being dead?"

Mingus was silent for a moment.

"I'm not ready to talk about that yet," she said. "Let me think it over. Maybe someday when I get to know you a little better, we can sit down and have a drink and talk about what it was like to die for that man you've got in your arms there."

"I'm going to make that up to you, Mingus," Spade said.

Mingus smiled at him. "Don't worry about that, Jace. I forgive you. Just don't let it happen again, OK?"

Lourdes Magna

The large screen at the front of the conference room flickered. Through the static, the image of a woman came into focus.

Her black hair was pulled back and braided tightly. The long black braid fell over one of her bare shoulders. She wore a white, sleeveless, low cut shirt with utilitarian pockets over her buxom chest. Her skin was a healthy, radiant brown. Her brown shoulders were smooth and taut, like those of an athlete.

"Greetings. I am Lourdes Magna, the mayor of New Taji City."

Vomica Nux paused the video. Lourdes Magna's face was frozen on the screen. Mayor Magna had high cheekbones and a severe but attractive face that radiated competence, confidence and authority.

The video transmission had been received only about an hour before Vomica Nux had called for this meeting.

"Lourdes Magna is the leader of the human colony on Biop," Vomica said to the staff and battalion commanders assembled in the conference room. Vomica turned to Spade who was seated at the front of the room next to Capt. Casey. "I sent her your transmission stating that we intend no harm and are only passing through their system, and that we plan to stay only until we are fully supplied for our journey to the Calli Sector."

Vomica turned and restarted the video.

"You say you intend no harm, and we would like to take you at your word. However, we have learned through experience that blind trust is unwise when dealing with spacefarers. I have discussed your wishes to traverse our system with the Taji City Board of Supervisors. After much debate, we decided unanimously to reject your request to remain in our system. If we detect any hesitation on your part, we will consider you malicious intruders."

Vomica paused the video. "I have compiled an intelligence estimate of their military capabilities." She handed Spade a flat screen display and he looked it over.

"They are no match for us," Vomica said. "A squadron of our interceptors could destroy their aircraft and aerial defenses pretty easily."

Spade placed the handheld display on his desk. "The Red Wrath could knock out all their aircraft and flatten their colony with one hand tied behind her back," he said.

Vomica restarted the video. "You are not welcome here. However, we are interested in a mate swap. We are seeking 96 mature human males of above average stature, with average to above average looks. We also seek three females, human or cyborg, of any body shape and appearance, but no Megalan women please. We can provide you with six of our females and one male for mating purposes. Once the mate swap is complete, we expect you to be on your way."

Capt. Casey looked up at Vomica Nux. "Mate swapping?"

Vomica paused the recording. "There are only 15,000 of them down there, and most are genetically related. It appears Mayor Magna is interested in increasing the genetic diversity of her community."

"Or maybe they're just lonely," Capt. Casey said.

"What does she have against our Megalan women?" Ramone Bombero asked.

Vomica restarted the video. "Please respect our wishes and depart from our system immediately after the mate swap. We do not want trouble."

The transmission cut out.

"I don't think we have anything to fear from these jokers," Lt. Col. Skyles said. "They've got no ships other than a handful of planetary airframes. Their atmospheric defenses are primitive. If we go in there with a show of force, then she'll know who's holding the stronger hand."

"Does she really think any of us is desperate enough to want to hook up with backwater colonists on her barren world?"

Capt. Casey asked. "I highly doubt anyone on Escalon is interested in this mate swapping business."

"I am above average in height and well above average in looks," Ramone Bombero said. "I will sign up if I get to mate with Ms. Lourdes Magna."

"We've got one taker," Spade said.

Spade turned to Vomica Nux. "What's your assessment of the situation, Vomica? How should we deal with Mayor Magna?"

"My recommendation, Captain Spade, is we set Escalon Station into orbit over Biop. We invite a delegation from the surface up to Escalon, and wine them and dine them, and give them whatever gifts we can spare that they would find of value down on the surface. Captain Spade, I am confident you can charm Lourdes Magna and win over their leadership so that we can remain in the system without the commencement of hostilities."

"OK, so we wine and dine Lourdes Magna and Ramone over there mates with her and we'll be golden," Spade said.

"I am Level 10 qualified in mating technique," Bombero said.

"I heard you were a six," Vomica said.

"Your friend was a Level 2 and I was drunk," Bombero said.

Doxy, the commander of the Escalonian refugees, looked over at Spade with her sullen brown eyes and caught his attention. Her blonde, stringy hair was pulled back from her downcast face. Doxy's skin was pale, almost translucently so. If one looked closely, a web of blue and green veins were faintly visible under the surface of her ivory skin. Her male cyborg companion sat silently next to her, attuned to her emotions. The cyborg placed his hand on hers and gave it a reassuring squeeze.

Doxy looked down at the surface of her desk. "The Escalonians are concerned about our impending voyage to the Calli Sector," she said. "It is a voyage of a thousand years. As you know, my people once drifted through the void for nearly that span of time. In our experience, petty quarrels and strife sometimes escalated with violent results. Over time, mental and emotional breakdowns took their toll. Over the centuries, our oxygen bled off into space until we nearly suffocated. A journey over so vast an expanse of space must be carefully planned. Humans must prepare themselves for the mental strains of isolation, boredom and claustrophobia. We must be robustly provisioned or we will suffocate or starve in the void."

"That's why I'm glad you Escalonians are coming with us, Doxy," Spade said. "You guys survived a journey this long and your experience is a valuable resource that will help us prepare. Remember, you did it without preparation after an unplanned flight from Diocon aggression. We're going to spend a year at minimum in orbit around Biop supplying this station, building the engines that will power this voyage and preparing ourselves for what's to come. I don't intend to go out there unprepared."

"A thousand years is a long time, Spade," Lt. Col. Skyles said. "We're going to get on each other's nerves."

"We probably will," Spade said. "But we're going to be ready for that circumstance. We have rules of conduct we know and follow. Your behavior as leaders will set the example, and as long as we stay cool and follow the rules, we'll do fine out there. A thousand years will go by in no time, and it will all be worth it when we reach the Calli Sector. There are enough uninhabited Earth-like planets out there for all of us. No more Craaldans. No more Diocons. We're going to live happily ever after once we get there. We will survive the void. Bottom line up front, we've got to get Mayor Magna to agree to let us provision Escalon before we depart."

"I don't know, Spade," the Paltran leader, Tarvey Rigo, said. Maybe we should rethink this journey. We might go stir crazy on this station before we reach the Calli Sector."

"Don't go soft on me, Tarvey," Spade said. "Just think of this voyage as a chance to do all those things you never had time for before."

"Like what?" Rigo asked.

"You'll have a chance to catch up on your reading, for instance," Spade said. "Maybe learn a new language or a musical instrument. There's chess and bridge. Old Earth movies. Working out. Karaoke."

"I am a big fan of 21st century video games," Rigo said. "I suppose I will have the time to play them all now."

"I'm putting together a zero-gravity ping pong league, if anyone is interested," said Jober Mope, the commander of the space drifter battalion.

"We'll be fine out there," Spade said. "And if you get too bored, there's always cryonic hibernation. First things first, we need to focus on the present. There is much work to do before our departure."

"Roger," said Pervez Anax, the station's mustachioed logistics and supply officer. "I am of the opinion that building two hydrogen fission engines and installing them onto this station is not going to be a spacewalk in the park. Completing the task in a year is overly ambitious. It will require round-the-clock work schedules to pull off, so ping pong and karaoke are going to have to wait until we're on our way."

"Perv is right," Spade said. "We've got a lot of work to do."

Jober Mope suppressed a laugh. Mope was a gaunt space drifter with hollow eyes and deep creases in the skin of his cheeks. He had a reputation for being tough as nails. As a lifelong space drifter, he knew a thing or two about long space voyages.

"He just called you Perv," Mope said.

"Yeah. So?"

"Perv," Mope repeated.

"It's my name."

"It's an unfortunate name."

"How so?" Anax asked.

"Oh, forget it," Mope said.

"It's not like you don't have a funny name, Jober," Vomica said.

"You're telling me?" Mope said.

Capt. Casey concentrated on her handheld display. "Um, Jace," she said.

"What's up?" he asked.

"I just got a message from Bruce in the control room. He's tracking a vessel that's closing in on our position at extreme velocity."

"What kind of vessel?" Spade asked.

She looked up from her display. "It's a Craaldan destroyer."

Infantry attacks

An alarm blared through Escalon Station. All the humans aboard scrambled in the zero gravity, rushing to their battle stations. Escalon did not have much in the way of defenses, but Lt. Col. Skyles had drawn up procedures in the event of an attack. Everyone knew their roles.

Word quickly spread that it was a Craaldan destroyer closing in and panic began to catch like a contagion. The fear was visible on the human faces. Some fled for the ships outside and tried to make a run for it.

Spade and Capt. Casey looked up at the main display screen in Escalon's control room. Technicians sat at their stations and watched their leader and their executive officer with worried looks.

"We'll be in range of the destroyer's laser cannon in thirty seconds," said Bruce Borneo, the operations officer. "We have no weaponry to strike them with at this distance."

Borneo was a tall space drifter with a bald head and a pockmarked face. He pushed over to his main control panel and fired the station's engines at full power with a heading set for the planet Biop. Spade and Capt. Casey braced themselves as the large station accelerated against its own inertia.

"It's a solitary destroyer," Spade said. "It must have been following us for some time."

"He's coming in fast," Borneo said. "He's going to hit us hard with his cannon to disable us. Then he'll release his fighter drones to pick off our ships and neutralize any defenses we put up. Craaldan infantry will board us and then massacre us all."

"It's like a recurring bad dream," Capt. Casey said.

The Craaldan destroyer emitted a kinetic pulse from its big gun.

"Hold on!" Spade yelled.

In an instant, the laser impacted and pulverized a large section of Escalon Station. The station lurched and shook violently as explosions rocked its superstructure.

"Direct hit!" Borneo said.

The screens throughout the control room displayed burning chunks of the station that were ripping away. Humans were sucked out into the void.

The human ships from the flotilla were taking flight in a frantic attempt at escape. Missiles streaked from the destroyer and impacted against the fleeing ships in brilliant explosions. Cargo ships, schooners and frigates disappeared in bright flashes of light.

"Here come the drones," Borneo said.

A squadron of drone fighters swarmed like angry wasps toward them through the blackness of space. Some of the human fighters in the flotilla made short-lived attempts at engaging the Craaldan drones, but were outnumbered and outgunned.

"Skyles, do you copy?" Spade said into his handheld communicator.

"Roger," Skyles said. "My guys are ready for the boarding party. We're not going down without a fight. Just like Heliac all over again."

"They will board with a company-size element," Spade said. "Concentrate fire on the company commander and his platoon leaders."

"That's what they'll be doing to us," Skyles said. "They'll be gunning for our leadership. That means you, Spade."

"On Gallos, when we massed our fire we could penetrate their armor," Spade said.

"Roger that," Skyles said.

"Keep your head down, Colonel," Spade said.

"I thought they would have come for us sooner," Skyles said. "When they didn't, I started to believe we had escaped them. You actually had me looking forward to a relaxing thousand-year cruise. But deep down, we all knew this was going to happen, didn't we?"

"We're not dead yet," Spade said.

"We've survived worse odds, I suppose," Skyles said. "In any event, I've got 300 Heliac Rangers under my command and we're going to give them all we've got. We'll take a few Craaldans with us."

"Here it comes," Borneo said.

A large black ship appeared on the main display screen. It was a menacing vessel, armed to the teeth, and carrying 1,000 fearsome Craaldan Expeditionary Troopers, in addition to the ship's crew.

"Fire the nukes," Spade said.

Borneo hit a red button and launched three nuclear missiles. The missiles shot out of tubes that extended from Escalon Station's launch bay. Once outside, their engines ignited and kicked out bright flames from their tails. The missiles arced and turned for the destroyer.

The destroyer's laser cannon quickly pulverized the first missile and then the second. Borneo punched a button on his control panel and the third missile detonated.

The detonation was too close. Many of the ships in the flotilla accompanying Escalon were vaporized by the blast. An immense shock wave slammed the station with such force that the entire structure twisted violently on its axis. A quadrant of the station peeled away in fiery pieces. The massive structure careened and cartwheeled through space as flames shot from its core.

Glass and shards of plastic flew about the control room like shrapnel. Capt. Casey and Spade were briefly stunned by the concussion, but recovered their faculties.

"Bruce, are you OK?" Spade shouted.

A few of the technicians had been knocked unconscious by the blast. They floated about the room, knocking against the walls and ceiling. The others scrambled out of the room as the station shook and vibrated as it spun about at great velocity.

Bruce Borneo's body drifted in the weightlessness and bounced off the main display screen.

Up on the screen, a Craaldan troop transport raced alongside the careening remains of Escalon Station. Rappelling cables shot out from the side of the transport and hooked onto the station's outer wall. Armored Craaldan infantry troopers zipped down the lines and boarded the station.

"Bruce!" Capt. Casey yelled.

"I've got him," Spade said.

He pulled down Borneo's body as the station shook and vibrated violently.

"Oh, no," Capt. Casey said. "Bruce."

His face was peppered with shards of glass. The back of his head was a bloody pulp.

"The blast threw him against the computer servers," she said. "I'm not getting a pulse." She looked up at Spade with worried eyes.

One of the control room's display screens depicted the firefight that was raging on board. Heliac Rangers were engaging the boarding Craaldan troopers with well-aimed fire from their M-929 assault rifles. Rounds pop-pop-popped. Grenades thumped. The interior of the station was being ripped to shreds.

The giant Craaldans were encased in black mechanized armor and armed with CX-649 weapons systems. Craaldan squads moved tactically with inhuman speed through the chaotic interior of the spinning, burning station. They moved insect-like in the weightlessness, propelling themselves through the corridors with air jets on their armor and with the assistance of hooks on their gloves and boots. The Craaldan troopers fired their weapons in coordinated volleys, chewing up the inside of the station and forcing Skyles' men to retreat down the transport tubes. The Rangers fired concussion grenades back at their pursuers.

"They're zeroing in on the control room," Capt. Casey said.

The main screen now depicted the planet Biop. The steel-gray planet grew larger as the station rushed toward it. The nuclear explosion from Borneo's missile had propelled the station directly toward the edge of the planet's atmosphere.

"We're being pulled in by the planet's gravitational field," Spade said into his communicator. "Evacuate if you can, Skyles. This station is going down."

"We just cornered a platoon leader and massed fire on him," Skyles said. "Blew his head off, hooah!"

Spade hit the main intercom button. "Evacuate this station. I say again. Evacuate this station. Save yourselves."

A siren blared and red and yellow lights flashed in the corridors. Air rushed down the hallways and transport tubes as it was sucked out into the vacuum of space through ruptures in the outer walls.

"We need to get to the main docking bay," Spade yelled to Capt. Casey over the roar of air. "If we reach the Red Wrath, we can make a run for it. Follow me!"

Crash and burn

Human bodies and electronic debris hurtled down the corridors as yellow and red warning lights flashed. The alarm blared. Capt. Casey and Spade were swept into a current of rushing air.

Spade held onto Borneo's lifeless body as they did their best to ride the air currents to the docking bay. They bounced off walls and were lashed with debris. They held onto each other as they skidded down corridors and up transport tubes.

Spade pulled himself against the flow of air. Capt. Casey clung to his back, gripping Borneo by the collar. Flying debris hurtled past them.

"Hurry, Jace!" Capt. Casey said. "There's a Craaldan behind us!"

Spade looked over his shoulder and saw a Craaldan soldier at the far end of a transport tube. The soldier peeked around a corner. Spade caught sight of its yellow faceplate before it ducked away.

"Not good," Spade said.

The Craaldan fired its weapon. The round struck Borneo and splattered his guts against a bulkhead. Capt. Casey lost her grip on the flayed corpse, which was whisked away by the powerful flow of air.

Spade kicked his leg up onto the edge of the passageway and pulled himself with all his might against the current of air. He could see a portal to the docking bay. It was sealed off due to the breaches in the station's outer walls.

Capt. Casey pulled a retractable cable from her utility belt as Spade held on against the windstorm that whipped at their bodies. She threaded the cable through her multi-tool and aimed it like a dart and then shot the tip toward the portal. The tip hit and embedded itself in the metal.

"Hold on, Jace!" she said over the roar of rushing air.

The Craaldan behind them popped out from the corner and fired its weapon. A huge blast of molten metal ripped through the ceiling above them, showering them with sparks.

Capt. Casey reeled herself toward the door with Spade holding on with one hand. The Craaldan came over the ledge and Spade fired his pistol. The rounds ricocheted off the Craaldan's faceplate.

The soldier ducked for cover behind the ledge.

"There'll be more behind him," Spade said.

Capt. Casey punched at the portal's control panel and the portal unlocked. They ducked inside the docking bay, closing the hatch behind them.

The Red Wrath was moored to the docking bay floor. Spade admired his red and black interceptor, with its mammoth engines and shark's teeth painted under its nose. Stenciled on its hull was the drop dead image of a nude female cyborg sitting atop a skull and crossbones, holding the ace of spades in her hand.

The ship was scorched and beat up, but still looked formidable, even anchored to the deck with several panels removed and scaffolding honeycombed over one of its enormous engines

"You're beautiful, Red," Spade said.

"Red, you old battlewagon," Capt. Casey said.

They pushed off the portal and dove across the bay in the zero gravity.

Suddenly, the station jumped and lurched wildly. The bay rotated around them. Spade and Capt. Casey smashed into a wall and bounced off it as the bay spun about them.

"We've hit Biop's atmosphere!" Spade yelled.

A deafening roar filled the docking bay. Centrifugal forces pinned Capt. Casey and Spade against the wall.

The portal door exploded off its hinges. Their Craaldan pursuer appeared in the entryway.

A long bayonet popped from its fist with a zing.

Spade grabbed Capt. Casey by the hand and shoved off the wall. They slammed into the hull of the Red Wrath. Spade punched buttons on a panel and twisted open a hatch. He shoved Capt. Casey inside and then clambered in after her, sealing the hatch behind him.

He pulled himself hand over hand as fast as he could to the cockpit. He strapped himself into the pilot's chair. The bay's outer doors were sealed. He punched at buttons on the control panel and armed the Red Wrath's pulse cannons. He pulled the trigger on the flight stick and the cannons fired, blasting a huge hole in the docking bay doors in a fiery explosion.

The air inside the docking bay rushed out into space. Three Craaldan soldiers hurtled head over heels out the blast hole.

Biop's gravity field gripped the station and pulled it downward. The massive station gained momentum and streaked down through the upper atmosphere. It ignited and a furnace-like blast of white and yellow flame engulfed it. Escalon began to rip apart into several huge fiery pieces. A hurricane of white heat blasted into the docking bay.

Capt. Casey strapped herself into the chair beside Spade. "Get us out of here, Jace," she said.

"Roger that," he said.

Spade fired the Red Wrath's engines. The interceptor ripped free of its mooring cables and scraped the docking bay's walls before bursting through a curtain of white flame that was blasting over the disintegrating remains of Escalon.

The Red Wrath raced out in front of the falling station, speeding straight downward toward the planet's surface. Friction caused flames to shoot up the Red Wrath's nose and lap at the forward screen. The interceptor streaked downward as Spade tried to outrun the falling station behind him.

"Look!" Capt. Casey said. The monitors on the control panel showed small ships and pods shooting from the sides of the flaming space station at intermittent intervals. "People are escaping."

"I need more speed," Spade said. "I've got to get some distance before I can turn away from her."

Capt. Casey looked forward through the flames that licked up the forward screen. "Pull up, Jace!"

"Just a little more speed before I can clear her," he said. Spade gunned the Red Wrath's big engines. "This is going to be close," he said.

Capt. Casey shrunk into her seat watching with wide eyes as the planet's gray surface rushed up at them. G-forces pulled at the skin on their faces and crushed at their torsos.

"Now!" Spade yelled. "Brace yourself!"

He yanked back on the stick and the Red Wrath veered off and zoomed around the leading edge of the flaming wreckage of Escalon. The station impacted the surface of the planet with a massive concussion that threw up an explosion of flames, metal and rock. The concussion smashed into the Red Wrath and threw it into an uncontrolled spin.

The g-forces from Spade's tight turn and from the spin pinned him and Capt. Casey to their chairs as the muscles in their necks bulged and strained. Blood rushed from their brains.

Spade struggled to regain control of the Red Wrath as it twisted and turned in the thick gray atmosphere.

"Hold on!" he yelled. "We're going down!"

The Red Wrath impacted the surface and bounced hard and then skidded and rolled as panels ripped away and the outer walls were shredded by rock and sand.

The Red Wrath skidded along for quite some distance before finally slowing to a stop.

Capt. Casey shook her head and blinked her eyes. "My heart's pounding," she said breathlessly. She looked over at Spade.

He sat in his chair staring forward. He ran his hand through his black hair and then reached into a pocket on his flight suit and pulled out a cigar. He popped the cigar into his mouth and lit it and puffed on it for a moment. He leaned back in his chair and exhaled a cloud of blue smoke.

"I thought you quit that dirty habit," she said.

"I thought so, too."

World of dread

"This is Captain Jace Spade," he said into the radio. "Does anyone copy?"

Spade looked out the forward screen into a heavy, gray haze. Visibility was less than a mile. The flat, featureless landscape faded behind a gray dust cloud that seemingly blanketed the planet.

The atmosphere outside consisted of about 50 percent nitrogen, 15 percent carbon dioxide, 10 percent methane, 10 percent argon, 5 percent oxygen, 4 percent xenon, 2 percent fluorine and a caustic mix of several other gases. The atmospheric pressure was higher than on Earth, and the temperature slightly hotter. Right now it was nearly 160 degrees Fahrenheit outside.

Wind whipped at the dusty surface. The ground and sky merged in the haze. The Cextos sun was a white disk in the steel-gray sky.

Biop was roughly the size of Earth, but it spun on its axis nearly twice as fast. Cextos had risen and set five times since Capt. Casey and Spade had crashed landed on the surface.

"This is Captain Jace Spade. Is anybody out there? Respond if you copy."

Static crackled over the radio.

"I say again. This is Captain Jace Spade."

"There's nobody there, Jace," Capt. Casey said.

"You're right," he said. He leaned back in his chair and gazed out into the gray. "If we head southeast we will eventually hit New Taji City," he said. "It's a long walk but we should make it there in about two weeks, depending on the terrain."

"We don't have a map," Capt. Casey said. "You're just making a rough estimate on the city's location from memory. With the low visibility out there, it will be hard to find any settlements. We could walk right past a city and never know it. Or we could walk off a cliff, or get lost in a boulder field. We could end up wandering around out there until our air runs out."

"We can carry a month's worth of air," he said. "We can walk for two weeks. If we don't find the city, then we just walk back the way we came."

"I don't know, Jace," she said. "Do really want to walk around out there?"

"It beats sitting around here talking to ourselves on the radio."

"Well, I do need to stretch my legs."

Spade and Capt. Casey began packing up gear for the trek. Spade rummaged around one of the Red Wrath's cargo bays until he found two crates that contained sets of Heliac tactical body armor. The white and blue armor was old and beat up, but it would have to do.

"I wish we had Craaldan mech armor," Spade said. "This low tech human stuff doesn't compare."

"Beggars can't be choosers," Capt. Casey said.

They put on the white and blue armor, helping each other out and fastening each other's snaps. They put on their white and blue Heliac battle helmets and clamped shut the black faceplates with a click. They each picked up an M-929 assault rifle and stepped into the decompression chamber.

The outer hatch opened and dust rushed into the chamber. They hopped down to the surface. Their boots landed on the gravel in puffs of ash.

Capt. Casey looked up at the sun through the dusty air. The brightness of the white disk ebbed and waned behind thick dust clouds that gusted overhead.

They walked across the flat surface. The lack of color, the featureless terrain and the close horizon made them feel as if they were walking beneath an iron dome.

"This planet sucks," Capt. Casey said.

They walked for hours through the haze until the giant white disk of Cextos disappeared below the horizon. The world turned black. Lamps on their shoulders shot out beams of light that illuminated the grainy air. They plodded along in the darkness.

The hours passed as they walked over the flat terrain. An oppressive darkness surrounded them, until slowly the dark gave way to a faint glow as dawn approached.

The black turned to gray. Then the sky turned a faint orange and then purple as the white disk of Cextos breached the horizon.

The blackness of night gave way to the monochrome gray of day. Spade and Capt. Casey walked in silence as Cextos rose higher in the morning sky.

"You've been quiet," Spade said.

"You too," Capt. Casey said.

They continued plodding across the featureless landscape.

"I'm sorry, Jace."

"Sorry for what?"

"I'm sorry for pressuring you to take charge of all those people."

They walked across the gray world in silence.

"Don't be sorry," Spade said. "It's me that screwed up. I keep thinking about what I could have done differently. Those people relied on me."

"No," she said. "This was my fault. I knew after we survived the destruction of Portogallos that you wanted to continue your search for Dr. Zander, to rescue him from whatever prison he's in. But I pressured you to go against your nature and take up an impossible task. I should never have done that."

They walked silently for a bit.

"Jace, do you remember back when we were dating, before you dumped me? I used to always say that you had the potential to be somebody, but your problem was that you were unwilling to apply yourself."

"I didn't dump you, Mina."

"Well, what I meant back then was that people looked up to you. People have this natural inclination to follow you. I thought back then that you had the potential to be a leader who could do good things for people. On Escalon, you proved me right. You were a great leader."

"Escalon is gone," Spade said. "Those people would have been better off if they hadn't followed me."

"I was selfish to put you in that situation," she said.

"You are apologizing to me, but I'm the one who let you down," he said.

"No. You did everything right. And it gave me so much hope for the future. But everything went wrong anyway. Like it always does. I'm not going to hope anymore."

She stopped walking.

He turned and faced her.

She stood in the dust in her beat up Heliac body armor with her M-929 rifle slung on her back. He could not see her face, only the expressionless black faceplate of her battle helmet.

"I'm tired, Jace."

"Don't give up on me, Mina."

She stood there for a moment. He extended his hand to her.

She took it and they began walking again. They walked in silence across Biop's gray desolation.

"Hey, look at that," Spade said, pointing forward.

In the distance, the silhouette of a huge pyramid appeared through the thick haze. More pyramids came into view. They were enormous, hundreds of feet high and spread across the plain.

Spade and Capt. Casey walked toward them, eventually reaching the first of the massive structures. They approached the gigantic base of a pyramid made of blocks of stone. The stones were stacked atop each other, reaching up into the gray sky.

"What is it with ancient civilizations and pyramids?" Capt. Casey asked.

Blast marks and rough craters scarred the sloping sides of the stone structure. Spade and Capt. Casey walked between the pyramids, which were arranged in a widely spaced grid. Rubble was strewn between them. Occasionally, they had to climb over boulders that were piled across what appeared to have once been boulevards.

"I read about this place in Vomica's report," Capt. Casey said. "This was Biop's capital city. Twenty million residents lived here. The Craaldans nuked them. That was 2,500 years ago."

As they walked, the pyramids became more densely spaced. The boulevards became narrow, dusty corridors between the towering structures.

"Get down!" Spade shouted.

He grabbed her by the hand and pulled her behind a boulder.

"What?" she asked.

Spade pointed upward. A Craaldan drone cruised over the tops of the pyramids. Spade and Capt. Casey remained still as the black drone passed overhead.

It was a menacing looking craft, with sharply angled wings and an insect-like form. Its nose was large and bulbous and packed with sensors that busily sought signs of life.

The drone turned and circled back and then picked up speed and headed straight for their position.

"It's got our number!" Spade yelled. "Run!"

Pyramids

Spade and Capt. Casey sprinted through the dust down a boulevard beneath the towering pyramids. The Craaldan drone dropped low between the stone structures, throwing up a cloud of dust and ash behind it as it accelerated toward them.

Capt. Casey stopped running. She pulled her rifle from her back and turned around and faced the approaching drone. She fired her weapon.

Her rounds struck their mark but bounced off the armored airframe. The drone fired its big gun, which chewed up the boulevard in a firestorm of metal.

Spade tackled her and they rolled in the dust as an explosion of rounds raced up the boulevard. The drone passed over them and then hovered and swung back around in the tight confines between the pyramids.

Spade grabbed Capt. Casey under the arm and pulled her through an arched stone entranceway. They entered a dark, cavernous room. Its stone floor was caked with ash. Spade pulled Capt. Casey up a narrow stairwell. The lamp on his shoulder cast a white beam through the darkness.

They emerged onto an open floor. Ledges jutted outside and looked down on the boulevard below.

"Get down," Spade said.

He low crawled to a ledge. The drone had set down in front of the entranceway to the pyramid. A ramp dropped down from the rear of the craft.

Three Craaldan soldiers trotted down the ramp. Spade took aim with his M-929 and fired off a shot.

His round struck his target in the head with a clang, knocking the armored soldier down. The soldier looked up from his back and pointed his weapon and fired.

Molten metal ripped through the pyramid's stone walls. Spade got up and sprinted toward Capt. Casey. He picked her up under her arm and they ran up the stairwell. They emerged onto another open floor.

"We can shoot them as they come up the stairs," Spade said. "If we both concentrate our fire center mass we might be able to penetrate their mech armor."

Spade looked over at her. She was seated, slouched against the wall, her weapon on the floor at her side.

"Get up, Mina," he said.

"I'm tired of fighting them, Jace."

"Don't give up now."

A burst of rounds exploded up the stairwell. When the burst ceased, Spade ducked into the stairwell and fired his weapon down it, before ducking back out.

Another burst of rounds exploded up the stairwell. Light flashed and shadows danced across the stone walls.

"Hey, Mina," Spade said.

She didn't respond.

"I want you to wear white at our wedding."

"I was thinking black leather," she said.

"Like that little black number you wore when we hit the town on Vacteria? I could go for that."

Spade stepped into the stairwell and fired a grenade down it and then ducked behind the wall. The concussion blasted pressurized dust up the narrow passageway.

Spade jumped up and stepped back into the stairwell and fired another burst before ducking back behind the wall.

He looked over at her. She sat there on the floor with her back against the wall, her weapon unattended by her side.

"Get up, Mina. Please."

"They won't stop until they've exterminated all of us," she said.

"Mina. I need your help."

"We can't beat them, Jace. It's no use."

"They're beatable. But I can't do this alone."

He stepped back into the stairwell and fired a long burst. A huge Craaldan rushed up the narrow passageway with bayonets unsheathed from its fists.

Spade's rounds bounced off the Craaldan's armored chest in sparks of flashing light. Spade fired a grenade. The round struck the Craaldan and exploded with a deafening crump.

The concussion hit Spade like a sledgehammer, slamming him against the wall at the top of the stairwell. He lost consciousness for a moment. His head rang loudly when he came to.

The Craaldan was on its back at the bottom of the stairwell. The big soldier pulled itself to its feet and ducked out of the narrow passageway.

Spade got up on his feet in time to see the Craaldan re-enter the stairwell with weapon blazing. The rounds exploded around Spade, who fired off another grenade, which exploded at the bottom of the stairs.

Spade dove out of the stairwell and slid across the ashy floor.

He checked his weapon. Only one grenade left.

A Craaldan pulled himself over the ledge behind him. Spade fired the last grenade, striking the Craaldan. The powerful boom knocked it off the ledge.

Spade picked up Capt. Casey's weapon and fired another grenade down the stairwell.

"We need to get out of here," he said. "Follow me!"

She didn't get up.

"Stay with me, Mina."

"Go," she said. "I can't do it anymore."

Spade leaned down and grabbed her by the shoulders and looked into her faceplate. "Listen to me! No matter what you think, no matter how you feel, you never give up! You drive on! No matter how bad it gets! You hear me, Mina? Always drive on!"

He picked her up and pulled her up the stairwell, stopping every few flights to fire a grenade behind them.

They emerged onto a platform at the apex of the pyramid. The tops of thousands of pyramids stretched into the distance around them, fading into the gray haze.

A giant Craaldan in black mechanized armor sprinted out of the stairwell with both bayonets drawn. Spade pushed Capt. Casey behind him and fired his last grenade. The Craaldan sidestepped the round which shot over the side of the pyramid and exploded harmlessly in the distance.

Spade fired a long burst from his rifle. His rounds sparked and bounced off the rapidly approaching Craaldan who thrust his bayonet at Spade's gut with lightning speed.

Spade dodged the thrust, but was tackled by the huge alien soldier. They tumbled to the floor of the platform.

"Jace!" Capt. Casey screamed.

The Craaldan gripped Spade by the throat and pinned him to the dust-covered stone floor. The giant armored soldier raised its fist to deliver the coup de grâce.

Capt. Casey picked up her rifle and fired it. The rounds bounced off the soldier's hard armor. Its head turned and it looked at her through the dim gray. The white disk of the sun was behind her.

With a flick of its wrist, its bayonet slashed her weapon from her hands.

It then looked down and in an instant punched its bayonet into Spade's gut.

Spade gritted his teeth in intense pain. The quick and forceful death blow cut into him and punctured his insides. Hot blood gurgled up his throat.

The Craaldan swiftly withdrew the bloodied blade.

"No!" Capt. Casey screamed.

She ran at the Craaldan and crashed into him. The Craaldan caught her and stood and lifted her like a rag doll, holding her by the throat with one hand. Its fist was cocked back with the long, bloodied bayonet pointed downward.

The Craaldan trooper was nearly 10 feet tall in its black mech armor. The thick metal of its armor was colored yellow at the joints. Its yellow faceplate looked into hers.

"Captain Mina Casey?" it said slowly in a gravelly and sulfurous voice.

Two more Craaldan soldiers emerged from the entranceway. They stood and watched their commander.

"Zeth?" she asked.

Spade was on his back looking up at them. Through spattered blood on the inside of his faceplate, he saw the giant Craaldan holding Capt. Casey suspended by the throat. The white disk of the sun was behind them. The tops of pyramids faded into the haze. Spade felt himself rapidly bleeding out. His consciousness collapsed into darkness.

The two Craaldan soldiers waited for their commander to deliver the final bayonet thrust to the human suspended by the throat. But suddenly, one of the watching soldiers' heads exploded in a cloud of pink mist. Its helmet split open and organic matter spattered around it. The headless soldier fell backward into the dust.

The soldier next to him dropped to a knee and looked up and caught sight of an aircraft zooming toward them. It was a gray, fat-bellied airframe with a rounded nose and rocket pods on its stubby wings. A sniper in the aircraft took aim from an open door and fired. The round struck the Craaldan in the chest and burst out its back, spraying guts and yellow blood across the platform behind it.

Zeth let Capt. Casey fall to the floor and sprinted for the stairwell. A rocket zipped off a rail on the approaching aircraft's wing and corkscrewed at Zeth.

The big Craaldan ducked into the stairwell as the rocket hit the entranceway and exploded with a boom.

The aircraft zoomed down and hovered above the platform, throwing down a powerful backwash of air and exhaust from its swiveling engines. A swirling cloud of dust whipped up from the platform. A line dropped down and a sniper in Heliac armor fast-roped down it, landing on his feet.

"Are you OK, Mina?" the sniper asked.

"Joe?" she asked as the dust swirled around her. She got to her feet. "Is that you?"

"Roger. It's me, your hero, Sergeant Joe J. Grimes." He pointed upward with his thumb. "Genie's piloting that bird."

Sgt. Grimes picked up Spade and threw him over his shoulder.

"Hang on!" he said, reaching out his arm to Capt. Casey. She grabbed a hold of him.

The line pulled them upward into the hovering aircraft.

DFAC 5

Glowing red lenses came into focus above him. He heard the snap of fingers at his ear.

"I hear you, Doc," Spade rasped.

"How are you feeling?" Dr. Viz Ebos asked.

"Not good," Spade said. "Cotton mouth. A cold beer would really hit the spot."

"That can be arranged," Ebos said. "Although, it is early morning and coffee would be the appropriate beverage."

"Roger. A cup of coffee then."

Spade was lying on a gurney in a plain room with tan walls. A light mounted on a jointed metal arm shone down on him.

He was shirtless. He sat up and rubbed the back of his neck. "How long have I been out?" he asked.

"Nearly a week," Ebos said. "That's an Earth week. Here on Biop it would actually be two weeks."

"Where's Mina?" Spade asked.

"We weren't expecting you to regain consciousness today," Dr. Ebos said. "Captain Casey is outside the wire with a search party looking for more survivors from Escalon Station. It is my opinion that we have found all those who could be recovered. But hope springs eternal, I suppose."

Spade looked at his gut. It was bandaged. A purple bruise could be seen spreading out on his skin from under the edge of the bandages.

"That Craaldan messed me up pretty good," Spade said.

"Yes," Ebos said. "The contusion was almost surgical in its symmetry. It was only a matter of cleaning up the lesion, replacing the most severely damaged tissues and then sewing you back together. I replaced much of your stomach with carbonitic mesh. Your own cells will replace the mesh over the next decade. I also gave you a new kidney. And you lost nearly all your blood so I filled you up with plasma."

"Thanks."

"You have remarkable healing powers, Captain Spade. I was unaware that a portion of your DNA is alien. Captain Casey tells me that your robust immune system is due to DNA from a Vomis nematode. Apparently, Dr. Zander acquired the DNA from a specimen he collected in the Roga System, and then integrated its DNA into your genetic makeup."

"That's me, the Vomis nematode."

"Did you know that 3 percent of your DNA comes from a German Shepherd? A canine!"

"Hey, Doc. Can we talk about something else? I'm trying to recover from being stabbed in the guts with a Craaldan bayonet."

"My apologies."

"Where are we, anyway?"

"We are in a medical clinic in Taji City," Ebos answered. "Sergeant Joe Grimes and a Tetrailani cyborg named Genie found you and Captain Casey atop an ancient Bioppian pyramid and brought you here."

"Joe and Genie?"

"If they hadn't found you when they did, that would have been the end of you and Captain Casey. Permanently."

"Hey, Doc," Spade said.

"Yes?"

Spade looked up at the doctor's glowing red eyepieces. "Was I dead?"

"You were at death's door, to be sure," Ebos said. "But you hadn't yet expired when Sergeant Grimes brought you to me."

"Grimes," Spade said. "I'm usually the one rescuing him. Where is that knucklehead, anyway? I thought he and Genie would be halfway to the Calli Sector by now."

"He and the cyborg Genie work for Mayor Lourdes Magna," Ebos said. "They've been residing in the northwestern quadrant. I sent a message to them that you have regained consciousness."

Spade rubbed his temples. "At least you're here for me, Doc," he said.

"Come," Ebos said. "Let's get that cup of coffee."

Spade stood from the gurney and put on his gray flight suit and boots and strapped his pistol to his leg. He and Dr. Ebos walked out of the clinic's narrow entryway into an airtight tube that enclosed a walkway barely wide enough for two people to pass.

Dust hung in the air in the dim passageway. Ebos walked along in his white lab coat. His red lenses were aglow in the dim light. Mechanical prosthetics over his thin arms and legs aided his movement. The gravity on Biop was much higher than on his home world of Paltros.

Windows on the wall of the tube looked out at the nebulous Bioppian night. The tube branched off every few yards and connected to rectangular metal buildings of various sizes.

Spade had to stoop to avoid bumping his head on the ceiling. He ducked behind Ebos every time a human passed them in the tight tubeway.

The humans here looked rough. They wore tan boots and cargo pants and utility shirts covered in pockets. The men were haggard and most had scraggly beards. The women were taller than the men and looked hearty and athletic. Everyone had stern expressions as they passed.

Parts of the gritty cement floor gave way to gravel. Metal planks covered the rougher sections. The tube opened to a larger walkway that could accommodate the crowd of humans walking to and fro. The ceiling was low, but as many as eight humans could pass without bumping into each other.

Spade followed Ebos who turned down different passageways until they came to a large entranceway. Over the entranceway, a metal sign read "DFAC 5" in black lettering.

"The acronym stands for dining facility," Ebos explained.

Spade followed Ebos into the DFAC. Hundreds of tables were lined up in rows inside the large building, which had a high metal ceiling. Groups of humans sat at some of the tables, but there weren't many here in the facility this early in the morning.

Ebos slid a card under a laser scanner and it beeped twice. "Breakfast is on me," he said.

He picked up a tray and a plate from a stack and then pulled silverware out of plastic containers. Spade followed his lead and walked to a serving line behind the doctor. A skinny, bearded cook wearing a white paper hat stood behind containers of food. He held a large metal spoon.

"Bacon and eggs," Spade said. "And waffles. This is awesome."

"I prefer the fruit bar," Dr. Ebos said.

The cook piled eggs and bacon onto Spade's plate. Spade signaled with a nod for him to add more.

"You don't want to know how they make the eggs," Ebos said.

They got coffee and sat at an empty table. Spade devoured his breakfast, shoveling large forkfuls of eggs into his mouth.

"So, Viz. Fill me in. What's the situation?"

Ebos sipped at his coffee and picked at a bowl of greenhouse fruit. "Out of five thousand of us, a thousand survived the destruction of Escalon Station and made our way to the surface," he said. "Our losses were horrible. The people of Taji City have reluctantly taken us in. They have been hospitable, although we are a great burden on their small colony. Some of them grumble that we are responsible for making the Craaldans aware of their presence here."

"Did Mingus make it?" Spade asked.

"Yes, but unfortunately Leonard Brute did not. He was killed aboard Escalon by a Craaldan trooper. His body was not recovered."

"Vomica?"

"Yes. Alive and well."

"What about Skyles?"

"No word from him. A few of his Rangers are here but the last anyone saw of him was on Escalon. He was engaged in hand-to-hand combat when the station broke apart and burned up in the atmosphere."

"Ramone?"

"Of your staff, Ramone, Pervez and Doxy survived and are here. Bruce and Jober are confirmed dead. Tarvey is missing and presumed dead."

Spade stopped eating. He looked across the tables and absentmindedly played with his food with his fork. "Mina and Tarvey were close."

"She is taking it hard. We have lost so many since Gallos. And now this. Over the last few days, Captain Casey has adopted a fatalistic outlook, as have many now. They know that Craaldans are here on the planet. The general consensus is that we will make a last stand and then die here. Many of the survivors of Escalon have become despondent. The locals are fearful."

"I'm surprised the Craaldans have left us alone this long," Spade said. "It's not like them. Why haven't they attacked? Especially with that destroyer orbiting up there."

"Their destroyer crashed onto the surface and was destroyed," Ebos said.

"What? How did that happen?"

"A ship appeared out of the void and achieved a direct hit on the Craaldan destroyer using a powerful pulse cannon," Ebos explained. "The Craaldans were caught completely by surprise and lost control of their ship, which was captured by the Bioppian gravitational field and pulled into the atmosphere, where it burned up on the way down. From what we can gather, about 500 Craaldans survived the crash and are on the surface. We assume they are regrouping for an assault on the city. The sneak attack on the Craaldan destroyer was quite an amazing turn of events, however. I believe it is the reason we are still alive here."

"Whose ship was it?" Spade asked.

"Captain Jack Winner is his name. He is a Heliac Ranger from Nebas. He has already become quite the heroic figure here in Taji City. Some are saying he can lead us to victory

over the Craaldans. I will have Captain Casey introduce you to him when they return."
"Return from where?"
"They are currently on his ship searching the planet for survivors."

The Blue Falcon

Spade got seconds at the food line and refilled his cup of coffee before sitting back down across the table from Dr. Ebos. More humans were filing into the DFAC now. The tables became crowded with people and the din of conversation filled the large facility.

Spade studied the many faces around him.

"What's with all the butch women?" he asked.

"If you notice, the women here are larger and more dominant than the men," Ebos said.

"They look healthy, like they all work out, but the men look like featherweight geeks," Spade said.

"I believe it's something in the water," Ebos said. "A parasite of some sort that stunts the men and invigorates the women. You'll notice that there are no children in Taji City. The local men have become infertile over the years. The last child was born here 30 Earth years ago. The father was a newly arrived space drifter. The males who arrived with us are concerned about all this and some refuse to drink the local liquids. I'm looking into it, but at this point it's all hearsay."

Spade gazed down into his coffee.

"I don't think it's anything to worry about," Ebos said. "The humans here are perfectly healthy. But to be on the safe side, I boil everything I drink."

"Tell me about this ship that defeated a Craaldan destroyer," Spade said.

"Captain Jack's ship is named the Blue Falcon. It's a remarkable vessel with advanced armaments that appear more sophisticated than even Craaldan weaponry. I've seen it up close and it is an impressive ship, as the Craaldans have duly learned."

"More impressive than the Red Wrath?" Spade asked.

"I hate to say it, but yes. Another thing, Captain Jack brought ammunition that can defeat Craaldan mechanized armor."

"Armor-piercing rounds?" Spade asked.

"Yes. He has cargo bays full of them. The rounds can cut right through their armor. Captain Jack has us pulling round-the-clock security at the city walls. We're conducting reconnaissance patrols outside the wire and setting up ambushes. He also brought an advanced missile defense system that we have set up to guard against indirect fire on the city. Captain Jack quickly took charge and has organized our defenses. Many of us are discouraged and morally defeated, but Captain Jack is telling us we have a fighting chance and he's trying to restore hope."

"This Captain Jack sounds like a real hero," Spade said.

"Yes. And now that you are back with us, Captain Spade, my morale is improving."

"Hey, look over there," Spade said. "I know that guy."

Spade pointed at a big Megalan man who was ducking through the DFAC entranceway. Spade recognized him as a member of Ramone Bombero's work battalion. Their eyes met, but the big man glanced away without acknowledging Spade.

"The Megalans are not having the best time of it here," Ebos said. "Taji males are intimidated by them. And the Taji females have been throwing themselves at the Megalan men, causing friction. The Megalans eat and drink double what a local eats, plus the infrastructure here does not accommodate their large frames. They can't fit in the transport vehicles or in many of the city's walkways, and the living quarters here are too cramped for them. They have begun constructing their own Megalan ghetto on the south side of town."

"Look over there!" Spade exclaimed. "It's Tanaka!"

A skinny man wearing green lenses over his eyes and mechanical prosthetics over his limbs was carrying a tray and walking with Vomica Nux. The two sat together at a table at the far end of the DFAC.

Spade stood. "Tanaka!" he called out waving. "Vomica!"

Everyone looked up at him from their tables. Tanaka and Vomica looked over and spotted him.

Tanaka stared blankly at Spade through his green lenses and then returned to his food. He whispered something to Vomica and she whispered back.

Everyone turned their gazes away from Spade and resumed their conversations, speaking softly.

"Captain Spade," Ebos said. "Please sit down."

Spade sat back down across from Ebos.

"What's up with everybody around here?" Spade asked.

"While you were incapacitated, there has been a question of leadership," Ebos said. "As you know, the mayor of this city is a woman named Lourdes Magna. The mayor realizes that she is ill-equipped to defend the city against a Craaldan attack. She is asking that we put forth a commander to take charge of the defense of Taji City. Captain Jack has stepped into the role, but he is new to us and is somewhat of an enigma. Mayor Magna has called for a public meeting where she and the Board of Supervisors will decide who will be our military commander."

"When is the meeting?" Spade asked.

"Two nights from now," Ebos said. "You are a candidate. Ramone, Capt. Casey and a few others, too."

"So how's it looking for old Jace Spade?" Spade asked.

"Not good," Ebos answered. "Since the destruction of Escalon Station, I'm afraid to say some have lost confidence in your leadership. Not me, of course. But word has spread across the city of Captain Jack's actions while you were out, and his popularity is soaring as more of us meet him and learn more about him. The talk lately is that the vote is expected to be unanimous."

Suddenly, a blaring alarm filled the DFAC. All conversation stopped and everyone looked around, their eyes searching each other's faces.

As the alarm blared, a metallic voice rang out, "Incoming! Incoming! Incoming!"

One man at the far end of the DFAC scrambled under a table, setting off a chain reaction as the entire crowd followed his lead and dove under the tables in unison in a great tumult of crashing plates, sliding chairs and jolting tables.

Spade ducked under his table. Dr. Ebos was across from him lying on his side in the cramped space. His glowing red lenses stared blankly at Spade.

"What's going on, Doc?" Spade asked.

"Indirect fire," Ebos said. "Inbound rockets, most likely. Craaldan. Possibly armed with nukes. The city's new missile defense system is tracking them."

The floor of the DFAC rumbled and loud booms rocked the building forcefully.

"That's the counter fire battery," Ebos said. "We will know in a moment if our defenses were effective."

The humans under the tables carried worried expressions on their faces. Spade was pressed up against a skinny, bearded man who was staring intently at the floor. Across from him, a woman with long tawny hair had her eyes shut tightly. Others were searching the faces around them. Their eyes showed concern or outright fear.

A series of booms rumbled from afar. Then silence.

"All clear. All clear. All clear," the metallic voice said over the citywide intercom.

After a moment of stillness, the crowd seemed to exhale as one. Then scattered cheers arose across the DFAC. Everyone got out from under the tables and sat in their seats and resumed eating and talking.

Spade sipped his coffee and studied the faces around him. Everyone appeared relieved.

"If Captain Jack's missile defense system had not been operational, that would have been the end of all of us," Ebos said. "We would have just been nuked."

A commotion arose at one of the DFAC's entryways. A tall, blonde man in a blue flight suit entered the DFAC. People mobbed him.

"Hey, it's Captain Jack!" Ebos said.

The name Captain Jack was repeated across the facility. Everyone craned their necks to catch a glimpse.

The tall, blonde man walked through the crowd wearing a big smile on his face. He shook hands and slapped backs. A cheer arose in the DFAC.

Spade craned his neck to get a better view of him. He spotted Capt. Casey. She was smiling and walking at the tall man's side.

Containerized Housing Unit

"Hey, hey, Captain Jack!" Dr. Ebos said, waving his skinny, prosthetics-covered arm.

Capt. Jack waved back and walked up to their table.

"How about the C-NAM 3000 missile defense system?" Capt. Jack asked, enthusiastically. "We can take anything the Craaldan can throw at us!"

"Your missile defense system worked like a charm," Dr. Ebos said.

Capt. Jack's Counter Nuke, Artillery and Mortar system had only recently been installed on cement reinforced dirt platforms around the city. Getting the system up and running had been his first priority when he arrived on the ground at Taji City, and he had immediately set about constructing it with great urgency.

Capt. Casey approached the table. Spade stood from his chair.

She was dressed in her tight-fitting black coveralls with an M2 pistol strapped to the side of her thigh. She looked up at Spade with her big, dark eyes.

"Hey, handsome," she said.

She hugged him. She closed her eyes and pressed her face against his chest and squeezed him tightly. "Oh, Jace," she said.

"I've been missing you," Spade said.

"I've been missing you, too," she said.

Their eyes met. Hers were teary and red.

"I've been missing you so much," she said.

"Captain Spade, I must introduce you to Captain Jack Winner, commander of the Blue Falcon," Dr. Ebos said.

Capt. Jack smiled broadly, flashing perfect white teeth. He extended his hand. "So this is the famous Captain Spade," he said. "I have heard a lot about you."

Capt. Casey was still under Spade's arm when Spade shook Capt. Jack Winner's hand. Capt. Jack had a crushing handshake.

Both men were tall, about equal in height, with Capt. Jack perhaps being the slightly taller of the two.

"I hear you are trying to take command of our ragtag band of refugees," Spade said.

"Not true," Capt. Jack said. "And I wouldn't exactly call them ragtag. These people here have shown a lot of heart under very adverse circumstances. They just lack direction. And they were in need of the right weaponry until recently. I've got a feeling this band of humans, with the right motivation, can drive the Craaldan menace from this planet."

"With your motivation, you mean," Spade said.

"Maybe," Captain Jack said. "But that's up to them."

"You're a Heliac Ranger?" Spade asked.

"Roger that," Capt. Jack answered. "You?"

"I was a fighter pilot with the Naos Lunar Militia," Spade said.

"I haven't heard of it," Capt. Jack said. "Mining colony?"

"Negative."

"Hey, Jace," Mina said, looking up at him. "I got us our own CHU. It's nothing special but it beats sleeping on a gurney in the clinic. Come on. Let's go get you cleaned up and settled in, OK?"

"Roger that," he said. "Hey, Doc, it's been a pleasure, as always. Captain Jack, nice to meet you. I'll see you around."

"No doubt," Capt. Jack said.

"Bye, Captain Jack," Capt. Casey said. "See you soon, Doc. Dinner tonight, OK?"

"It would be a privilege," Ebos said.

Capt. Casey held Spade tightly around the waist, pressing her body against his as they walked out of the DFAC. They walked together down a crowded corridor. Dust hung below buzzing lights that were set in the low ceiling.

"You don't know how good it feels to have you back," Capt. Casey said. "I've been so down in the dumps lately, going over everything again and again in my mind. But I don't want to think any more. All I want is to be with you."

Spade held her close as they walked in the busy corridor. They came to a platform above a set of tracks. Humans stood on the platform awaiting a tram.

"You're not mad at me, are you?" she asked.

"Mad at you for what?"

"You needed me and I was just deadweight."

"Mina, I could never be mad at you," he said.

"What about that time I was playing with your pistol and accidentally shot a hole in our bedroom window and your Naos home video collection was sucked out into space?"

"OK. I can be mad at you. But I got over that."

"You're over that?"

"I mean, I might get over that someday."

A long tubular tram rolled up on the tracks and eased to a stop at the platform. Its doors slid open with a whush and humans exited the car.

"If you want to know the truth, I'm worried about you," Spade said. "I'm worried that you're giving up on me. When I saw you with that jerk Captain Jack, all kinds of evil thoughts ran through my brain."

"Don't be silly, Jace," she said. "Captain Jack isn't a jerk."

They boarded the tram and sat together on a bench with their backs to the window. Spade had his arm around her. She rested her head on his shoulder.

The tram accelerated down the tracks through a dark tunnel. The speeding tram shot out into Biop's atmosphere.

Outside the window, the world was a dull gray. The buildings of Biop were a jumble of rectangular cement structures, the tallest reaching only three stories high. Steel-reinforced, concrete blast walls twelve feet high were lined up end to end around the buildings. The city was sectioned off by these walls. Each section of wall resembled an inverted T when viewed in cross-section. The high concrete walls protected the smaller structures somewhat from the powerful blasts of wind and sand that often ripped through the city. They also provided some protection from flying rubble during meteor strikes.

Spindly radio towers pierced into the haze above the flat roofed buildings of the cityscape. A huge boxy DFAC dominated the jumble of buildings that surrounded it. To the east was the city's airfield where massive aircraft hangars were silhouetted against the gray haze. The hangars were easily the largest structures in the city.

The white disk of the Cextos sun shone faintly through the gray distance beyond the hangars.

The tram clickety-clacked over the tracks. It entered another dark tunnel and slowed to a halt at a platform. Passengers exited and boarded. The tram slowly accelerated through the tunnel before emerging outside into the gray once again.

Outside, big six-wheeled vehicles with knobby tires rolled down canyon-like gravel roads lined with blast walls. Behind the walls were cement buildings and stacks of large, rectangular metal containers.

Humans walked around outside between the containers or along the T-walls. They wore heavy boots, thick khaki coveralls, helmets and air masks that covered their faces. Tubes extended from the sides of the masks and connected to backpack air filters.

Capt. Casey pulled out her handheld display and studied a map for a moment. "You know what's weird, Jace?" she said as she looked at the map.

"What?"

"Captain Jack has this uncanny resemblance to you," she said. "Sometimes when I'm talking to him I forget and I think I'm talking to you. Then I'll snap to and realize it's him, not you, and it really weirds me out. I mean, you're tall, dark and handsome. He's taller, blonde and…"

"Handsomer?"

She looked up at him and studied his face curiously. "No, that's not what I meant. He reminds me of you, but he's different than you in many ways. It's just weird, that's all."

He glanced at her skeptically from the corners of his eyes.

She put her head back on his shoulder and squeezed him around the waist.

The tram clack-clacked over the tracks. The rectangular block buildings outside gave way to metal containerized housing units, called CHUs by their residents. The tram was now traveling through one of the city's residential districts where most of the refugees now resided. In some places the containers were stacked three high. Tube walkways connected them. The CHUs were organized in pods surrounded by blast walls. Block numbers on the cement walls distinguished one pod from another.

Each CHU had at least one window. The metal blinds were drawn shut on most, but some were open. A bluish glow emanated softly through the metal slats. Humans could be seen inside moving back and forth in their small quarters, or sitting in front of glowing screens. Spade saw a man standing at a window looking out at the passing tram. A woman with black hair and fair skin stood behind the man with her arms wrapped around him as she gazed over his shoulder into the gray.

The tram entered a tunnel and shot downward and slowly clacked to a stop. The tram's doors opened with a whush.

"This is our stop," Capt. Casey said.

She stood and pulled Spade by the hand from his seat. They ducked out the tram doors and stepped onto the platform.

They rode an escalator up a narrow, dusty tunnel for what seemed like an eternity. Capt. Casey pulled Spade by the hand down a cramped, dimly lit walkway until they came to a metal ladder that went up a narrow tube. He followed her up the ladder until they came to a small corrugated steel platform where a gray metal door was set into the side of a steel container. Faded white paint was flaking off the side of its banged up walls.

Capt. Casey pulled a set of keys from her utility belt. She stuck a key into the bolt lock and opened the door.

"Home sweet home," she said.

Blast from the past

Her arms were wrapped around him as he lay in the bed in her CHU. The CHU was nothing more than a storage container that had been converted into living quarters.

Its walls were covered in faux wood paneling. A gray fiber carpet covered the floor. Two dressers were pushed up into the corners. A desk faced out the CHU's only window. A tiny bathroom with a cramped shower stall filled a sectioned-off corner across from the bed.

Capt. Casey had added some female touches. Lamps on end tables cast a soft light; a painting of a sunset and sailboats hung from a wall; and tiny glowing aquatic creatures swam in a small aquarium on the desk. The room was free of dust. The bed was warm and cozy.

Capt. Casey's head was on Spade's chest. She gazed out the window into the haze. Red lights blinked on the wings of two aircraft that cruised low over the gray horizon. They were large utility aircraft flying in formation, off to some mine or greenhouse out there.

Capt. Casey watched them until they disappeared into the gray.

"Jace?" she asked.

"Yeah."

"I'm not going to make it off this planet," she said.

"Of course you will," he said.

"I know I'm going to die here. I am at peace with that. I want you to know this because I don't want you to feel responsible when it happens."

"Don't talk like that, Mina. What's come over you, anyway?"

"I have been unable to escape war, no matter how hard I try or how far I flee," she said. "I hate war."

"Nobody likes war, Mina. We have to survive it as best we can. That's all we can do."

"The Craaldans like war," she said. "It's all they live for. They will never stop attacking us. We can't beat them. And we've tried to escape. I don't want to live like this anymore."

"We almost escaped them," he said. "We will escape them. We'll get through this. Just stick with me, Mina. I'm going to find you a planet with oceans and sunsets and warm sand."

She turned and studied his eyes for a moment. "I know what happens next. They will attack us and it's going to be horrible and we will all be killed. But maybe somehow you will survive. If you do, you will leave us and disappear into the Inner Galaxy, searching the void for Dr. Zander."

"Let's find him together," he said. "When we do, we can run away to some friendly star far away from Craaldans and Diocons and their wars. Come with me, Mina."

"I can't do it anymore, Jace. I'm done drifting through the void. This planet is my last stop."

"Mina, don't talk like that. I need you. I can't live without you."

"That's not true," she said. "I know you. You're not the dying type."

She kissed him and held him.

The hours passed as they lay together in the bed in the small CHU. They dozed, slipping in and out of consciousness, talking for a while about their dreams and about people they had known, before falling back asleep in the warmness of the bed.

A loud alarm awoke them and filled the inside of the CHU with a rising and falling blare.

"Indirect fire," Spade said.

"No," Capt. Casey said. "That's the meteor shower alarm." She reached over and turned on a screen on an end table and pulled up a data page.

"Fragments of Biop's moon are going to impact 120 clicks to the southeast of the city," she said. "Looks like some pretty big ones are coming down."

She got up and pulled a sheet over her nude form and stood in front of the window. He got up and put his arms around her and looked out into the gray.

"There," she said, pointing to the southeast.

Eight fireballs with long sparking tails streaked across the gray sky. The blare of the alarm continued to rise and fall.

The meteors shot across the haze and disappeared below the horizon. Sonic booms rocked the CHU. A huge dome of light expanded in the distance at the point of impact, followed by seven more eruptions of fiery light. The haze above the horizon glowed red, green and orange. Lightning lit up the roiling atmosphere and flashed electric webs across the sky.

The floor rumbled as booms rocked Taji City. The blare of the alarm changed tone and beeped rapidly.

Capt. Casey shut the metal blinds. "We better get down," she said.

They both lay on the floor. Rocks began to pepper the outside of their CHU. The rocks hit the metal like heavy rain, tinging and pinging and knocking against the outside walls.

A loud crash shook the CHU as a large rock banged off its metal roof. Then a ball-bearing size rock blasted through the wall with a zing and bounced off the metal door. Gray dust filtered into the CHU through the puncture hole.

Two more ball-bearing size stones punctured through the CHU like bullets, hitting the back wall and bouncing onto the carpet.

"I wanted a top CHU for the view," Capt. Casey said. "Now I understand why people like the lower CHUs behind the blast walls."

Gray dust filtered in through the puncture holes. The acrid stench of the outside atmosphere filled the CHU.

Capt. Casey coughed. She stood up and grabbed a can from one of the dressers. Rocks were still peppering the roof and the outside walls with increasing intensity.

"Mina, get down," Spade said.

"I have to seal the holes," she said.

She attached a nozzle to the can and sprayed foam into the puncture holes, sealing them. She turned on an air filter and then got back down on the floor next to Spade.

A large boom rocked the CHU. A boulder had impacted the surface nearby.

"I hope nobody got hit by that one," Capt. Casey said. "If they did, they're goners for sure."

The sound of rocks pinging against the CHU slowed and then stopped. The citywide intercom system then announced, "All clear, all clear, all clear."

Capt. Casey got up from the floor and opened the metal blinds. One CHU three pods over was on fire. A large stone had punctured the center of its flat roof. The interior was engulfed in blue and orange flame. Black smoke curled up from the puncture hole.

Capt. Casey and Spade caught sight of where the large boulder had landed. It had impacted on a dirt road, leaving a large crater and knocking over several blast walls. A CHU near the crater had been tipped over on its side.

Capt. Casey and Spade got dressed and then cleaned the CHU, wiping up the dust and making repairs to the puncture holes.

"Nice planet," Spade said as they worked.

"It's not exactly the worst planet I've lived on," Capt. Casey said. "But it's not heaven."

Someone knocked on their door. Capt. Casey put down her rag and wiped her hands. She opened the door. A man with spiky blonde hair, almost white in color, stood on the metal platform outside the door. A striking female cyborg with iridescent eyes and silver skin stood behind him. The cyborg wore a cap pulled low over her eyes. Khaki coveralls covered her perfect female form.

"Hi, Joe," Capt. Casey said. "Hi, Genie."

Sgt. First Class Joe Grimes smiled. He looked over his shoulder at his cyborg companion. "Do you smell that, Genie?"

"I sure do," she replied.

"I think I smell…" Grimes looked over the top of Capt. Casey's shoulder. His pale blue eyes met Spade's. "A Vomis nematode."

Spade stepped through the doorway and gave Grimes and Genie big, happy hugs.

The Biop Bop

Capt. Casey, Spade, Grimes and Genie left the CHU and walked together down the cramped tube walkways. They boarded a crowded tram.

Capt. Casey and Genie sat together on a bench talking while Spade and Grimes stood holding onto the hand grips with their gloved hands.

Spade was a head taller than Grimes. Spade was hunched down under the tram's low ceiling. His black hair was slicked back, and his dark eyes had a twinkle as he looked down at his old battle buddy.

Grimes, with his spiky hair and his pale blue eyes, had the rugged face of a battle-hardened soldier. He spoke matter-of-factly to Spade.

"The Craaldans have encamped on Mount Mactus on the opposite side of the planet," Grimes said. "There are about 500 of them. Three hundred are heavy infantry and the rest are the surviving crew from their destroyer. They've got about 50 attack drones that they've salvaged from the wreckage. They've been raiding us, but with these new armor-piercing rounds that Captain Jack supplied us with, we can keep them at arm's distance."

"What are they up to?" Spade asked.

"They are preparing to assault Taji City," Grimes said. "It will come any day now."

"These people don't have a chance against them," Spade said. "Why is everyone hanging around?"

"The locals have lost most of their spaceflight capabilities," Grimes said. "They've put all their effort into surviving on the surface, and their technological development has been dedicated to that. They have a few low-orbit vehicles but are, for the most part, landlocked. But they do have some sophisticated atmospheric flight capabilities. It's how they get around the planet to collect the resources they need to survive here. The few spaceships on the surface are mostly owned by recent arrivals, but there aren't enough to evacuate the planet to make a run for it."

"So they're trapped," Spade said.

"Roger," Grimes replied. "But Genie and I have been working on that. Genie gave the mayor schematics for space transports for evacuation. Genie designed them so they could be constructed with the present resources and labor available here on Biop. We showed Lourdes the plans and she got right on it and put a work crew together to build the ships, but it's going to be several weeks until the transports are ready for lift off."

"Will they be ready before the Craaldans attack?" Spade asked.

"The probability is low," Grimes said. "You know what's funny? After the mayor found out that Genie could draw up plans for constructing just about anything—from cement factories to water purifiers to supercomputers—she began shoveling money at us. Lourdes is taking precautions and planning an evacuation if worse comes to worst, but she's holding out hope that her city can survive an attack."

"The mayor is paying you for access to Genie's hard drive?" Spade asked.

"Roger. That's why Genie and I are lounging in a villa on the north side of town while you and Mina are in a CHU. We've got a wine cellar and a hot tub. I've been trying to convince Mina to move in with us, but she said she wanted her own place. She took a job at the water treatment station to make money for rent, and she's been spending all her free time flying around with Captain Jack looking for survivors from the Escalon crash."

"What are you and Genie doing here, anyway?" Spade asked. "I thought you guys would be halfway to the Calli Sector by now."

"We got here about a month before your arrival. We've been stocking up our ship and retrofitting it for our journey, trying to make it as comfortable as possible before we head out. But now we've got all this cash from the mayor, so basically we've been hanging out, spending T-bucks. We spend most of our time at the wave pool and then hit the night life some. They've got good beer here. The last thing I was expecting was for you guys to show up with a bunch of Craaldans on your tail."

"How'd you and Genie find me and Mina on top of that pyramid?" Spade asked.

"Genie picked up a beacon from a crashed ship and recognized that it was from the Red Wrath. I couldn't believe it. I should have known better than to stick around one place too long. Sooner or later you always turn up."

"So what's the plan, Grimes?" Spade asked him. "Are you and Genie leaving or are you going to hang around for the big show this time?"

"I haven't decided yet," Grimes said. "I'm going to see what Captain Jack says tomorrow night at the town hall meeting. I'll make up my mind from there."

"Captain Jack," Spade repeated.

"This Captain Jack has people believing they have a chance against the Craaldans," Grimes said. "He's got Lourdes believing. He's motivating these people to put up a fight. He's nuts, but at least he's giving them hope."

"Do you remember him from Heliac?" Spade asked.

"Negative," Grimes said. "I know most of the Heliac Rangers I run into. But none of us here on Biop remembers him, which is odd since as a captain he would have been a company commander. Lieutenant Colonel Skyles would have known him for sure. But he's not around."

"Captain Jack might be a phony, then," Spade said.

"It's hard to say," Grimes said. "There were 11 billion humans in the Heliac System. There were 600,000 Heliac Rangers before the Craaldan destruction. I didn't know everybody."

The tram rolled to a stop at a crowded underground platform in a busy section of Taji City. The four friends exited the tram and rode an escalator up a dusty tunnel, stepping off into an open area where corridors branched off in every direction. Spade followed Capt. Casey, Grimes and Genie down a corridor lined with small shops selling all manner of utilitarian contraptions, such as CHU sealant containers, dust vacuums, air masks and air tanks, and heavy outdoor clothing with internal cooling systems for wear out in the thick Bioppian atmosphere. Some shops sold games and different forms of electronic entertainment, such as old movies and electronic books. A plant shop sold ancient Earth flowers and wilted potted plants from Nebas, and other vegetation from planets that humans had colonized or visited.

Humans sat on stools in front of counters at tiny family-owned restaurants that lined the corridor.

Taji City had a lively economy that used a medium of exchange backed by units of water, oxygen and food, called Taji Credits, or T-bucks for short. T-bucks were the dominant currency on the planet and were issued by Mayor Magna. She doled out her T-bucks to the city's residents in exchange for their labor. So long as the food, water and oxygen kept flowing, Mayor Magna and her T-bucks were popular with the city's citizens, who were happy to work for her in her greenhouses, H2O stations and mines.

But with the recent influx of refugees, the city's resources were being strained. To pay for food and shelter, the majority of the new arrivals took out loans from Mayor Magna. To pay back these loans, the mayor put them to work expanding food production and building new residences. The mayor also had plans to use her new surplus labor to more fully exploit the planet's mineral wealth. However, Craaldan raids had started soon after the refugees had arrived and most human effort was being concentrated on defense.

Capt. Casey, Spade, Grimes and Genie walked down a tightly confined corridor until they came to a glowing sign that hung above a shabby entranceway. The red and green letters of the sign read: "The Biop Bop."

Fliers advertising various music bands were plastered around the doorway.

They walked through the entranceway into a large darkened room with a low ceiling. Glowing faux stars decorated the ceiling and walls. A live band played up on a stage in front of an empty floor. Humans ate meals and sipped drinks around tables.

Spade followed his friends to the bar where Dr. Ebos sat on a barstool eating a plate of synthetic salad. His red eyepieces glowed in the dim light. He looked up from his plate and smiled when he recognized them.

"Would you like a beer, Captain Spade?" Ebos asked.

"Do Vacterian women emit fungal spores?" Spade answered.

"They most assuredly do," Ebos said. "Bartender, four beers. This round is on me."

The place started to fill with humans who crowded around the bar. Big Megalans were hunched down under the low ceiling. Paltrans moved about with their limbs encased in mechanical prosthetics and their eyes covered with glowing lenses. Heliac humans, both male and female, looked tough and fit and like soldiers even while wearing civilian attire and not their typical uniforms or armor. Gaunt space drifters mingled with pale Escalonians. Bearded Taji City men and tall Taji City women made up the majority of the crowd. The brown skinned, tawny haired Taji City women mingled with the Heliac males, but especially gravitated toward the big Megalan men.

The band up on the stage was made up of four bearded locals. They were somewhat unrehearsed and a little heavy on the drums and synthesizer.

"Don't worry," Dr. Ebos said. "Doxy is up next."

The local band wrapped things up to sporadic applause from the crowd. The band packed up its gear and stepped off the stage.

The next band walked onto the stage. Spade immediately recognized all the band members. Doxy adjusted the microphone stand. Her stringy blonde hair fell over her fair face. She was dressed like a Taji City resident, wearing heavy boots and khaki cargo pants. The sleeves on her utility shirt were torn off at the shoulder, revealing her ivory arms. Tanaka was squatting down on the stage—his glowing green lenses stared into an amplifier that he was fine tuning. He was carrying an electric guitar on his back. Vomica Nux adjusted her microphone. The lights shone off her rainbow colored hair, highlighting its purple tint on her crown. She carried a bass guitar. On the drums was Doxy's silver cyborg companion. He sat with a straight back and twirled his drumsticks like a pro.

"Testing, testing, one two three, testing," Doxy said softly into the microphone.

Tanaka looked at her and gave her a thumbs up.

"Hello, Taji City," Doxy said to the crowd. "I'm Doxy and these are the Space Drifters. We're your entertainment for the evening."

"And thus," Dr. Ebos said with great anticipation as his red eyepieces glowed brightly, "the night begins."

Rock star

Doxy spoke softly, gripping the microphone with two hands while looking down at her feet. She introduced her band. People sat at their tables eating, or mingled at the bar.

Then the cyborg started off with a thumping drumbeat. Vomica stepped up and joined in on the bass. Skinny Tanaka was looking down at his guitar through his green eyepieces. He stood perfectly still as his long skinny fingers began playing his instrument with incredible skill. Vomica watched him and smiled, visibly enjoying the rhythms he was creating while she strummed along with her bass.

Doxy began singing a melody about butterflies and rainbows and hummingbirds and a magical lover who had obviously knocked her socks off in more ways than one.

"She's got a beautiful voice," Capt. Casey said to Spade. "You guys dated, right?"

"We had a fling. She dumped me for that cyborg drummer."

"Serves you right," Capt. Casey said.

The music was pumping and the crowd was now on its feet and gathered in front of the stage. More humans filed into the Biop Bop.

The crowd was hopping to the cyborg's beats. Tanaka's riffs, Doxy's catchy melodies, and Vomica singing back up put everyone in high spirits. The drinks flowed and the floor in front of the stage grew crowded with bodies that swayed together under Doxy's spell.

Spade, Capt. Casey, Grimes and Genie moved up through the crowd. Heads bobbed and bodies moved to the rhythms of Doxy and the Space Drifters.

"These guys rock," Grimes said over the music. "Genie, can you play the drums like that?"

"Yes, but I prefer the cello," Genie said.

Doxy shifted gears and the music slowed. She began singing a haunting song about a human longing for a companion on a lonely space station.

Spade returned from the bar with drinks and handed them to Capt. Casey, Grimes and Genie. Genie had her arms over Grimes' shoulders and she was smiling mischievously while telling him something. Grimes smiled broadly and laughed and then said something into her ear.

"Aren't they romantic," Capt. Casey said, sipping her drink. "Get a room," she called over to them, "or I'm gonna barf."

Spade pulled Capt. Casey close to him and he held her as they swayed to the music with the crowd.

"Genie learned how to make him laugh," Capt. Casey said. "That was the one advantage I had over her with Joe. She used to be so serious, and I could always make that dumbbell smile."

"Now you're the serious one," Spade said.

"Don't worry about me, Jace."

She looked up at him in the dark. The faux stars set in the ceiling glowed above him. The band played and Doxy sang her sad melody.

When the song finished, Doxy looked out into the crowd, searching for someone. "Captain Casey?" she said into the microphone. "Mina, are you out there?"

Everyone looked around. A light shone down from above the stage onto Capt. Casey.

"Mina," Doxy said. "Will you sing us a song? That song you sometimes sang on Escalon Station. You know the one."

Capt. Casey blushed and shook her head, but the crowd clapped and urged her on.

"Please, Mina," Doxy said. "I love that song."

Doxy reached her hand down. Capt. Casey was reluctant but Spade gave her a shove and she walked over and took Doxy's hand and jumped up on the stage. Doxy smiled at her.

"I hate you, Doxy," Capt. Casey said into the microphone.

Doxy moved over to the keyboards and the band began to play. Capt. Casey sang about a love lost on a beautiful planet that had pink skies and a purple sea.

She stood under the lights in her form-fitting black coveralls with her M2 pistol strapped to her side. She ran her hand through her cropped black hair and closed her dark eyes for a moment as she sang. She sang that even if the silence were to take her, her love would live on forever and ever.

She opened her eyes and the song got faster and the crowd got into it, jumping up and down as she sang. Spade caught her eye and he winked and she smiled as she sang.

She sang about a lover who would live forever because he never gave up and never gave in no matter what the universe threw at him. That's what she loved about him; the chorus repeated, as the crowd chanted along to her words. The song ended on an upbeat note and the crowd broke into loud applause. Capt. Casey jumped down from the stage and ran up to Spade.

"Wow," Doxy said into the microphone. "Is she hot, or what?" The crowd hooted and whistled. "You're a rock star, Mina."

Doxy and the band broke into a fast-paced song that kept the crowd jumping. The floor started shaking when two big Megalan females began stomping their feet. Vomica walked back and forth on the stage, bobbing her head while playing her bass.

Capt. Casey and Spade moved into a dark corner. She held him tightly in the dark as they watched the crowd while the band played up on the stage.

"Tell the truth, Jace," Capt. Casey said. "You put her up to that, right?"

"I ain't telling," he said.

She hugged him tightly and looked up at him. "I love you," she said.

"You better."

They watched the show from their dark corner.

A big Megalan woman stumbled through the crowd, which parted in front of her. The huge woman was hunched down under the ceiling. She bumped people as she lumbered across the floor.

"Hey, watch it, beefcakes," an annoyed Taji City female said.

The big Megalan woman ignored her and stumbled up to Capt. Casey and Spade.

"Mina, that was so cool," she said in a hoarse, husky voice. "You are so amazing."

Capt. Casey and Spade recognized her in the dark by her square jaw and long pony tail that flopped over her bulging shoulder. It was Mingus. Her eye shadow was smeared across a cheek.

"You are so gorgeous, Mina," Mingus said. "That song was awesome. I swear, Jace is so lucky to have you. I hope he knows how lucky he is. He better never leave you again, Mina. I swear, he better never let you go if he knows what's good in this universe."

She gave Capt. Casey a crushing bear hug. Then she turned to Spade.

She started to cry. "Oh, Jace. I'm drunk. I am so drunk."

She stood in front of Spade in the dark with her eyes closed and she started sobbing. She blubbered loudly and the tears rolled down her cheeks.

"I'm so drunk, Jace."

Spade took her big hand. "I'm sorry about Leonard," he said. "Is there anything I can do? Tell me, Mingus."

She pulled her hand away and wiped the tears from her cheeks and shook her head no. She looked at Capt. Casey and leaned down and gave her another hug.

"Can I buy you a drink, Mina?" Mingus said. "I want to buy you a drink."

A wiry man wearing a tight shirt that revealed his cut muscles walked up in the dark. Capt. Casey and Spade recognized him. They had seen him fight in a combatives tournament on Gallos. His name was Ripper and he was a Heliac Special

Forces soldier who had been in Lt. Col. Skyles' work battalion on Escalon Station.

"Mingus," Ripper said. "You've had too much to drink. I'm taking you back to your CHU."

Ripper took Mingus' big hand and nodded at Capt. Casey and Spade. Mingus turned and gave Ripper a crushing hug. "I'm going to love you forever, Ripper," she blubbered. "Even if the silence takes me, I will love you until the end of time!"

Ripper winked at Spade and led Mingus by the hand out of the Biop Bop.

"If I know Mingus, she gets frisky after a few drinks," Spade said. "She's going to tear that man apart tonight."

"Good thing he's a combatives expert," Capt. Casey said. "He's going to need all his skills to survive a night with that woman."

They stood together in the dark and watched the show. Spade held Capt. Casey as Doxy sang. He watched Tanaka up on the stage, and thought about Mingus and about his former copilot Leonard Brute.

The silence had taken old Brute. He and Brute had not always gotten along, but big Leonard Brute was a good man, and Spade regretted not doing more to get him off Escalon Station alive. He had let the man down twice.

There were so many who had relied on him but didn't make it off Escalon. Brute was one more in a long line of humans he had known who were no longer with him.

Spade squeezed Capt. Casey and held her tight. She snuggled up to him in his arms.

"Hey, look," she said. "There's Captain Jack."

Capt. Jack Winner was at the bar talking with Dr. Ebos. A tall woman approached them. She had brown skin and a long tight braid of black hair that fell down her back. She handed Capt. Jack a drink and spoke into his ear, placing her palm on his back, rubbing it up and down.

"Who's that woman?" Spade asked.

"That's Lourdes Magna, the mayor of Taji City," Capt. Casey answered. "It looks like Captain Jack and Lourdes have gotten to know each other."

Political machine

He walked behind her as she entered a cavernous aircraft hangar. Nearly all the city had assembled here under its high ceiling, which was crisscrossed with steel girders and air ducts. An immense metal fan turned slowly above a stage, circulating air through the vast structure.

The hangar was enormous. Thousands of the city's residents were inside seated in fold-out chairs that faced the empty stage at the far end of the interior of the huge metal building. Capt. Casey and Spade walked past the disassembled hulks of Bioppian aircraft that had been moved to the back of the hangar to make room for so many humans.

They were all here; locals and refugees, at the largest assembly since the beginning of the human settlement of Biop three hundred Earth years ago.

The hangar was packed and as warm as a hothouse. Conversation buzzed. Human voices echoed off the giant metal walls and girders. Taji City locals and the new arrivals spoke to each other in animated debate as they sat in their chairs or stood in clusters in the aisles.

Capt. Casey and Spade moved through the crowded aisles. The stage was distant and could barely be seen over the heads of so many people. The big bodies of Megalans protruded up from the mass of humanity. Capt. Casey and Spade found two open chairs and took a seat in the dense, elbow-to-elbow audience.

"I spent four nights in this hangar after Joe and Genie rescued us off the top of that pyramid," Capt. Casey said. "While you were in the medical clinic, I was sleeping in a cot in here until Mayor Magna got us CHUs on the south side of town."

At the far end of the hangar, a skinny bearded man at a table in front of the stage spoke into a microphone.

"Please rise for the mayor of Taji City and the Board of Supervisors."

Mayor Lourdes Magna walked up the steps onto the stage, followed by four tall women. The mayor was dressed in a white shirt and white slacks while the Supervisors wore black cargo pants and utility shirts. The mayor sat at a table at the center of the stage while the four Supervisors sat at a table to her right.

"Please be seated," Mayor Magna said into her microphone.

A great rustling and commotion filled the humid hangar as everyone took their seats.

"Vice Mayor Malva Fung," the bearded man said.

"Here," said a stern-faced woman at the table.

"Supervisor Halex Page."

"Here," said the grave woman next to her.

"Supervisor Regina Vulgaris."

"Here."

"Supervisor Nector Zink."

"Here."

"Mayor Lourdes Magna."

"For the record, Tom, we're all here," Mayor Magna said. Her voice carried through the enormous hangar and reverberated with feedback over speakers placed up on girders.

She looked at the Supervisors. "Do any members of the board have opening comments before we begin?"

The Supervisors shook their heads as they adjusted their clothing or jotted down notes. Their faces carried expressions of seriousness.

"I have something to say," Mayor Magna said.

She looked out at the crowd. Her severe face, with its high cheekbones and intense eyes, carried an expression that underscored the gravity of this meeting. Her dark eyes studied the faces of the people assembled in front of her. She was dressed in a tight white long-sleeve shirt with an open collar that revealed the smooth brown skin of her chest. Her black hair was pulled back into a tight braid that ran down her back.

She leaned into the microphone. "I was born on this planet," she began. "I've lived here all my life. I've never left it."

She paused for a moment and flipped pages on a notepad before returning her gaze to the audience.

"Over the years, I have often heard new arrivals complain about Taji City and about Biop. I have heard them say that our air is too dusty. I have heard them say our food is too greasy and our homes are too plain. Maybe it's true. I wouldn't know any better because Biop is all I know. Taji City is my home. I have spent my life improving this town and making it a place where we can live prosperous lives without want for air, water, food and shelter. I have worked hard. Every last citizen of Taji City has worked hard."

The mayor stood up from her chair and walked to the edge of the stage.

She was a stunning woman, tall and athletic with radiant brown skin and shining ebony hair. She stood before them in her boots and white slacks and tight white shirt. Her large dark eyes looked out at them as she held the microphone in one hand. She stood in thought for a moment.

"In all my years, there has never been a time on Biop like the present. Our lives have been turned upside down. Many of you are fearful. Some of you are angry. You have not been happy with our new guests. You think they have brought disaster upon us. I share these thoughts and emotions. But the events that have brought us to this point cannot be undone."

She looked out at them, searching their faces.

"You all know me. I know you. I trust you and believe in you. Now trust in me and hear me out. Now is the time to put our differences aside and look forward. We must join together to save Taji City. These are desperate times, it is true. But I will do everything in my power to get us through them."

Mayor Magna paused for a moment and walked up and down the edge of the stage.

"I need all of you to prepare yourselves for more difficulties. Over the last several hours, Craaldan raiders have destroyed the Tasra Greenhouse Complex, the Malsu Mine Base and the Baruz Water Station. The Halill Nuclear Power Plant may be the next to fall."

This revelation caused a great commotion in the hangar as the humans reacted with surprise and worry.

"We have suffered casualties in these raids," the mayor said. "For now, no new supplies will be entering Taji City from the outside. Food and water must be conserved. This will be achieved through rationing. Each person will receive sufficient supplies to sustain themselves. I expect your full cooperation until the threat has passed."

The mayor walked back to her chair and sat down. She looked at her notes for a moment and then leaned into the microphone. "Vice Mayor Fung. What is the next item on the agenda?"

"The matter at hand for discussion is the defense of the city," Fung said.

Malva Fung's skin was also a radiant brown, but she had a shock of tawny hair that flowed wildly over her shoulders and down her back.

"We must be prepared for the Craaldan attack if and when it comes," Fung said. "For that, we need a military commander. Several names have been put forward; however, all but two have dropped out. Captain Jack Winner and Captain Jace Spade are the two remaining candidates. At this point, we have heard nothing from Captain Spade."

The mayor looked out at the crowd. "Captain Spade, are you present?"

Capt. Casey elbowed Spade in the ribs.

"Captain Jace Spade?" the mayor repeated. "Are you here?"

Spade stood up. "Right here," he called out over the crowd to the distant stage.

A great rustling filled the hangar as all eyes turned to Spade.

"Step forward so I can see you," the mayor said.

Spade squeezed past the humans in his row and then walked toward her down the aisle for what seemed like an eternity. He vaulted up onto the stage and stood in front of the mayor and the Board of Supervisors.

The severe-looking women of the board looked him up and down. The mayor gazed at him with her steely dark eyes for a long moment. Then she leaned into her microphone.

"You are a fine looking man," she said.

"You're not so bad yourself," he said.

"Please tell us, Captain Spade, why we should select you to lead the defense of Taji City."

The bearded clerk climbed up on the stage and handed Spade a microphone. Spade turned and faced the crowd.

All eyes were on him. Many had their arms crossed over their chests. Some shook their heads disapprovingly. Others looked away.

He looked out at them. There were thousands in this hangar. He could hear them grumbling. It was becoming evident to him that he was facing a hostile crowd.

In the front row looking up at him expectantly was Capt. Jack Winner. Sitting next to Capt. Jack was Dr. Ebos.

Ebos leaned over and said something in Capt. Jack's ear. The tall, blonde man in the blue flight suit nodded and then they both looked up at Spade waiting for him to speak.

Capt. Casey stood in the aisle looking up at Spade. She waved and smiled hopefully. She nodded for him to begin.

Dark horse

"I am Captain Jace Spade, commander of the Red Wrath."

His voice echoed through the vast hangar as he spoke to the crowd of thousands.

"I was also the commander of Escalon Station up until recently."

Capt. Casey stood in the aisle looking up at him, her arms hugging her own chest as she watched him.

"You're going to have to bear with me, folks. I wasn't prepared to speak here tonight."

He gathered his thoughts as he stood at the front of the stage as thousands of onlookers seated before him waited silently. "I got to know a good many of you on Escalon. We came together on that station during some hard times and I think we ran a tight ship. If you want to know the truth, the times we had together on Escalon were some of the best I have known since my home world was destroyed decades ago."

"Sit down, Spade!" a voice yelled out from the crowd.

Spade looked out at the audience but couldn't pinpoint the source of the yell. He continued.

"As your leader, I learned a lot about you, a lot about myself, about human nature in general, and about all the complexities that come with leadership and with being a commander."

"You had your chance to lead!" another voice called out. "You failed!"

Captain Casey looked over her shoulder searching for the source of the call. Spade's eyes fell on Capt. Jack, who was watching him closely. Spade got the feeling that Capt. Jack was assessing his reaction to the hecklers.

Spade looked out at a hostile audience and took a deep breath.

"We're all friends here. I consider all of you my friends," Spade said. "Now hear me out."

Spade looked out and sighted Mingus watching him. She looked apprehensive. He saw Tanaka in the crowd seated next to Vomica Nux. Tanaka had his arms crossed over his chest as he watched Spade through his glowing green eyepieces. He had a look of disapproval on his face. But Vomica sat with a straight back and watched him hopefully. Spade smiled at her and she smiled back.

"I've been in a few scrapes in my time and I've got some ideas on how we can get out of this predicament we've found ourselves in."

"Why are you here?" another voice yelled out. "A captain is supposed to go down with the ship!"

"He did go down with the ship!" Capt. Casey yelled back. "Let him speak!"

"Things went bad real quick up there," Spade said. "I wish I could have done things differently. I keep going over it in my mind. I did my best. I hope you understand that."

"Take a seat already!" a voice called out.

Mayor Magna banged a gavel three times.

Spade turned around and faced the mayor and the board. "Mayor Magna, Board of Supervisors." He turned and faced the crowd. "Citizens of Taji City. You have shown us hospitality during a dark time for us. You have taken us in at our time of need. I will repay you with anything you ask. If you need a military commander, I can be that person. I am at your service."

"No thanks!" a voice called out.

"Captain Spade," Mayor Magna said into the microphone. "What is your plan to defend the city?"

Spade walked up and down the stage in thought. He saw Capt. Jack from the corner of his eye. The tall man was jotting notes in an electronic tablet.

"From what I've been able to gather, the Craaldans are about 500 strong on the surface," Spade said. "We have them outnumbered, but they know they've got us outgunned and they've got us outmatched in a straight up fight. Our best bet is to prepare a strong defense on their most likely avenue of approach, which is the eastern plain. When they make their initial foray, we throw nukes at them so they keep their distance. In the meantime, we've got to finish constructing the evacuation transports. We need to double the construction efforts before the Craaldans can breach the city walls."

"Your plan is to stall for time so we can evacuate the planet?" Mayor Magna asked.

"Roger," Spade said. "It's the best hope we have of survival. If we slug it out with them in the city, we will suffer heavy casualties with a low probability of victory. And if we were to defeat them, it would come at great loss of life. All we will get from a victory is a visit from their reinforcements—a brigade at the minimum, and there's no way we can stand up to that."

"Reinforcements?" Mayor Magna asked.

"My estimate is that the Craaldans have already set up a beacon on that mountain they've encamped on, and their higher command is aware of the situation here. They follow a strict top-down hierarchy and are predictable in that regard. Our best bet is to hold them off as best we can until our evacuation spacecraft are built. When they are ready, we pop smoke before more of those butchers drop in on us."

"Where will we go?" the mayor asked.

"We skirt the galaxy perimeter for as long as our supplies hold out, on the lookout for a safe solar system where we can acquire the resources we need to build a ship for a deep space voyage. Then we head out for the Calli Sector."

"You are asking us to drift through the void for the rest of our lives?" Mayor Magna asked.

"It's about a thousand Earth-year voyage to the Calli Sector. It will be a long journey, but there are habitable worlds out there, and we would be out of reach of the wars of the Inner Galaxy."

The Supervisors talked amongst themselves at their table. Mayor Magna looked at Spade for a moment in contemplation. She jotted down some notes.

"Thank you for your time, Captain Spade," Mayor Magna said, without looking up.

A low buzz of conversation filled the hangar as the humans discussed Spade's pitch. He looked down from the stage at Capt. Casey, whose arms were still tightly crossed over her chest. She had a hopeful smile on her face, but it was tinged with worry.

Spade stood in front of the mass of humanity assembled before him. He began to speak again.

"You know that I am not perfect," he said to the crowd. "I am human and I make mistakes. But know that I will never give up on you. I would give my life if it means your survival. You have my word on that. Don't give up on me. Follow me. I will find a friendly star and take you there."

"You have had your say, Captain Spade," the mayor said.

"Understand that I carry your best interests in my heart. I want you to get through this. I want it more than you could ever know."

"Your time is up, Captain Spade," Mayor Magna said. "Please take a seat."

Spade jumped down from the stage and walked up to Capt. Casey. She took his hand and they walked down the aisle back to their seats.

"You said you would give your life for them," Capt. Casey said.

"I did," he said.

Mayor Magna banged her gavel three times.

"Captain Jack Winner," she said. "Come forward."

Landslide

Capt. Jack stood from his chair and strode to the stage. He jumped up onto the platform and stood tall in his blue flight suit and looked out at the vast audience. His hair was golden blonde and his eyes were a piercing blue.

Some in the audience clapped and others whistled.

"We heard what Captain Spade had to say," Mayor Magna said into her microphone. "It's your turn."

Capt. Jack nodded at her and turned to the crowd.

"I am Captain Jack Winner, commander of the Blue Falcon."

People clapped and hooted. Capt. Jack raised his hand, patting it downward to calm them, before bowing his head pensively.

"Before I begin, I want to say thank you to Captain Spade for his willingness to take on the burden of leadership in these uncertain times. First off, I want everyone here tonight to know that my purpose is not to prove to you through rhetoric that I am a better man than Captain Spade, or that I am somehow a superior commander on the battlefield. Captain Spade is a capable leader who was loved by most who knew him on Escalon Station. The fact that Escalon was destroyed should not cause you to lose confidence in his ability as a leader or lose respect for his judgment. We all know that the Craaldan is a formidable foe. What happened to Escalon was a tragedy and was no fault of his.

"My purpose here tonight is to offer you a choice. It is up to you to choose whether you want to follow Captain Spade, and give up on Taji City and on your homes and on all that you have built here, and flee forever into the cold, unforgiving dark."

All eyes were on the tall man standing on the stage. Everyone listened intently. Mayor Magna sat in her chair with her elbow on the table and her chin in the palm of her hand as she listened to him.

"Or you can choose my way."

Capt. Casey sat next to Spade and watched Capt. Jack with puzzled curiosity.

"It's strange," Capt. Casey said. "His mannerisms. The way he carries himself. That look in his eye. It reminds me of you. I mean, I just watched you up there and now he's up there. I can't quite put my finger on it. It's weird."

"What are you trying to say?" Spade asked her.

"I don't know. I get this feeling in my bones when he talks. It's the same feeling I get from you."

Spade raised an eyebrow and looked at her from the corner of his eye.

"It's a weird resemblance is all I'm saying," she said. "But his hands are thicker, and his boot size is much larger. His nose and ears are fuller. It's like he's a composite of you and someone else. I'm not sure who."

"He doesn't look like me at all," Spade said. "You're imagining things."

"Maybe you're right," she said. "Forget it."

Capt. Jack strode up and down the edge of the stage. "We humans have been beat down," he said. "We've been herded like livestock and hunted like beasts. We've been chased off just about every planet we've set foot on.

"In our time, we've had our share of sorrow. We've all lost family. We've all lost friends. We've been hurt and humiliated. We have all suffered."

He stopped at the center of the stage and looked out at them with flashing blue eyes.

"I say enough!"

He paused for a long moment and bowed his head. He turned and continued to pace the edge of the stage.

"Captain Spade said the probability of victory here is low, and that even if we were to repel the Craaldan aggressor, we would be destroyed by more numerous reinforcements.

"Captain Spade is wrong on both counts. You see, I have just returned from the Inner Galaxy where I witnessed for myself the cataclysmic war that is raging there. The Craaldan is being assaulted on all fronts by the mighty Diocon Empire. The Inner Galaxy is in turmoil and the Craaldan is on the receiving end of the Diocon blade. The Craaldan Empire has its hands full and cannot afford to reinforce a small shipwrecked crew at the far edge of the galaxy, and this gives us our opening. I've got an ace card up my sleeve, my friends."

Capt. Jack stopped pacing.

"I have seen battle. I have served with good soldiers and I have served with bad. I've seen cities rise and I've seen them fall.

"What I see here in Taji City tonight are the best of our species—pioneers, adventurers, soldiers—the builders of a new civilization. I see survivors. You here are a heroic people on the verge of greatness, if you would just make the decision not to turn and run, but to stand up and fight."

His eyes were alight.

Mayor Magna was watching him closely. Vice Mayor Fung followed along to his words with nods of approval. Supervisor Vulgaris appeared enthralled.

"People of Escalon, you have tried to escape the Craaldan war machine but it pursued you here to destroy you. People of Biop, you have built the beginnings of a great city, but all your work is threatened by a handful of shipwrecked cutthroats. If you turn and run, the Craaldan will pursue you relentlessly in his mission to exterminate you. I say we make a stand here and fight them! This is a time to stand tall and be bold!"

Capt. Jack paused for a long moment. He paced the stage.

"I understand that some of you want to flee. There is no shame in that. Nobody here is going to stop you if you have the means to leave. But for those of you who are tired of running, tired of being stalked by these inhuman killers, tired of drifting aimlessly through the void, stay here with me. A victory now will secure this planet for us at a time when the Craaldan Empire is collapsing in on itself in a destructive war. We can achieve victory here. I know it."

He stood at the center of the stage. His piercing blue eyes looked out at them, studying their faces.

"When I look out at you now, I see fighters and survivors and a people who can win this battle if they would just seize the moment. I feel it in every fiber of my being. I have weapons that can give us the edge we have always wanted against them. We have them outnumbered. We can save this city."

Mayor Magna watched him intently.

"But be forewarned. They will come at us hard. That is their nature. We must prepare ourselves. There is no time to rest, no room for second best. This is a case of do or die. We have to hang tough with an iron will and a steely resolve and face down the Craaldan threat. More than that, we need a plan and we need leadership. I can provide that for you. The Craaldan can be defeated. I've seen it done. Follow me, and there'll be some action spent."

He looked down out at them and stood tall in a posture that exuded strength and total confidence. "Let me tell you this, if the Craaldan thinks I'll sit around waiting for him to put a bayonet in my brain, he better think again. He's got another thing coming.

"People of Taji City, this is where the talking ends. I ask you to make your choice. Don't give in. Defend your homes. Stand tall with me and I swear to you that I will not rest, I will not doubt, I will not falter, until every Craaldan on this planet is a smoldering corpse.

"People of Taji City, this is a time for heroic action! This is a time for heroes! This is your time! Stand with me and fight!"

"I'm with you Captain Jack," a voice called out from the audience.

"We can do it!" someone said.

"Hear! Hear!"

Capt. Jack turned and looked at Mayor Magna. "Make your choice."

"Hey, hey Captain Jack!"

They repeated his name. A chant filled the cavernous hangar. "Captain Jack! Captain Jack! Captain Jack!"

They hooted and hollered and stomped their boots on the cement floor.

Mayor Magna banged her gavel three times, but the chanting continued. She banged her gavel again and again.

Capt. Jack stood in front of them smiling triumphantly.

A battle scarred Heliac Ranger jumped up on the stage and wrapped an arm around Capt. Jack and pumped his fist. Another Ranger took the stage and did the same. The crowd mobbed the stage and lifted him from his feet.

"Take your seats!" Mayor Magna said into the microphone. She banged her gavel until the crowd calmed and order was eventually restored.

"He's got a band of partisans," Capt. Casey said.

On the hangar wall behind the stage, a large screen came alight. One half of the screen depicted the face of Captain Jack and the other of Captain Spade.

The bearded clerk spoke into the microphone. "The Mayor and the Board of Supervisors will select a commander to take charge of the defense of Taji City against the Craaldan aggressors. A simple majority determines the winner. Madam Mayor, Honorable Supervisors, please cast your vote."

The mayor and the supervisors pressed buttons in front of them on their tables. Up on the screen, five green checkmarks appeared under the face of Capt. Jack Winner.

The crowd erupted in cheers.

"Unanimous," Capt. Casey said.

"Not a single vote," Capt. Spade said.

She looked over at Spade seated next to her. He displayed no emotion as he watched the action at the front of the hangar. She squeezed his knee.

A mob formed around the new military commander of Taji City. The hangar shook as they chanted, "Captain Jack! Captain Jack! Captain Jack!"

The Plunge

Spade and Capt. Casey rode a tram through Taji City. The tram clack-clacked over the tracks as it sped through the thick gray haze. The cityscape outside was a jumbled mix of cement residential dwellings and metal CHUs that were organized in pods sectioned off by wind-scoured blast walls.

Tube walkways connected the buildings. Spindly radio antennae punctuated the skyline. Large, cylindrical water towers stood in the corners of the pods. Dominating the cityscape in this section of town was a large warehouse-like building. It was a DFAC that served the residents of this neighborhood.

Six-wheeled vehicles sped over the gravel roads that ran between high blast walls. Humans wearing air masks and heavy outdoor gear sat in the rugged looking vehicles as they zipped up and down the roads through the dusty, gray haze.

The tram sped through a section of town where the pods enclosed cement dwellings. The flat-roofed structures were quite large, a few reaching three stories high.

The tram entered a tunnel before slowing to a stop at a platform. The doors whushed open.

A handful of passengers entered the car. Sgt. Grimes and Genie stepped aboard and greeted Capt. Casey and Spade with smiles and hellos. Grimes and Genie sat on the bench across from Capt. Casey and Spade as the tram rolled forward.

Genie wore fingerless black gloves, black boots and a tan cap pulled low over her iridescent eyes. Her form-fitting black shirt and tight pants outlined her drop-dead figure.

Genie looked at Capt. Spade with concern. "Are you feeling OK, Captain Spade?" she asked.

"I'm fine," Spade said.

"You look glum," Grimes said.

"He feels rejected," Capt. Casey said.

"You win some, you lose some," Spade said.

"You're better off not leading this cluster," Grimes said. "Why did you want to be in charge of a backwater military on a dead planet, anyway? It's not your style."

"Yes, Captain Spade has always been the lone wolf," Genie said. "The pack only slows him down."

"You guys aren't making me feel any better," Spade said.

"Will you now continue your search for Dr. Zander?" Genie asked.

Spade looked at Capt. Casey sitting next to him. "No," he said.

Grimes squinted his pale blue eyes and studied Spade curiously. "Hmm. I think he's serious about you, Mina. I saw it back on Gallos and I see it now."

"When he figured out he couldn't have Genie back, he settled for me," Capt. Casey said.

"Don't be mean, Mina," Spade said.

"Did you know he asked me to marry him?" Capt. Casey said.

Genie's iridescent eyes were alight. "Mina, that is wonderful news."

"Our lone wolf wants a mate?" Grimes said. "Now I've heard everything."

"Jace is not a lone wolf," Capt. Casey said. "He's more a Labrador Retriever, or a German Shepherd."

"Did you say yes?" Genie asked her.

"Not yet," Capt. Casey said. "I'm making him sweat it out."

"Joe hasn't asked me to marry him," Genie said.

"So what's the hold up, Joe?" Capt. Casey asked him.

Grimes waved his hand across his throat signaling for Capt. Casey to cut her line of questioning. He looked at Genie from the corner of his eye with an uncertain smile.

Genie crossed her legs and folded her arms over her chest. "Joe is skilled in many areas, romance not being one of them," she said.

The tram approached the edge of the city and then sped out a gate. The gray haze was thick and visibility was low as the tram clacked on the tracks as it raced through a junkyard filled with broken down vehicles, wrecked aircraft and half-collapsed containers. The tram shot out of the junkyard and onto a featureless plain. The tram followed tracks that extended into the thick gray haze that saturated everything on this dusty, monochromatic world.

"I've noticed you two are not planning to depart Taji City any time soon," Spade said.

"We've decided to stick around and see how it goes," Grimes said.

"I'll tell you right now how it goes, Grimes," Spade said. "The Craaldans are going to level this place."

"That was my thinking until recently," Grimes said. "But Captain Jack has made me a believer. I think we can win this time, Spade. We've got the numbers and the firepower. We can really stick it to them and give those Craaldan killers a taste of their own medicine for once."

"He's brainwashed you," Spade said. "Tell him, Genie."

"I estimate the probability of a victory over the Craaldan force on Biop at 58 percent," Genie said. "But your point that the enemy will soon send reinforcements is accurate, in my estimation."

"Captain Jack asked me to be an infantry training instructor," Grimes said. "I've accepted. Genie and I are going to train up these yokels and then we're going to lock and load and kick some Craaldan ass."

"You're serious," Capt. Casey said. "I thought you two were dead set on voyaging to the Calli Sector."

"We are," Grimes said. "But this is my last chance for a little payback for what they did to Heliac, for what they did to me when I was their prisoner. I've heard Captain Jack's plan and it's doable."

"You are taking a gamble with your life when you could be on your way, safe and sound," Capt. Casey said.

"Those Craaldans have beat us down for so long, Mina. If I can be part of just one victory over them, I can leave this place with my head held high. If that comes to pass, I will hold that feeling with me for the rest of my days."

The tram slowed as it approached a rocky outcropping. It clacked around boulders and up an incline before coming over a ridge and then descending into a large crater. At the center of the crater's floor was an enormous concrete dome.

The tram sped across the crater floor toward the dome. Several six-wheeled vehicles were parked in a gravel parking lot in front of the huge structure. A few aircraft were parked on a landing pad nearby. Walkways from the parking lot and the landing pad led to an entranceway in the dome. Above the entranceway were large cement letters that read: "The Plunge."

The tram clack-clacked into a tunnel that dropped under the dome.

The tram slowed and came to a stop at a platform. The doors whushed open and the four friends exited with the other passengers. They crossed the platform and walked through glass doors and into the interior of the dome.

Inside was an enormous deep water pool that seemed as large as a small sea. The pool filled nearly the entire interior of the dome. Lamps embedded in the ceiling cast light that reflected and refracted off the clear, turquoise water. Shimmering reflections of light danced across the dome's curved cement walls.

The air inside the dome was humid and smelled of chlorine. Splashes and human voices echoed through the structure's hollow interior.

Humans walked on the cement floor in bare feet near the water's edge. The men wore swim trunks. The women wore bikinis or one-piece bathing suits.

Some humans were carrying surfboards. Muscular Megalans carried longboards. A few humans were swimming or floating in the water. The pool was about a thousand yards across to the far end of the dome.

"This seems like your kind of place," Spade said to Capt. Casey.

"It's almost as cool as the real thing," she replied. "It's too bad the mayor is closing it down due to the planetary crisis."

Capt. Casey placed her bag on a bench and then kicked off her boots. She unzipped the back of her coveralls and slipped out of them, revealing a slick black bikini that she had been wearing under her clothes.

She stood in front of them in her bikini with her hands on her hips.

Grimes and Genie whistled enthusiastically. Spade smiled at her and shook his head.

"The surfboard shack is over there," she said. "Come on, guys. Hurry up. Let's go surfing."

Surf City

The four friends stood in their swimsuits on a peninsula of cement that extended out into the glassy water. They held surfboards under their arms.

Grimes' spiky, platinum blonde hair and pale blue eyes made him look every bit the surfer dude as he stood in his trunks with his board under his arm. However, his wiry torso was striped with scar tissue from war wounds and torture sessions with his Craaldan captors, marking him for all to see as a soldier who had survived the horrors of war.

Genie stood next to him in a blue bikini holding her surfboard. Her sleek, silver form was a perfect vision of female sexuality, custom designed by her makers to get a rise out of the human male. Men who caught sight of her held their gaze—the polite ones unintentionally, while the more shameless males stared at her sometimes with mouths agape.

Even Capt. Casey found herself sneaking peeks at the sexy cyborg.

"I don't know how to surf," Spade said.

"You're gonna love it," Capt. Casey said.

"Just go with the flow," Grimes said. "No pressure. Wipeouts generally are not fatal, but they are captured on video. The best wipeouts are replayed every night in the city's watering holes."

"Great," Spade said.

"About 60 years ago, one guy had such a spectacular wipeout that they still play the video today," Grimes said. "Don't be that guy."

A tall woman wearing a white bikini and carrying a surfboard under her arm walked toward them. Her black hair was braided tightly down her back. Her white bikini accentuated the golden brown tone of her smooth skin.

"Well hello, Madam Mayor," Grimes said.

"Aloha," Mayor Lourdes Magna said. "It was an island greeting on Earth. Polynesian, if I remember my ancient Earth history correctly."

"Aloha," they repeated.

The mayor looked up at Spade. "It is good to see you here, Captain Spade. I would like you to know that I value your input and your insights and it was difficult casting my vote for a military commander. But in politics, we must make choices. I hope you understand."

"Understood."

Capt. Jack was standing at the water's edge speaking to Dr. Ebos. Mayor Magna waved him over.

The tall, blonde man walked toward them with his surfboard under his arm. He had an athletic gait and was well-muscled, similar in proportion to Spade's physique.

Capt. Jack's blue eyes sparkled. He flashed a smile.

"Hey, hey Captain Jack," Mayor Magna said.

"Ladies," he said.

The three ladies all smiled up at the tall man.

"Sergeant First Class Grimes," Capt. Jack said, slapping him a friendly handshake. "The most skilled and fearsome Ranger on the planet."

Capt. Jack turned to Spade. "No hard feelings, Spade?"

He made eye contact with Spade and their eyes locked for a long moment. Capt. Jack's eyes were friendly, and seemed a window into an honest soul. Uncannily so.

"No harm, no foul," Spade replied.

Capt. Jack ran his hand over the rail of the surfboard under his arm. The board was a thruster with three fins under its tail. Flames were airbrushed along the rails and the image of a screaming blue bird of prey was stenciled on its bottom.

"Will you surf with me?" Mayor Magna asked him.

"With this surfboard in my hand," Capt. Jack said, "I will be your surfing man."

"The best you can," Mayor Magna said.

The mayor looked at the group. "The pool will be drained this evening and the water will be pumped into storage tanks under the city. The Plunge will close indefinitely, so make the best of the next few hours."

The mayor turned and looked up at the back wall of the dome where the windows of a control room overlooked the pool. She raised a finger and circled it in the air.

A large engine beneath the floor hummed and rumbled to life. The crystal clear water along the cement peninsula began to flow in a swift current. The current jetted into the center of the pool where the surface of the water bulged and swelled and formed a rising wave.

The swell jumped up and reached 20 feet in height. It crested and its lip crashed forward in a roar of exploding whitewater.

The current rushed up the wall of water and curled and rolled forward forming a huge liquid barrel that churned and spit spray in great gusts of compressed air.

Mayor Magna turned back to the control tower and gave a thumbs up in approval. The giant wave collapsed and the water in the pool went flat. Its clear waters were no longer glassy and calm as before. The surface of the water threw off reflections of shimmering light that jumped and danced across the inside of the dome.

Mayor Magna waved her hand forward and the current started up again and a swell began to rise in the center of the pool. The mayor ran across the cement and leaped with her surfboard held in front of her. She hit the water and landed on her belly on her board and immediately began paddling as she was swept forward in the current.

She hit the swell straight on and jumped up to her feet as she shot up the cresting wave on her board. She hit the breaking crest with the flat of her surfboard and snapped it around, throwing up a fan of water off the top of the wave.

Everyone watching at the water's edge cheered and hooted and hollered.

"That was hot," Grimes said.

The mayor dropped down the face of the wave into the trough and broke into a tight bottom turn, kicking up spray. She slid up the wave's face and then pulled into the barrel as the lip of the wave broke over the top of her. She disappeared into a tube of water before being spit out in a gust of air and spray.

The crowd cheered as she slid her hand across the smooth face of the wave and tucked back inside the churning cylinder of water.

"She's so groovy," Capt. Casey said.

"Wow, where did she learn how to surf?" Spade asked.

"She comes here every afternoon," Capt. Casey said. "She designed this place. I couldn't have designed it better myself."

Capt. Jack ran across the cement and leaped, landing in the current on his board. He paddled hard and popped up to his feet and shot up the face of the curling wave. He crashed into the crest and launched into the air above the wave in an explosion of spray. He twisted in the air with his feet still on his board, holding its rail with one hand. He hit the landing smoothly and slid back down the wave's face, turning back up it before sliding at an angle just below the crest. He dragged his hand along the inside wall of the barreling wave and looked over his shoulder, catching sight of Mayor Magna inside the barrel behind him.

The mayor pumped her board up and down the wall of water that churned and crashed and spit spray around her. She surfed gracefully up to Capt. Jack and the two surfed together, crisscrossing tracks and riding up and down the wave face, throwing up spray off the crest and making tight bottom turns in the trough. The crowd cheered their every turn and trick.

The wave flattened and rolled forward. Mayor Magna and Capt. Jack pumped their boards on the dissipating wave and rode it to the water's edge. They let their bodies fall into the water and were smiling from ear to ear as they chatted and floated on their backs in the clear water.

"OK," Capt. Casey said. "You're up, Genie."

Genie turned and gave a thumbs up to the control room. She ran like quicksilver and leaped into the current with hardly a splash.

Dream surfer

Genie paddled into the rising wave and popped up to her feet. She rocketed up the wall of water and smashed the lip of the wave with a wallop, launching into an aerial spin. One 360-degree turn came after another as she soared high above the top of the giant crashing wave.

She reached the apex of her climb. Gravity took hold and pulled her down as she spun round and round. She hit the landing effortlessly, and slid onto the face of the wave.

Onlookers at the water's edge oohed and aahed and cheered.

Genie leaned forward and jetted out over the trough before digging the rails of her board deep into the water. She carved into a powerful bottom turn, throwing up a rising curtain of spray in her wake.

She traced her silver fingers over the liquid surface as she skimmed over it and then around onto the wave face, leaving deep tracks in the water. She leaned back and tucked into the tube, disappearing into the tunnel of crashing water.

"How does she so perfectly surf?" Capt. Casey asked.

"I've never seen the girl wipeout," Grimes said.

They watched her in awe as she carved and turned and slapped her board off the lip. At one point on her ride, she hit the top of the curling wave and launched outward, floating on the crashing curtain in freefall. She stuck the landing at the bottom and bounced up in an explosion of white water, before effortlessly shooting back onto the smooth wave face to cheers from the crowd.

"I want to go surfing with her," Grimes said.

Grimes ran and jumped into the current and hopped to his feet. He launched off the lip of the curling wave, and shot upward into the air with one hand held out for balance and the other gripping his rail. He reached the apex and paused in the air for a second before dropping in on the wave and sliding up next to Genie.

"He's not so bad himself," Capt. Casey said.

"He's OK," Spade said.

Genie and Grimes rode the wave together until it subsided. They pumped their boards on the dissipating swell as they rode it in to the water's edge.

"OK," Capt. Casey said. "The moment we've all been waiting for."

Capt. Casey twirled her finger in the air and the current started up and a swell began to rise in the center of the pool. She ran barefoot over the wet cement and leaped and landed on her belly on her board with a splash.

She hopped to her feet and eased up the wave face, making a smooth turn off the top before sliding in on the cresting wall of water. The rising swell was double overhead as it crested and broke. Capt. Casey tucked under the falling curtain of water and disappeared into the barrel.

She traced her hand over the glassy surface of the wave face as the water glistened and churned around her and spit gusts of spray. She pulled deeper and deeper inside the hollow tube of water.

She loved being in here, inside the calm eye of a liquid tornado. She slid through the watery tunnel ducking down as it spun around her.

This perfect wave reminded her of the best times of her life on her home world of Nebas. As a teenager, she had learned to surf on the Nebas sea. Sometimes the waves of Nebas broke as perfectly as this artificially created one.

Back on Nebas, the water was colder but the scenery was far more enchanting. Nothing was better than the real thing, but riding this wave came close.

The barrel of the wave collapsed behind her, spitting her out of the tube in a gust of spray. She skimmed along the wave face as the crowd cheered. They knew the skill and experience it took to negotiate the roiling waters inside the tube for that long without wiping out and being swallowed up and pulled under. Capt. Casey wasn't an aggressive or flashy surfer, but a smooth and graceful one, and a joy for the crowd to watch.

Capt. Casey looked over her shoulder and signaled for Spade to join her with a nod of her head.

"Here we go," Spade said to himself.

He ran and jumped into the current which swept him toward the monstrous, crashing wave. He jumped up to his feet with one hand extended forward and the other back in an attempt to maintain his balance.

Capt. Casey slid along the wave face and watched as Spade shot right past her. He hit the lip, which caught his board and flipped it out from under his feet. His riderless board flipped away through the air.

Spade was caught in the crest as it pitched and threw him forward. He was 20 feet above the surface and in freefall. His arms and legs flailed as he fell backwards, embedded in the crashing liquid curtain.

Capt. Casey watched as he went up and over her head and then hurtled downward. He hit the bottom of the wave in an explosion of whitewater. He bounced off the surface, rolling head over heels in the crashing wall of water.

The powerful, swirling current pulled him deep down below the surface. His body was tossed and flipped and yanked around and around as he was pulled downward into a cloud of roiling white bubbles.

He kicked and pulled desperately, not knowing which way was up. He finally burst through the surface and gasped for air.

The wave had dissipated. Capt. Casey was sitting on her surfboard watching him.

"Are you OK, Jace?" she asked.

He treaded water and shook his head. "I think half the water in the pool went into my ears and up my nose."

"That was an epic wipeout," she said.

Capt. Casey looked to the water's edge and gave a thumbs up. The crowded broke into applause, whistling and clapping.

"Come on," she said. "Let's paddle over to the kiddy pool. I'll teach you how to surf."

Capt. Casey coached Spade on the smaller waves at one end of the pool. Soon he was surfing alongside her, pumping his board up and down the smooth wave face and turning off the top.

They surfed together. She was all smiles as he hot dogged around her, impressed at his progress.

"Hey, look," Capt. Casey said, pointing to the main wave in the center of the pool.

Ramone Bombero was surfing on a longboard on a giant wave. The huge seven-foot tall man was wearing red swim trunks. His pectoral muscles were massive slabs of beef. His arms and legs bulged with rippling muscle. A thick mat of curly black body hair covered his muscular arms, legs, shoulders and back.

Ramone walked up and back on his board. He walked to the nose and stood up straight and arched his back and hung ten as the onlookers cheered.

Vice Mayor Malva Fung surfed out of the tube behind him. The brown-skinned woman with tawny hair wore a tan bikini. She surfed up next to Ramone and stepped off her board and onto his. Her board whizzed away riderless over the breaking wave.

Ramone lifted her up with his hairy, bulging arms and held her over his head. She bent her knee and arched her back and raised her arms as they tandem surfed on the giant wave.

The onlookers clapped.

Back at the far end of the pool, Capt. Casey surfed away from the smaller wave she was riding until her momentum slowed. She let herself fall backward into the water.

She floated on her back looking up at the high concrete ceiling of the dome.

Spade swam up behind her and wrapped his arms around her. She turned around and faced him and wrapped her legs around his waist and placed her arms over his shoulders.

He stood on the bottom in the neck-high water. Capt. Casey's face was wet, and her short, jet black hair was slicked back.

"Do you want to try the main wave again?" she asked.

"Let's do it," he said.

"You're a quick learner," she said.

"That's because I've got a great teacher," he said. "I can't take my eyes off her."

Spade looked into her dark eyes as he held her in the water. She was happy. It made him happy.

She kissed him and looked into his eyes. "Yes," she said.

"Yes?" he asked.

"Yes. I will marry you, Captain Jace Spade."

Spade smiled from ear to ear. "Awesome," he said. "Things are looking up for Captain Jace Spade."

He planted a big kiss on her wet lips.

Affection

Spade sat on a barstool at the bar at the Biop Bop. Dr. Ebos sat next to him eating a meal off a plate. His red lenses glowed in the dim light as he ate his dinner.

"What is that stuff?" Spade asked him. "It looks disgusting."

"They call it Biop slop," Dr. Ebos said.

Spade ordered a beer.

"After the Craaldans destroyed the Tasra Greenhouse Complex, the quality of the food in Taji City has taken a precipitous dive," Ebos said.

A few small groups of humans sat at the tables out on the floor below the low ceiling that was decorated with a galaxy of glowing faux stars. A large screen in the front of the room played video of surfers at the wave pool.

"Here it comes," Dr. Ebos said.

The screen depicted Capt. Spade being flung and crushed by a giant wave. Everyone in the bar cringed and groaned. The screen showed it again in slow motion to more groans. Then it showed close-ups of Spade's face at different stages of his wipeout. His eyes were bulging and teeth were gritting while he was suspended in freefall. The screen showed the wipeout several more times from different angles.

"That had to hurt," a Megalan man said.

"That poor man," a Taji female said.

Spade ducked his head hoping not to be recognized.

Capt. Casey entered the bar and walked up to them and put her arms around Spade.

"Hi, Viz," she said.

"You look ravishing, as always," Dr. Ebos said. "Congratulations on your engagement."

"Why, thank you," she said. She held up her left hand and showed him the silver band on her ring finger.

"You're famous, Jace," she said, nodding to the screen.

"I am surprised you weren't injured," Dr. Ebos said.

"Only his pride," Capt. Casey said.

"How was work?" Spade asked her.

"Busy," she said. "We've secured the water supply. There's about a year's worth of H2O distributed in tanks around the city and in reservoirs underground. No more wave pool, though."

A group of five Taji City males approached them at the bar. The skinny bearded men in khaki cargo pants and utility shirts were grinning broadly.

"What's up, guys?" Spade asked them.

"We want to meet the doctor," one of the men said to Spade. The man turned to Dr. Ebos. "It's an honor to be standing here with you, Dr. Ebos."

Ebos turned from his meal and looked at them through his glowing red eyepieces. "The honor is mine," he said.

The men were fidgeting like schoolboys.

"How are you all feeling?" Dr. Ebos asked.

"I feel fantastic," the first bearded man said.

"I feel like a million T-bucks," said another.

"I feel like I could whip the whole Craaldan Empire myself."

"I feel like I could impregnate a Megalan female."

"I feel like impregnating five or six of them tonight."

"Hey, guys," Capt. Casey said. "That's gross."

Spade looked at them closely. "You guys look different, like you've been working out. You all look healthier, more energetic."

"It's Dr. Ebos' doing," one of the men said. "He discovered that a microscopic parasite in the water supply had made us infertile. He has invented a vaccine that inoculated us to the parasite. Our masculine powers have been restored."

"Yes, we have regained the power to impregnate women."

"I wish to exercise this power."

"Oh, brother," Capt. Casey said.

"This is a very important development for us and for the city," the first man said. "Our women have no interest in us. They throw themselves at any new male arrival because of our deficiency. After all, reproduction is a cornerstone of life. Now we are back in the game."

"First of all, guys," Capt. Casey said, "they are not your women. Second of all, your game is going nowhere if you don't change your attitudes. Try being gentlemen. Make a girl feel special and maybe you'll get somewhere."

"Is that how you won Captain Casey's heart?" the bearded man asked Spade. "By being a gentleman?"

"Nice guys finish last," Spade said, and winked.

Capt. Casey elbowed him in the ribs.

"Captain Spade," one of the men said. "Have you ever impregnated Captain Casey?"

"Not yet," Spade said. "Maybe tonight."

"Hey, cool your jets, flyboy," she said.

"You are a hero to us, Dr. Ebos," one of the men said. "May I shake your hand?"

Each one of the men shook the doctor's hand. Dr. Ebos invited them to visit him at the Taji City Clinic whenever they liked. They thanked him profusely and returned to their table.

"There's a parasite in the water?" Spade asked.

"Not anymore," Dr. Ebos said. "It took some doing, but I was able to solve the mystery of why the men on Biop had become infertile."

"Explain, Doc," Capt. Casey said.

"I was searching through old records in the clinic and found an encrypted file. Tanaka unlocked it for me. The contents of the file were the research of a genetic engineer who had secretly constructed an elusive microorganism that devitalizes the men it infects. Apparently, shortly after Taji City was founded, the humans here struggled with division and strife as they fought over the limited resources at their disposal. They needed to work together to survive, but factions had arisen and the colonists were constantly at each other's throats. The men outnumbered the women and rivalries for mates escalated to bloodshed. The genetic engineer blamed the violence on the male of the species and her solution was to engineer an organism that sapped the reproductive drives of the men. She never told anyone of her scheme, knowing that they would rebel against it."

"It worked, though," Capt. Casey said.

"In some respects," Dr. Ebos said. "The men became less prone to fighting over women, but they then fell under the rule of a tyrannical gynarchy. Meanwhile, the colony expanded as more resources became available, but the birthrate slowed. The parasite mutated over the years and finally the men became completely infertile and the colony's birthrate dropped to zero. To make matters worse, the parasite intensified the reproductive drives of the females who longed to reproduce, causing a new set of frustrations."

Spade looked over at the five bearded men seated around a table. They were ogling a tall Taji City female who was chatting up a Megalan man who stood holding a drink, hunched down under the low ceiling

"Those poor knuckleheads," Spade said.

"Oh, I wouldn't feel too badly for them," Dr. Ebos said. "They have done quite well here considering the severity of the environment. And since Lourdes Magna ascended to the mayor's office 50 years ago, the colony has been well governed and has thrived. In fact, it is one of the best administered colonies I have visited."

Suddenly, the lights went out and the bar went dark. An alarm went off.

"Incoming! Incoming! Incoming!"

Everyone hit the floor.

In the darkness, all that could be seen were Dr. Ebos' red eyepieces and a feint bluish glow from the galaxy of faux stars embedded in the ceiling.

The floor rumbled and loud booms rocked the building.

"There goes the counter fire," Ebos said. "Cross your fingers."

Three distant booms could be heard. Shockwaves rattled the city.

The lights flickered back on.

"All clear, all clear, all clear," said a metallic voice over the city-wide intercom.

Everyone rose to their feet and got back in their seats.

"What a planet," Capt. Casey said.

Capt. Casey and Spade attempted to eat but only picked at the food on their plates.

Doxy took the stage and sat on a stool. Her cyborg companion sat next to her holding a guitar. He strummed it and she sang a melancholy song.

Dr. Ebos called it a night and headed back to his pod leaving Capt. Casey and Spade alone at the bar. They sipped their drinks and listened to Doxy in the dim light of the Biop Bop. A few couples had migrated to the floor in front of Doxy. The male and female forms held each other, swaying together as she sang her sad song.

Capt. Casey pulled Spade by the hand out onto the floor and they slow danced with the crowd. Near them, a bearded Taji City male chatted up a Heliac female. The woman was a battle-hardened soldier and slightly taller than the male. The man leaned in and said something to her. She slapped him hard across the face and walked away.

"That sorry sap," Spade said.

"Dr. Ebos has awakened a monster," Capt. Casey said.

She looked up at Spade and smiled.

He smiled back.

She put her head on his shoulder.

"I've had a good life, Jace," she said. "I really have."

"What do you mean?" he asked.

"Oh, you know," she said. "I've been feeling down lately."

"I've noticed," he said.

"It's been hard for me since Heliac fell," she said. "For all these years, I've had this feeling of loss, and a longing to find another place where I could feel happy again. My hope was restored on Gallos, but that didn't last. I've accepted now that I'll never find the place that I've been dreaming of. I know

now it's only a dream, and that's made me sad inside. But even through all the hard times and the loneliness, when I look back on my life, I would still do it all over again."

"Cheer up, Mina," Spade said. "I'll find your place in the sun. We'll find it together."

She looked up at him. "Do you think we'll be OK, Jace?"

"Mina," he said. "We're gonna live forever."

Part II

Man up

Sgt. First Class Joe Grimes marched through a vast hangar alongside a formation of 40 armored soldiers. Grimes sang a cadence as he marched them. The soldiers marched in step in their old Heliac armor with their M-929 weapons systems held in front of them.

The formation was made up of a motley collection of refugees from Meglos, Paltros and Heliac. Space drifters, Escalonians and several Taji City locals were in the mix. They were males and females; all marching in lock step with Grimes. They wore blue and white Heliac armor, or variations of it manufactured here at Taji City, tailored to fit the sizes of the varied human forms here.

"Hey, hey, Captain Jack," Grimes sang.

The marching soldiers repeated the line.

"Meet me down by the railroad tracks."

They marched in step to the rhythm.

"With this weapon in my hand, I'm gonna be a shootin' man. A fightin' man, the best I can."

Grimes marched the formation past column upon column of soldiers lined up in the enormous hangar. Thousands and thousands of them stood at stiff attention.

Marching a formation of soldiers and calling out the cadence sparked a fire inside him. The sound of his own voice singing out the cadence in this hangar as the boots thumped on the cement made his blood run hot.

"Your left, your left, your left-right, your left."

"You got it," they called back.

"Left. Yo-o left. Left-right, yo' left."

"You got it!"

"Left. Right, o' left."

"Pump, pump, pump, pump it up!"

"Right face, march!" he bellowed. "One, two, three, four!"

"Hoot, pick it up, your left!"

"One, two, three, four! Mark time! March!"

The formation marched in place. Their boots pounded the cement in unison. The clomps from the boot steps reverberated through the dusty air and echoed metallically off the far away walls, trestles and ceiling.

"Platoon! Halt! Left! Face!"

The soldiers turned in unison and faced Grimes who stood at attention facing them. He had on blue and white Heliac armor that he had buffed and polished so that it gleamed brightly in the artificial light. His weapon was slung on his shoulder. His gloved hands held it around the butt stock and barrel.

His platinum blonde hair stood up on his head. His pale blue eyes sparkled.

This platoon in front of him was his baby. These 40 soldiers were the city's new Quick Reaction Force, or QRF. Grimes had taken special care to train up these soldiers to respond with haste to any combat emergency. Each soldier in the QRF was ready to strike hard and fast and take on the Craaldan foe without hesitation and wherever needed.

To Grimes' right and left stood three brigades in formation. About four thousand humans were in each brigade. They all stood at attention facing forward.

Supervisor Halex Page stood facing forward at the head of a combat aviation brigade. The Heliac Special Forces fighter, Ripper, stood at the head of the heavy infantry brigade. Ramone Bombero stood in front of Third Brigade, which consisted of one infantry battalion, an artillery battalion and an engineering battalion.

Grimes pivoted around on his heels and snapped a salute.

"Sir!" Grimes bellowed, as he held the salute. "The Taji First Armored Infantry Division is all present and accounted for!"

Capt. Jack strode in front of the mass of assembled troops. He was wearing polished royal blue armor. Two silver stars were centered on his chest. His weapon was slung on his back.

His hair was slicked back, and a blonde mustache was maturing above his lip.

He stopped when he reached Grimes and turned and faced him and squinted his piercing blue eyes. The tall, blonde man in royal blue armor snapped a salute.

Grimes dropped his salute.

Capt. Jack leaned down. "Excellent work, Sergeant First Class Grimes. What you've built here is a thing of beauty."

Grimes nodded and turned and trotted away and returned to the front of his formation.

"At ease!" Capt. Jack bellowed.

Over 12,000 humans shifted their boots and locked their hands behind their backs.

"Outstanding!" Capt. Jack said.

He walked in front of the formation examining the troops. Ripper snapped Capt. Jack a salute as the tall man walked past.

"You soldiers make my heart proud!" Capt. Jack said. "Look at you! You are a beautiful sight to behold! A deadly sight! I see in front of me a force that will restore pride and respect to the human species, and rain death and destruction down on our enemy. The death hammer will be brought down upon the Craaldan! Hooah!"

A roar filled the vast hangar as thousands yelled, "Hooah!" and cheered.

Mayor Magna stood at the back of the hangar looking out at the huge formation. She appeared pleased, but awed as her eyes followed Capt. Jack who paced in front of the armored soldiers.

Capt. Casey stood in parade rest with her hands behind her back at the head of a squad in the combat aviation brigade formation. She had been assigned to be the pilot of a Bioppian aerial utility vehicle, called an AUV-60.

Spade stood next to her in the formation. He had volunteered to be her crew chief.

"These next few days are going to test each and every one of us to our personal limits and beyond," Capt. Jack said. "I need you all to be at your best. I need you to maintain a laser focus on our mission. That mission is to crush the heinous Craaldan, without fear, without hesitation and with a willingness to fight to the death with relentless tenacity.

"There is an immutable law in this universe," he continued. "For every action there is an equal and opposite reaction. Your actions here will mean something. Not only here, but across the galaxy. We must be willing to take heroic action even if it means the sacrifice of our own lives for a greater good. Even if death comes, know that our victory over the Craaldan here on this planet will live on. Our victory will live on forever, and the reaction to it will change the course of time, and echo eternally across the void. Our day of reckoning approaches! We're going to kill the heinous Craaldan with extreme violence and bathe this planet in his blood! Be prepared to stand up, fight and kill!"

"Good grief," Capt. Casey said to herself.

"Who gave him the two stars?" Spade asked her.

"He had the mayor give them to him," she answered. "He's Major General Jack Winner now."

"The training continues," Winner said. "Stay sharp. Stay focused. Keep your head in the game. And let's kill the Craaldan with prejudice, without contrition, and with malice aforethought! Hooah!"

"Hooah!" they thundered back.

"I must say," Spade whispered to Capt. Casey, "this is impressive. Grimes and Captain Jack have built an army to be proud of. Even the Taji City guys look sharp and squared away."

"Like lambs to the slaughter," Capt. Casey said.

Murder board

Spade walked down a dusty corridor. Its cement walls became glass and he could see the outside world. The Cextos sun was a white disk in the bleak, Bioppian sky.

The sun was setting behind a flat-roofed, blockish building that was three stories high. Spindly antennae and microwave dishes stuck up from various points on its roof. The building was known to everyone in Taji City as the Mayor's Cell.

Spade walked in the glass corridor and pushed through a glass door and entered the building.

The ceiling was low and the air was dusty. The plain walls were without decoration except for framed photo portraits on the opposite wall.

A large portrait of Mayor Magna centered the wall. Her stern expression was confident and authoritative. Beneath her photo were four smaller portraits of the members of the Board of Supervisors. They each held similar expressions to the mayor.

Soldiers were everywhere in the halls. They wore boots and armor. Their weapons were slung at their sides. Their helmets were either held under their arms or hooked onto their belts. Their faces were grimy and their hair was sweaty and mussed. Most had just come off some kind of battle drill designed by Grimes, and were here at the Mayor's Cell in between training missions to take care of mundane tasks, such as putting in work orders to get air filter units repaired in their dwellings, or replace lost keys, or pay their water or oxygen bills.

They stood at counters or at windows as clerks assisted them.

Spade approached a kiosk where a bearded Taji City man sat reading an electronic military field manual. It was an infantry squad tactics manual. The bearded man was wearing armor and his weapon was standing in a rack next to him.

"I've got an appointment with the mayor," Spade said.

The man looked up at him and appeared to recognize him. He pushed the button to an intercom. "Captain Spade is here, ma'am," he said.

"Send him up," a female voice replied.

"Upstairs, second door on your right, conference room three," the bearded man said to Spade.

"Roger that." Spade turned and walked toward the stairs.

"Captain Spade," the man said.

Spade turned. "What's up?"

"This is our home," he said.

The bearded man at the kiosk looked at Spade for a moment. "I'm glad that I am staying to fight and not running away."

Spade looked at him. He was wearing second-hand armor sitting at his station at the kiosk. He was a small man with little training and wearing armor that offered virtually no protection against even the smallest caliber Craaldan projectile. But his face displayed confidence and betrayed no fear at the prospect of a fight with battle-hardened alien soldiers who had been killing their way across the galaxy for millennia.

Spade knew at a glance that this man was no match for any Craaldan.

"I understand," Spade said. "I'm staying here with you."

"I'm glad," the man said. "I know you have been beaten by them in the past, but we're going to defeat them this time."

"Roger," Spade said. "Keep your head down, OK? Remember your training and listen to your commanders. Don't be the hero out there and you might survive all this."

"This is a time for heroes," the man said.

Spade looked at the little man for a moment. "Roger that."

Spade turned and walked up the stairs. He walked down a carpeted hallway and came to a conference room door. He knocked on it.

"Enter, Captain Spade," a female voice said.

Spade entered the conference room. Three females were seated at a long table at the far end of the room. He recognized them.

Vice Mayor Malva Fung and supervisors Nector Zink and Regina Vulgaris were looking up at him. Supervisor Halex Page was absent.

Spade walked up to the table and stood in front of them. They were tall women with golden-brown skin and wild hair. They wore boots, black cargo pants and sleeveless utility shirts.

Fung had wild tawny hair and dark eyes. Zink's hair was long and also tawny, but her eyes were a deep blue. Vulgaris had brown eyes and black curly locks that fell over her smooth, brown shoulders. All had severe expressions. They looked up at him gravely from their seats.

"I thought I was here to see the mayor," Spade said.

"You are," Fung said. "But first we have questions."

"You were born on a moon called Naos in the Roga System?" Zink asked.

"Roger," he replied.

They closely scrutinized his response and body language and took notes.

"You were an artificial birth. Your father was the scientist Dr. Zander who created you by splicing his DNA with various non-human life forms."

"Roger that."

"Dr. Zander founded the human colony on Naos and you served in the Naos Lunar Militia as a fighter pilot," Vulgaris said. "Your interceptor is called the Red Wrath."

"That's correct."

"You are the lone confirmed survivor of a Diocon attack on the Naos Colony?" Fung asked.

"That was a long time ago," Spade said, shifting uncomfortably in his boots.

"You have spent most of your life piloting the Red Wrath through the Inner Galaxy, searching for Dr. Zander, not knowing if he is alive or dead. You have taken extreme risks in your search, and in so doing, you have seen much of the Inner Galaxy. You are a living witness to the annihilation of vast sectors of space committed by both the Diocon and Craaldan empires," Zink said.

Spade nodded.

"You have been a prisoner of the Craaldan. You have had contacts with the Noctish," Vulgaris said.

"You've done your homework," Spade said.

"You survived the Craaldan destruction of Portogallos and led the exodus of survivors here as the commander of Escalon Station," Fung said.

"I enjoy a cold Paltros Space Ale after chow," Spade said. "I like playing spades with friends, poker with foes. Until recently, my greatest pleasure was a good cigar on the flight deck before a night out at whatever backwater spaceport I happened to find myself in. I play a little piano but I don't dance."

The supervisors took notes.

Fung looked up at him sternly. "You are in love with Captain Mina Casey, a former Heliac Defense Forces fighter pilot. You wish to leave Biop with her but you stay because she refuses to go. You are worried about her well being and fearful of the fatalistic attitude she has adopted since the destruction of Escalon."

Spade stood silently. He looked down at his boots. "Can I ask you a question, Ms. Fung?"

"No," she answered.

"You are a capable commander with experience leading deep space voyages," Zink said. "You are a skilled engineer and you understand the workings of spaceships."

"Why are you ladies giving me the third degree?" Spade asked.

"Please respond to Supervisor Zink's query, Captain Spade," Fung said.

"Her query?"

"Do you have engineering know-how and do you understand the intricacies of spaceship design?" Zink asked. "Specifically, do you have expertise in the areas of life support systems, propulsion and navigation; and do you have the capability to construct deep-space transports using limited resources, an untrained work force while under serious time constraints?"

"That depends on who wants to know," Spade said.

Fung looked at him gravely with her dark eyes. His eyes locked with hers and he held the stare.

Her eyes exuded seriousness and confidence. Her expression gave the impression that she was determined to do her job to the best of her ability. But, unexpectedly, Spade detected vulnerability behind her hard eyes. Not fear, but uncertainty.

"Mayor Lourdes Magna and the Supervisors would like to know," Fung said.

"Tell the mayor I will build her the space transports," Spade said.

The three women nodded. Fung pushed a button to an intercom microphone in front of her. "We have completed our questioning. Captain Spade is ready to see you now."

"Send him in," Mayor Magna replied.

Fung stood up. "Follow me," she said.

"Lead the way," Spade said.

She led him down the carpeted hallway.

"Hey, Malva," Spade said. "How's Ramone?"

She looked over her shoulder at him but didn't reply.

"I miss that big lug," he said. "Maybe you, me, Mina and Ramone can get together for drinks."

"I would like that."

She came to a door at the end of the hallway.

"Captain Spade?" Fung asked. "When was the last time you saw Dr. Ebos?"

"Two nights ago," he said. "Why?"

She nodded. "The mayor will see you now."

Contingencies

Spade entered the mayor's office. It was a large carpeted room full of shelves that were filled with white binders. Potted plants were set in the corners. Purple flower buds and blue leaves sprouted from the thick stems.

Mayor Lourdes Magna stood behind a large faux wood desk that was in front of a window that looked out at the monochrome skyline of Taji City.

The city behind her was a jumbled collection of flat-roofed buildings, water towers, antennae, and warehouse-like DFACs—all under a thick, gray blanket of dust and gas.

Trams zoomed between blast walls. Halogen street lamps glowed through the gray.

"Good afternoon, Captain Spade," Mayor Magna said, extending her hand to him. She wore a white long sleeve shirt and white slacks. Her black hair was tightly braided down her back.

Spade shook her hand.

Her hand was soft. Her handshake was feminine. This somewhat surprised Spade because the mayor projected an aura of authority, and she was so tall and fit. He had expected a firmer grip.

"Good afternoon, Ms. Mayor," he said.

"Please have a seat," she said. "Would you like some tea?"

He nodded and sat in the seat in front of her desk.

She came around the desk and stood in front of him and poured steaming tea from a metal thermos into two metal cups.

She handed him a cup and leaned against the desk and took a sip of her tea, watching him.

He took a sip.

"Good stuff," he said. "How is it made?"

"We recycle the waste water from the laundry facility and filter it through the compost heap in the barley greenhouse.

The water is then piped from the greenhouse to the city. While in the pipe, solar radiation heats it to a boil."

"Laundry water?" Spade asked.

"For years, the laundry waste water was used to wash down the greenhouse floor, but then this process was discovered and now Taji Tea is one of the city's most popular beverages."

"Never ask how it's made," Spade said to himself.

He sipped his tea.

"H20 is a valuable commodity on Biop," she said. "This tea will run through you and through me and it will be recycled again. Would you like to know the next step in the water cycle?"

"Negative," he said. "Ignorance is bliss."

He looked up at her as he sipped his tea. Her white clothing accentuated her coal black hair and her golden brown skin. Her V-neck shirt displayed the smooth brown skin of her buxom chest.

Her face was stern and serious, but attractive. Her ebony eyes, high cheekbones and radiant complexion conveyed a regal impression. Yet to Spade, she did not in the least seem intimidating or unapproachable.

She walked back around the desk and sat down across from him. She adjusted the papers and pens in front of her.

"When I cast my vote for a military commander to lead the defense of Taji City, I had no doubt that my judgment was sound," she said. "But lately, I have often found myself thinking about the things you said before the vote. Since then, I have come to the realization that maybe emotions got the best of me that night, and cooler heads may have voted differently."

"Captain Jack has built an army to be proud of," Spade said. "What he and Grimes have done is an impressive achievement. It never would have happened if you and your board had voted for me."

"General Winner has fully militarized our colony in a very short period of time," she said.

She was spinning a pencil in her fingers, absentmindedly. She looked up from the pencil and looked at him.

"What would have happened if you were in charge, Captain Spade?" she asked.

"We would be halfway to the Calli Sector by now," he answered. "And everyone on the voyage would have blamed me for retreating when they wanted to stay and defend their homes."

"You are right, of course," she said.

She seemed unsure of herself for a moment. She rearranged the pens and papers on her desk, distractedly.

She leaned back in her chair and began spinning the pencil in her fingers again. "What do know of General Winner?" she asked him. "His past, I mean."

"The first I heard of him was after I arrived here."

"None of the Heliac Rangers knew him before his arrival here," she said.

"It's a big galaxy," Spade said.

"When the supervisors were questioning you a moment ago, I was watching you closely on my monitor," she said. "Your answers came naturally. The narrative of your past can be verified with others."

"What are you trying to say?" Spade asked.

"I'm not sure," she answered. "It's a big galaxy."

"If Captain Jack is lying about being a Heliac Ranger, it wouldn't be the first time a fast-talking stranger showed up at a spaceport making false claims and telling tall tales," Spade said. "Even so, he is proving himself to be a capable leader. He's charismatic. People like him and they follow him. He knows what he's doing."

"Yes," she said. "He has given us hope and a newfound pride. Everyone loves him."

She paused and looked down at her desk.

"He has seduced us," she said. "He has seduced me."

She looked up from her desk and their eyes met.

"He does things to me physically and emotionally that cause me to let down my guard. My body surrenders to him and new emotions take hold and I am swept away. I have become emotionally vulnerable."

"It sounds like you are in love with him," Spade said.

"He says the city will be defended with strength and honor and we will defeat the Craaldan aggressors. When I ask what happens after, his answers fill me with hope and promise. I feel excitement and great hope not just for our city, but for all humanity. He has made me believe that together we can do anything. But upon further reflection, the future remains vague in my mind, and when I press him for specifics, he deflects and is evasive. All efforts are focused on the moment and on the upcoming battle. I do not believe he has a plan for what happens next. I have no plan."

Spade studied her face from across the desk. Mayor Lourdes Magna possessed personal grace and a confident authority. She was obviously a woman of ability. But he saw the uncertainty and worry in her eyes.

Spade had seen many types of leaders in his day. He had seen the conmen, the striving busybodies, the ambitious privilege seekers, the power-hungry egomaniacs and the control freaks. He had seen incompetents and bumblers.

But Mayor Magna was one of the rare good ones. She was a woman of ability selected by her people because they trusted her to promote their best interests. She was a true leader who was not a person apart, but was of her people. All the best qualities of these backwater colonists were evident in this beautiful woman sitting before him at her desk. The gray skyline behind her turned red and purple as the Cextos sun set on the horizon. Her face was lost in thought.

In the end, Lourdes Magna was only the mayor of a small, isolated outpost, and she was trying to defend it from a relentless war machine that was millions of years old and hundreds of billions strong.

Mayor Magna turned her chair sideways and gazed out the window at the humble cityscape that stretched into the haze.

"What happens next, Captain Spade?"

"Let's say Captain Jack, or General Winner, I should say, is successful and we defeat the Craaldans here on Biop," he said. "Best case scenario, half the city is destroyed and maybe 60 percent of the population is killed. After the battle, we'll have about a month or two before Craaldan reinforcements arrive. Their game is extermination so they will come down here and swarm us with hunter-killer teams to make sure they've gotten us all. Then they will bombard the planet to sterilize it, or re-sterilize, as is the case with Biop. Their fighters, cruisers and destroyers will hunt down those of us who flee into space. It won't take them long to pick us all off since we won't have much lead time."

The mayor turned her chair toward him.

"Genie designed space transports for an evacuation," she said. "Our work crews are working round the clock to complete them. The shipbuilding operation is called the Zephyr Project and it is my backup plan. General Winner says it is a waste of manpower and resources that should be put to better use preparing our defenses. But I have been insistent that the project continue despite his objections. However, our workers are unskilled and lack experience. Sergeant Grimes has been calling Genie away to the hangars to assist him in training the troops, and the work crews would rather be training at the firing range and out on the battle drill lanes. Without Genie's expertise and supervision, the construction of the transports has slowed."

She stood and walked around the desk and stood in front of him. She leaned back on the desk and crossed her arms over her chest and looked at him sternly.

"I am asking you to take the lead on the Zephyr Project, Captain Spade. Build us the transports before half our city is destroyed and 60 percent of our people are lost."

"I'll build them for you, Mayor," he said.

Her hard eyes softened as she looked into his. "Thank you," she said.

"Now I have a favor to ask you," he said.

"Go ahead."

"I want to salvage my ship, the Red Wrath. It's stuck out on a plain by a huge ghost city."

"Yes, you abandoned your ship on the Mesolatium Plain."

"I need a fully supplied team of mechanics. It should take us about eight hours of work to get her flying again."

"OK. But first, take the lead on the Zephyr Project. Show me a timeline for completion and then I will give you your team of mechanics."

"Roger that."

He stood from his chair. She reached out her hand and he shook it. Her grip seemed firmer now.

"Captain Spade?" she asked.

"Yes?"

"Have you spoken with Dr. Ebos today?"

"Negative," he answered. "Why?"

"Dr. Ebos concluded an investigation I had asked him to conduct for me," she said. "He was supposed to present his findings this morning, but he did not show up at the scheduled time."

"That's not like him," Spade said.

"If you see him, please tell him that I am looking for him," the mayor said.

"Roger that."

Firing range

Sgt. Joe Grimes walked up and down the firing line. Through the display in his helmet, he closely monitored the shots fired by the troopers lying prone in the gravel in front of him.

The troopers were wearing white and blue Heliac body armor. They fired M-929 rifles at humanoid-shaped targets that popped up from behind berms on a flat expanse of gravel. The berms had been bulldozed at various intervals on this featureless plain, which stretched into the hazy distance.

"Lane 14," Grimes said. "Watch your shot grouping. Tighten it up. You're all over the place."

The targets snapped up and down in the distance as the shots from the soldiers pop-pop-popped. Waves of heat shimmered above the gravel as rounds streaked at the targets up on the berms.

Grimes walked over to Lane 14 where an armored soldier was lying in the dirt with his weapon pointed downrange. Grimes squatted down beside him. The soldier was a Taji City man.

"Don't splay your elbows. Pull them in." Grimes gripped the soldier's armored elbows and pulled them in tight. "Don't forget to breathe. Let the optic find the target. Squeeze the trigger at your respiratory pause, just like you did in the simulator. Let me see you hit the 1,000 meter target."

A humanoid-shaped target popped up from behind a berm 1,000 meters out. It was barely visible through the dust and through the waves of heat that were rising up from the gravel, but the soldier's optic sight quickly acquired it. The soldier fired a burst from his weapon. The glowing rounds streaked over the gravel at nearly the speed of light. Only one round in the three-round burst hit its mark high up on the shoulder. The target remained upright on the berm.

"You're high and to the right," Grimes said.

He took the soldier's weapon, aimed it at the target from the standing position and fired quick three-round bursts. The rounds struck the target in a tight shot group, knocking it down behind the berm.

"Definitely high and to the right. Your weapon needs to be re-zeroed."

The soldier hopped to his feet. He was watching Grimes closely from behind his black face plate. "Roger that, Sarge."

Grimes handed him the weapon.

"What's your name, soldier?" Grimes asked.

"Private Lopes," he answered.

"OK, Private Lopes. Take this weapon to the zeroing range and get it squared away. I need you to hit your target every time you squeeze that trigger or else this battle is going to be a short one, for you and for the rest of us. Every shot counts. One shot, one kill. Tracking?"

"Roger that."

"Good. Move, Private."

"Moving, Sergeant!"

Private Lopes ran off to the zeroing range, his boots crunching on the gravel as he disappeared into the haze.

Grimes walked the line as the targets popped up and down at various distances out on the range. The soldiers fired bursts from their weapons while in the prone.

Another experienced marksman walked up and down the line supervising and assisting. He was the platoon sergeant and a Heliac Ranger.

"Cease fire, cease fire, cease fire!" Grimes said into the radio net. "First platoon. Police your area and then report to Sergeant Genie at Lane 42. She'll be evaluating you on Battle Drill Number Three: Break Contact. Remember your training and make Sergeant Genie proud. Hooah?"

"Hooah!" the platoon replied.

"Second platoon, lock and load. You're up," Grimes said.

First platoon trotted off the range and the soldiers of second platoon took their places on the firing line.

"Fire when ready," Grimes said.

Bursts of rounds spewed out of their weapons, knocking down the pop-up targets out on the range.

Grimes stood back and watched. This platoon had some shooters.

"Hey there, drill sergeant."

Grimes turned his head and saw an armored form walking up to him through the waves of heat.

"You think these boys can win a war?"

"Not a war," Grimes said. "But this battle? Maybe."

The armored form stopped and stood next to him on the gravel and watched as the soldiers on the line lit up the range with rapid bursts from their weapons.

"Are you here to practice shooting, Mina?" Grimes asked.

"Roger that," she said. "I'm feeling rusty with my pistol and was hoping you could give me a little one-on-one instruction."

"Any time."

Pvt. Lopes ran up to them and stood before Grimes. "My weapon is zeroed, Sergeant Grimes," he said.

"Roger. Report to Sergeant Genie at Lane 42. Once you finish on the lanes, report back to me and we'll see if you can hit those targets out there. Copy?"

"Copy that, Sarge."

"Move."

"Moving!"

The soldier ran off.

"Sergeant Genie?" Capt. Casey asked. "I don't think that rank fits her."

"What rank do you suggest?"

"How about Your Royal Highness Genie, Cyborg Queen of the Galaxy?"

"Too wordy," Grimes said. "This ain't a fairy tale."

"OK. How about Genie, Robot Overlord?"

"Sergeant Genie works fine for our purposes."

"At least make her a second lieutenant," Capt. Casey said.

"Humph. Do you think she's too good to be an NCO?"

"Testy, aren't you?" Capt. Casey said. "How about a chief warrant officer? That rank suits her."

"Sergeant Genie," he said.

"OK. Sergeant Genie it is."

Grimes turned his attention to the firing range. "Specialist Batner," he said into the com system in his helmet. "I don't want to see any more head shots. Center mass. Copy?"

"Copy that, Sarge."

"On Gallos, you said you were done with war," Capt. Casey said. "You were dead set on voyaging to the Calli Sector and never looking back."

"Funny, isn't it?" Grimes said.

"I had this romantic vision of you and Genie heading out into the unknown and starting over on some peaceful planet out there. Now here you are playing the hero again, training a bunch of green recruits to withstand a Craaldan infantry attack."

"It's crazy, I know," Grimes said. "But I feel like we have a chance to beat them for once. Just once before I go."

"You and Genie should have kept going, Joe. Winning a minor battle here won't change the past. It won't bring back Heliac."

"Understood, Mina. But I've decided to stay and fight it out. Win or lose, live or die, for better or for worse. I know I should leave but I can't help myself. A victory here won't matter much in the grand scheme of things, but it will mean a lot to me personally. And I take consolation in the thought that what I am doing here might save the lives of some of these Taji City bumpkins. They are coming along really well. They're soldiers now."

"More of their lives would have been saved if we had listened to Jace," she said.

Grimes was silent for a moment. "They chose this course of action, not me. No changing that now. It is what it is."

"Roger," she said.

"Mina, we both learned to hate war through bitter experience. But I was born for it. We both were. Whether we are at war or at peace, you are still a pilot. For me, it's the infantry that runs through my veins. When I close my eyes, I dream about being a soldier. I can't help myself. But I hope you understand that I am no conqueror. I am a defender. It's in my blood. It's what I am."

"I understand, Joe," she said. "I just wish you felt differently. I want you and Genie to get through this and make it to the Calli Sector."

"I don't see you making a run for it," he said.

"No. I'm done running."

"And Spade?" he asked. "I thought you lovebirds were getting married. He's not the type to sit on one planet for too long."

"Jace has an instinctual trait for loyalty that is deeply ingrained in his character," Capt. Casey said. "That trait has driven him all over the galaxy in search of Dr. Zander. But on Gallos, I convinced him to stop searching, and he let go of Dr. Zander. His sense of loyalty then fixated onto me."

"That hound dog can't take his eyes off you."

"Lucky me," Capt. Casey said.

"Isn't that what you wanted?" Grimes asked.

"Yes," she said. "It really was."

Grimes turned his attention to the firing line. "Cease fire, cease fire, cease fire! Outstanding shooting, second platoon! Police your areas and report to Chief Warrant Officer Genie at Lane 42. Hooah?"

"Hooah!"

The Zephyr Project

Three giant space transports were docked inside an immense crater, the top of which was covered by a thin tarp. From above, the tarp blended into the gray landscape. But from below, the taut covering was an airtight roof that kept the dust and gas of the Bioppian atmosphere out of the spacious crater while keeping life-giving oxygen in.

Lights set atop booms illuminated the rocky surface of the crater floor. Huge robotic arms, cranes and scaffolding bracketed the space transports, each in different stages of construction. The gray spaceships had massive, curved hulls set atop three squat, bell-shaped fission engines. The huge ships were big enough to carry 5,000 humans apiece.

The inside of the crater was abuzz with activity. Industrial-sized robotic arms operated glowing welding torches that emitted sparks which cascaded down the hulls of the ships. Humans in hard hats walked about the crater floor. A pair of cyborgs climbed the scaffolding like silver spiders. Cranes lifted titanium beams and engine components. Forklifts moved parts and containers from huge stacks that were piled across the crater floor.

Generators chugged and hummed. Beeps and bangs and crackles filled the crater with noise.

"Commo check," Spade said into a handheld radio. "Perv, do you copy?"

"I'm here," Pervez Anax answered. "Go ahead."

"How are the fission engines coming along?" Spade asked as he walked through a dusty corridor inside one of the partially constructed spaceships. He was in Zephyr One, the ship nearest to completion. Mingus followed behind him holding an electronic clipboard. Both wore hardhats.

"Once the uranium cylinders are loaded, the engines will be good to go," Anax said.

"Outstanding," Spade said.

"Tanaka, give me an update," Spade said.

"The Zephyr One work crew is wiring the superstructure and we will begin installing the supercomputers this evening," Tanaka said over the radio.

"Excellent."

"Let's check up on Work Crew Six," Spade said to Mingus.

"Our problem children," Mingus said.

They walked through the ship's corridors which had yet to be paneled. Wiring and cables ran along exposed beams.

"Do you think the fission engines will work, Jace?" Mingus asked as they walked. "I mean, we're just slap dashing these spaceships together. I'm afraid the engines are going to incinerate us all."

"Genie designed this ship," Spade said. "She knows what she's doing."

"I know that," Mingus said. "But we're throwing these crates together with amateur labor and provincially manufactured industrial robots."

"These guys are doing a great job, considering," Spade said.

"When those engines ignite, the only thing that's going to be left where Taji City is now is a radioactive skid mark," Mingus said.

"That's right. So we need to double down and complete Zephyrs One, Two and Three pronto and get everyone on them as soon as we're ready to blast off."

They walked through the dark corridors turning right and left and clambering up transport tubes.

Spade too worried about the fission engines. Each ship had three of them. Basically, the engines would simultaneously set off channeled nuclear blasts and the big ships would ride the explosions up out of the atmosphere.

Fission engines were an old technology that had been used for interstellar flight for millennia. But they were not normally used to launch a ship off a planet. If your ship wasn't built right, instead of blasting off, it just vaporized inside a mushroom cloud. Also, anything on the ground near the point of launch gets incinerated in the nuclear explosion. You don't blast off with a fission engine from a place you plan to return to.

Spade and Mingus found Work Crew 6 atop Zephyr One's hull. The crew was made up of several bearded Taji City males and one hard-faced female, who was their supervisor.

Spade and Mingus checked in on their progress and then spent several hours helping them repair a malfunctioning industrial robot.

"It's up and running now, Captain Spade," the female said. "Our section of Zephyr One can be completed in about three hours."

"Outstanding," Spade said. "Let me know when you're done. Then we will assign your crew to Zephyr Two."

"Roger, sir."

Spade and the crew stood atop the giant curved structure watching the robotic arm rapidly piece together a section of the hull.

Big, muscular Mingus was nearly a head taller than Spade. Her long black pony tail was slung over her bulging shoulder. The Taji City men stole glances at her as they worked alongside the robotic arm. The men were somewhat intimidated by her size but were checking her out and looking her up and down. She would catch their eyes and they would quickly avert their gazes.

Spade admired the ships and all the activity inside the crater. Zephyr One was just about done. Zephyr Two stood next to it. It was half complete. Zephyr Three was just a skeleton of a ship inside a latticework of scaffolding.

"Captain Spade?" Pervez Anax said over the radio.

"Go ahead."

"Will you join me on the bridge for a smoke?"

"We'll be right up."

Spade and Mingus left the work crew and climbed atop the curved hull toward the bridge. Zephyr One's bridge was a bubble-like protrusion atop the highest point of the huge ship.

"Those Taji City guys think I'm hot," Mingus said as they walked.

"I noticed them checking you out."

"The other night I had six of them in my CHU. I rocked their worlds."

"Mingus," Spade said, shaking his head. "I hope you didn't hurt the little guys."

"There were some bumps and bruises but nothing permanent," she said. "I'll tell you what. Those little fellows are eager."

They entered a hatch and emerged on the bridge where they found Pervez Anax in a chair with his boots up on a control panel. Anax was one of those space drifters who liked to wear black. He had on black pants and a black imitation leather jacket. His jacket was covered with metal studs. He had a thick black mustache and a shaggy black mullet of hair. He twirled a cigar in his fingers as he looked out at all the activity way down on the crater floor.

"Hey there, Pervy," Mingus said.

"Greetings, Mingus. Captain Spade." He handed them cigars.

"You know I quit, right?" Spade said as he sat in a chair next to Anax. Spade smelled the cigar, running it under his nose.

Anax signaled for him to put the cigar in his mouth with a nod of his head. He flicked his flameless lighter which hissed. Spade was tempted, but pulled the cigar away without lighting it.

"I'll keep it as a memento," Spade said, twirling it in his fingers.

"As you wish," Anax said. He leaned over and lit Mingus' cigar.

Spade leaned back in his chair and looked down at the Zephyrs under construction. "I thought the Craaldans would have attacked by now, but they've been holding off. Now it's looking like we might actually get off this rock."

"The fission engines concern me," Anax said.

"Me too," Mingus said.

"Wear your seatbelts because it's gonna be a hell of a ride," Spade said.

Anax watched Mingus puff on her cigar. "I like the way you smoke," he said. "It's erotic."

Mingus smiled. Her cigar appeared tiny in her thick fingers. She slipped the cigar into her large fleshy lips and puffed on it. She gave Anax a wink.

Spade called Tanaka over the radio and invited him up. A few moments later, the skinny Paltran man clambered into the bridge with help from the mechanical prosthetics on his limbs. Vomica Nux entered behind him. They stood at the window next to Mingus. Anax handed them cigars and lit them. Tanaka puffed on his cigar, looking out at the activity below through his glowing green lenses.

"Hey, guys," Spade said. "I'm glad that we're working together again. It's good having you all back."

"Back from the dead," Tanaka said.

"Your zombie crew," Mingus said.

"Are you feeling emotional, Captain Spade?" Vomica asked.

"Frankly, I thought you all had dumped me for Captain Jack," Spade said. "Vomica, back on Escalon you were really something. Perv, you always had my back. Mingus, Tanaka. You guys were the best crew the Red Wrath ever had."

"Minus one," Mingus said.

They sat silently for a moment. Anax pulled a flask from a pocket in his jacket. He filled three metal cups and handed them out.

Anax lifted his flask. "To Leonard Brute," he said.

"To Leonard Brute," they repeated, and downed their drinks.

"Captain Spade," Anax said. "I will fly with you anytime."

"I'm going to remember that," Spade said. He looked out at the activity below.

"Now all I need is old Red."

Tactical Operations Center

Six-wheeled armored cars with large knobby tires crunched over the gravel roads that funneled between high blast walls. The gray armored vehicles were each big enough to carry a squad of infantrymen. Their headlights pierced the haze with bright beams of fluorescent light.

Spade walked along a blast wall in his self-contained Heliac body armor. Visibility was low from the haze and the dust being kicked up by the cars. When an armored car got too close, Spade stopped walking and pressed his back up against one of the walls to avoid being crushed.

Spade's boots crunched on the gravel as he approached an imposing walled building made of gray concrete. The building was known as the Tactical Operations Center, or TOC as it was called, and it was the new military headquarters for the Taji First Armored Infantry Division. An armored Megalan guard stood at a guard shack at the entranceway.

"I have an appointment," Spade said to the guard through the com system in his helmet.

"You have ID?"

Spade transmitted his electronic ID to the guard who then radioed it into the Tactical Operations Center.

"OK, Captain Spade. You're good, sir," the guard said, and snapped a salute. He opened the door to the guard shack and Spade entered a walled gravel courtyard that fronted the imposing Tactical Operations Center.

Atop the arched doorway was a triangular yellow crest centered with a hand drawn painting of a screaming blue falcon.

Spade entered the decompression chamber at the entranceway. The dusty Bioppian air was flushed from the chamber. Spade removed his helmet and entered the building.

Inside the lobby, a large banner centered on the back wall displayed the same screaming blue falcon as outside. Also on the wall was a large framed picture of a stern faced Mayor Lourdes Magna. Beneath her were smaller pictures of the Board of Supervisors.

Next to the picture of the mayor was a similarly large picture of General Jack Winner, looking commanding and heroic in his royal blue armor. Beneath his portrait were pictures of his brigade commanders.

Armored soldiers carried binders and electronic tablets as they walked about briskly. Very few were lower enlisted. Most were high ranking officers—majors and above.

Spade walked down a dusty hallway lined with offices where officers sat behind desks while talking into communicators or drawing up battle plans on computer screens.

Spade came to the end of a hallway and entered a room where an armored Heliac female sat at a desk. She was a second lieutenant. The room was centered by a conference table. A bar with barstools stood at the far end of the room. Heroic paintings of Heliac Rangers at war lined the walls.

"I'm here to see Captain Jack," Spade said to the lieutenant.

"You mean Major General Winner," the lieutenant said.

"Roger. Major General Winner."

"He's expecting you, sir. Please have a seat."

Spade sat down in a large imitation leather chair across from her.

"Would you like a cup of Taji Tea?" she asked.

Spade nodded.

She poured him a cup and handed it to him. She was a fit, attractive blonde.

Spade waited, sipping his tea as he sat silently in his chair.

"What did you do in the Heliac War, LT?" Spade asked, finally breaking the silence.

"I was still in training when the Craaldans attacked," she answered. "At the last minute, the HDF integrated all us cadets into infantry platoons. It was a total cluster. We were green and separated from our friends and just thrown into squads with people we didn't know. I was on Smythe when it was bombarded. Me and three survivors from my squad barely made it off the planet alive, escaping on a troop transport. We drifted through the void for about 60 Earth years before we were picked up by a Megallan interstellar freighter. As far as I know, I'm the only surviving cadet from my class. There were over a thousand of us."

"Did you know General Winner back at Heliac?" Spade asked.

"No," she said. "He was a Ranger doing top secret special operations stuff, so nobody around here really knew him. But you should hear some of the stories he tells. I'd love to meet some of the Rangers he ran with. I bet they could talk for hours about the crazy things he did back in those days."

"I bet."

"LT Horgas," Gen. Winner said over the intercom. "Send in Captain Spade."

"Roger, sir."

She stood and Spade followed her to the door of Gen. Winner's office. She poked her head inside and then looked at Spade.

"The general is ready to see you now, sir."

Spade entered the office. Its walls were covered with maps of the planet. A model of Biop centered the room, with Taji City and the Craaldan positions marked in relief.

Gen. Winner stood from behind his desk and smiled, reaching out his hand. Winner's perfect teeth were pearly white. His eyes were bright blue. His golden blonde hair was cut short in military fashion and his blonde mustache had come in nicely. It was impeccably groomed.

Spade walked up and shook his hand.

"Have a seat, Spade," Winner said, motioning for Spade to sit in the chair in front of his desk.

Spade sat and Winner sat at his desk across from him.

"Would you care for something stronger than tea?" he asked.

"I'll have what you're having."

"LT Horgas," Winner said into the intercom on his desk. "Two whiskeys. On the rocks."

Winner leaned back in his chair and looked at Spade in a relaxed and friendly manner. "How goes the Zephyr Project?" he asked.

"Good. It's coming along."

"You know I am opposed to it," Winner said. "The project, I mean. It's consuming manpower and resources that would best be used in preparing our defenses. But the mayor was dead set on building those ships. She can be insistent."

LT Horgas entered the room and delivered the two whiskeys and then quickly departed.

"The mayor was also insistent that I meet with you today and comply with a request you have for me," Winner said. "So what is the request?"

"I need an aerial utility vehicle to transport myself and a work crew to my ship, the Red Wrath, which is out on the Mesolatium Plain. We can get her up and running in eight hours, max. But I need cover while I'm out there. I'll need air support."

"I can't authorize that," Winner said. "Every aerial vehicle in this city is accounted for—either in repairs or being used for training, transport or reconnaissance patrols. Besides, a bunch of aircraft buzzing over a flat expanse of gravel will attract Craaldan drones and anti-aircraft missiles by the hundreds."

"The mayor and I had a deal," Spade said.

"I can spare an armored car," Winner said. "It's all I've got."

"That will put me out there for days," Spade said.

"I don't recommend you go out there at all," Winner said. "You'll be gambling with your life and the lives of your work crew. Why don't you conduct your salvage operation after we defeat the Craaldan?"

"The mayor and I had a deal, Jack," Spade said.

"One armored car," Winner said. "That's what I can give you. If you get in trouble out there, call for air support. That's all I can do."

Spade began to stand from his chair when Winner put up his hand and signaled for Spade to remain seated.

"I'm afraid I have terrible news," Winner said.

Gen. Winner's piercing blue eyes met Spade's with a look of deadly seriousness. The look stopped Spade cold in his tracks.

"What's up?" Spade asked.

"Dr. Ebos," Winner said. An expression of grief crossed his face. "There was an accident."

"What?"

"Dr. Ebos had been running tests on the city's water supply," Winner said. "He spent hours every day traveling to every corner of the city to collect samples from water storage locations. If you recall, the winds have been severe over the last few days. Apparently, he was climbing a ladder on one of the water towers in the northeast quadrant. The fall was about forty feet. A work crew found his body on a rock pile early this morning."

"How bad is he injured?" Spade asked.

"He was killed on impact."

Spade's face turned white. "It can't be."

"This is a severe blow to all of us. He was beloved by everyone on Escalon Station and had quickly befriended hundreds of citizens here in Taji City. This tragedy couldn't have come at a worse time for us. That is why I want to keep his death quiet for now. It would be bad for morale for the news to get out. I have ordered that there be no mention of his death until after the battle. Once the Craaldan is defeated, then we can hold a funeral with full honors."

Spade's eyes drifted around the room. He couldn't believe what he was hearing.

"I know Dr. Ebos was your friend. In the short time I knew him, he earned nothing but respect from me. He will be missed. But in times like these, as leaders, we must not let an unfortunate tragedy like this detract us from our duties. We must be prepared for all adversities. We must remain strong and maintain a laser-like focus on our mission, which is defeating the Craaldan. That is what Dr. Ebos would have wanted."

"Does Mayor Magna know about this?" Spade asked.

"Yes. She has been under a great deal of pressure these last few weeks. Dr. Ebos was an invaluable advisor to her when she was dealing with the sudden influx of refugees from Escalon, and she had come to rely on his judgment. He was a shoulder for her to lean on. The news of his loss was devastating to her."

"Where is the body?" Spade asked.

"It is at the morgue. It is scheduled for cremation any moment now."

Spade stood and downed the last of his whiskey. He set the glass on Winner's desk. He turned and walked quickly out of the office.

Ennui

Dr. Ebos lay naked on a gurney in the morgue. The skin of his face had been mostly eaten away. Flaky black flesh clung to his bleached skull. His white teeth were exposed in a ghastly smile.

"The Bioppian atmosphere is highly corrosive to human skin," the coroner said.

The coroner was a portly, bearded Taji City man.

Dr. Ebos' eyepieces had been removed. His eye sockets were empty. The atmosphere had eaten away his eyeballs.

"He landed flat on his back on a pile of gravel," the coroner said. "His helmet cracked open when he hit the ground and the back of his skull was crushed. His spine broke in three places and most of his large bones were cracked. He probably died on impact. He had been dead about ten hours when the corrosive effects of the atmosphere began to accelerate and eat away at his tissues."

Spade looked down at the naked, badly decayed body of his friend. Ribs were exposed through blackened skin. Spade was used to seeing Dr. Ebos wearing his red lenses and white lab coat, with spindly mechanical prosthetics running up and down his long arms and legs. Here on the gurney, his corpse looked alien. His arms and legs were long and skinny. His long torso and large head were typical of humans from Paltros. His body was adapted to life on a low gravity planet. Back on his home world, he may have survived a fall from such a height.

"Who ordered the body cremated?" Spade asked.

"General Winner, sir," the coroner said. "We have limited facilities here and we are expecting to be busy once the battle commences. General Winner said when a fatality comes in, as soon as an autopsy is completed, the corpse should be immediately delivered to the crematorium. He wants to avoid hygiene issues if we begin to fill to capacity."

"I want you to hold off on any cremations," Spade said. "Do you understand?"

"But sir, I am under direct orders to remove all corpses to the crematorium as soon as my autopsies are complete."

"No bodies go to the crematorium!" Spade snapped. "Do you understand me?"

The coroner nodded, his face showing his uncertainty.

Spade helped the coroner load Dr. Ebos' body into a refrigerated compartment and then turned to leave.

"Captain Spade," the coroner said. "I worked closely with Dr. Ebos over the past few weeks. He was a good man."

Spade nodded and walked out of the morgue.

He walked through the narrow, dusty corridors to a tram station and caught a tram across town. He exited at a station near the airfield. He walked through narrow underground tunnels, emerging into a spacious aircraft hangar.

Spade's mind was spinning as he walked past rows of parked aircraft. So many humans had been lost in the destruction of Escalon, but the death of Dr. Ebos pained him acutely. He couldn't shake the feeling that something was horribly wrong.

He walked through the large hangar with its high ceiling ribbed with metal support beams. The hangar was filled end to end with row upon row of parked aircraft. The large airships were painted in a digital gray camouflage pattern. The ships had rotating scramjet engines that allowed them to hover, cruise slowly at low altitude, or scream high above the planet at the edge of space. Until recently, the aircraft had rarely been armed, but the ships had all been retrofitted for armaments.

The hangars that lined the Taji City airfield housed mainly four models of locally constructed aircraft.

The most numerous model was the AUV-60, which had a rounded nose and the look of a giant, flying mechanical bull. The AUV-60 was an aerial utility vehicle that could carry up to 18 humans, or haul light loads. It had a crew of two pilots and two crew chiefs, and was armed with flash missiles fired from missile pods by the pilots, and two heavy machine guns operated by the crew chiefs.

The largest model of aircraft in the hangars was the ACV-47 aerial cargo vehicle, which was a squat, fat-bellied beast of an aircraft which could carry a platoon of troops and haul heavy loads of up to 100,000 pounds. It had a crew of five, with a heavy machine gun on its tail and guns on its left and right side windows.

The small, fast-flying AOV-58 was an observation scout vehicle with a crew of one. It was armed with a heavy machine gun on its nose and could carry flash missiles in detachable pods.

Then there was the AAV-64 aerial attack vehicle flown by a crew of two: a pilot and a gunner. The aircraft was a mean machine that had the look of a fierce metallic hornet. It was armed with missile pods and a large chain gun under its nose that could tear through a mountainside or rip through structures and machinery with extreme violence. There had only been a few of them up until Gen. Winner took command of the city's defenses. He had ordered the immediate production of as many AAV-64s as possible.

Teams of mechanics climbed over the large aerial vehicles, checking them over and making repairs. The flight crews ran checks in the cockpits or assisted the mechanics.

The aircraft appeared primitive to Spade, especially for the purpose of modern warfare. They were planetary vehicles only and could not leave the atmosphere. They seemed a throwback to an ancient pre-Space Age era.

The Red Wrath could target and destroy any of these aircraft from the safety of orbit. As soon as one of these vehicles lifted from the ground, old Red could easily zap it with her pulse cannon—no defensive measures necessary.

That being said, these aircraft seemed to work well when it came to flying the thick skies of this planet. The people of Taji City had lost the desire for space voyaging and had developed technology to suit their specific purposes.

These ships seemed somewhat inadequate for a fight against the Craaldan war machine, but they would have to do.

Spade walked up to an AUV-60 parked in a row of aircraft. Capt. Casey was up on the tail, straddling it while using a multi-tool to turn a bolt inside a panel.

Spade stood under her, looking up, watching her work. She moved slowly and methodically, as if in a dreamlike state. Her eyes were focused on her task, but her mind seemed far away.

She finished with the bolt and slipped her multi-tool into a case on her belt.

"Jace. I didn't see you down there."

She slid down the tail and walked along the edge of the aircraft's gray hull before hopping down next to him.

Her eyes were sad and Spade knew instantly that she had already heard the news about Dr. Ebos.

"Oh, Jace." She hugged him, holding him tightly.

"How did you hear?" he asked.

"Tanaka," she said. "He picked up the transmissions when they found the body this morning. I can't believe it, Jace."

"I can't either."

He looked into her face. Her eyes and nose were red.

"This galaxy is cold and cruel," she said.

"No. Dr. Ebos wouldn't think that way," he said.

She sniffled. "You're right. I need a drink. Will you have a drink with me?"

He held out his arm and she took it and held it tightly.

"I'm heading out to retrieve the Red Wrath first thing in the morning," Spade said as they walked past the rows of aircraft. "All General Winner would give me is an armored car, so I'm going to be out there for a few days."

"I'm coming with you," she said.

"No. You stay here," he said. "I might need you to come rescue me in that flying jalopy back there."

A loud alarm blared through the hangar. "Incoming! Incoming! Incoming!"

Everyone in the hangar stopped what they were doing and froze.

"Where's the counter fire?" Capt. Casey asked.

"Better get down," Spade said. He pulled her under the belly of an ACV-47.

A loud braaap, braaap, braaap rattled the hangar.

"That sounds like counter mortar fire," Spade said.

The deafening sound repeated. Braaap, braaap, braaap!

A loud cement crunching crumph shook the ground violently.

Crumph! Crumph! Crumph!

Shrapnel shredded through the hangar wall and peppered the parked aircraft. Dusty air and gray gas flowed inside the hangar through the tears in the wall.

CRUMPH!

"Getting closer!" Spade said.

KABOOM!

Capt. Casey's eyes were closed. She held Spade's arm tightly.

Braaap! Braaap! Braaap!

Friendly artillery cannons unleashed an outgoing barrage from within the city walls. The barrage was thunderously loud but brief.

Then all was still. The air inside the hangar got progressively thicker and grayer and harder to breathe.

Spade and Capt. Casey lay together in silence under the fat belly of the heavy-lift airship. After several minutes, people started to move about the hangar.

"Seal the walls!" someone shouted. "Get those air pumps going!"

"You're not leaving me here by myself," Capt. Casey said. "I'm coming with you in the morning. No arguments."

Salvage team

News spread quickly that a Craaldan scout team had probed the city's defenses, easily evading the early warning sensors that ringed the terrain around the city. The scout team had set up mortars and a small mechanized field gun in a boulder field to the northwest and began lobbing in rounds.

The C-NAM defense system intercepted most of the rounds, but because they were fired at such close range, several had slipped through before a counter fire battery chased off the Craaldan scouts.

Three incoming mortar rounds impacted on the airfield leaving large craters. An artillery shell landed in the center of a road and exploded with tremendous force, knocking down several blast walls, spraying shrapnel and causing damage to surrounding structures. One mortar round impacted inside a residential pod and had vaporized 16 CHUs, killing 36 people and wounding another 50.

The deafening power of the bone rattling blasts had traumatized the city's residents and left them feeling vulnerable. If the scout team had been armed with a tactical nuke, that would have been the end of Taji City.

However, the city's first responders had reacted swiftly, putting out fires and tending to the injured.

Immediately after the shells stopped landing, Spade and Capt. Casey made haste to Zephyr Crater. No rounds had come close to the construction site and work continued unaffected.

After spending the remainder of the day at the crater, Spade and Capt. Casey rode a tram to downtown Taji City. He had rounded up a team of volunteers for his salvage operation and had asked them to assemble at the Biop Bop for a mission brief.

The tram came to a stop at a downtown station and Spade and Capt. Casey exited and walked the narrow corridors past closed up shops and restaurants. They walked through the main door into the Biop Bop.

The lights were on and the stage was empty. No music played. A coat of gray dust covered the floor. The place was empty except for Grimes and Genie. Grimes stood at the bar and Genie stood behind it mixing a drink.

Spade and Capt. Casey approached them. Genie leaned over the bar and gave Capt. Casey a hug. Then Grimes gave Capt. Casey a hug, embracing her for a long moment.

"The last time I was in here, Viz was sitting on that barstool," Capt. Casey said.

"He was a kind man," Genie said. She poured Spade and Capt. Casey drinks.

"You sure you want to go outside the wire tomorrow?" Grimes asked. "That scout team showing up means they're getting ready for their attack. They could have a whole company out there already and you might drive right into the main body. Then you're toast."

"I figure I still have time," Spade said. "They've just started probing us. They didn't expect to lose their interstellar destroyer to humans and they've only got a small force, so they'll probe us a few more times to find out what our capabilities are. They'll send in teams over the next few days before the main assault. If we can get out to the Red Wrath quick, we can repair her and jet back here before it starts. Once I have Red back, I'll feel a lot better about my prospects here."

"Are you sure you want to go out there, Captain Spade?" Genie asked.

"Positive," Spade said.

"Genie and I will monitor your progress," Grimes said. "At the first sign of trouble, we'll send in air support and pull you out of there."

"Will General Winner allow that?" Spade asked.

"I will allow it," Grimes said. "I've already saved your life once on this planet. The odds are good that I'll have to do it again."

Mingus, Pervez Anax, Tanaka and Vomica Nux entered the establishment and walked up to the bar.

"Your salvage team is all present and accounted for and reporting for duty," Mingus said.

Spade led them to a table and briefed them on the plan. They would leave first thing in the morning in an armored car and head for the Mesolatium Plain. Their route would take them over rugged terrain with good concealment until they reached the ruins of Pyramid City. They would drive through the city and then emerge onto the plain. They would be most vulnerable out on the flatland and would speed across it as fast as the vehicle could go. Once they reached the Red Wrath, the clock would be ticking to get her flight worthy. As soon as she could fly, they would jet back to Taji City. If everything went according to plan, they would be back in two and a half days at most, Spade said.

"As usual, you haven't thought this through," Tanaka said. His glowing green lenses turned on Spade. "Don't you think the Craaldans will be watching for someone to return to your ship? They're going to ambush us."

"That's a possibility," Spade said. "But the plain is strewn with wreckage from Escalon. I doubt they've noticed my ship with all the wreckage out there. I think their efforts right now are in preparing for an assault on the city, not setting up ambushes in the middle of nowhere."

"You doubt they've noticed your ship," Tanaka said. "I think they will be waiting to ambush us."

"In the event you are right, we've got to be prepared for an ambush and ready to respond," Spade said. "This mission is risky, I admit. I understand if any of you decide to back out."

"The way things are looking now, we are probably going to die on this planet one way or another," Anax said. "I just ask that if we survive this salvage operation, you save me a seat on the Red Wrath when you rocket out of here."

"Don't talk about dying," Spade said. "It's bad luck."

"I didn't take you for the superstitious type, Captain Spade," Anax said.

"It's a primitive quality of his," Tanaka said. "He enjoys games of chance and he has superstitious notions about luck, fate and death."

"That's right," Spade said. "So no jinxing us with death talk."

"Jinxing? You're killing me with your superstitions," Anax said. "Hey, Genie. I'm dying for a drink. Bring me another one, before I die of thirst over here. All this death talk is making me thirsty. Deathly so."

"Not cool, Perv," Vomica said. Her skinny arm was draped over Tanaka's shoulders. The fluorescent light that illuminated the club highlighted the purple tint of her hair. "But seriously, Captain Spade," she said. "The probability of us getting hit out there is high."

"I've got my fingers crossed that we'll make it out and back without incident. But you're right, Vomica. We need to be ready for contact."

They sat around the table and went over the equipment and weapons they would need, and discussed the various scenarios they might find themselves in and how they would react. They discussed at length what measures to take in case of an ambush.

Grimes gave them pointers and then had them get up and stand on the main floor in the positions they would be in inside their vehicle. Spade and Capt. Casey stood on the floor as if they were in the front cab of the vehicle. Tanaka and Vomica stood behind them. Mingus was in the center where the machine gun would be mounted on the roof of the vehicle, and Anax stood next to her. Grimes had them rehearse the defensive actions they would take if the vehicle got hit. He showed them how to pull 360-degree security and then coordinate their actions to accurately return fire.

"If you get caught in an ambush and react properly, these new armor-piercing rounds will give you a good chance of getting some kills," Grimes said.

Grimes pulled a magazine out of a pocket and flipped out a round with his thumb. He held the round in his fingers. It was black and shiny and about four inches long.

He handed it to Spade who examined it. "These rounds can stop them?" Spade asked.

"Roger," Grimes said. "They are made of armonium. They've got plenty of stopping power. They cut through their armor like butter, and then, pop! Blood and guts everywhere, like a tomato can exploding. These rounds will give us a fighting chance."

"Where'd Captain Jack get them?" Spade asked.

"Beats me," Grimes said.

Tanaka snatched the round from Spade and examined it in his long fingers.

"They are Diocon manufactures, specially designed for use in human weapons," Tanaka said.

"Diocon?" Grimes asked, skeptically.

"Roger," Tanaka said. "It is curious."

"Why would the Diocons design a bullet for human weapons?" Spade asked.

"Why don't you ask General Winner?" Grimes said. "All I know is they work."

After several more walkthroughs of a react to contact battle drill, they sat back down at the table.

Spade put his hands behind his head and leaned back in his chair. "We've got a good crew here," he said. "I'm feeling confident right now."

"Incoming! Incoming! Incoming!"

They all dove down and took cover under the table.

Drive on

The armored vehicle rolled out of the city gate and sped across a gravel field. A gray haze blanketed the field. The haze hung thickly above the rocky surface, or swirled in eddies of wind.

Spade was driving. Capt. Casey sat in the passenger seat next to him.

The big, six-wheeled vehicle was cramped. The rear compartment was crammed full of gear. Sensors mounted atop the vehicle scanned the surrounding terrain for threats and fed data to the vehicle's computer. Tanaka and Vomica sat in the rear compartment, hunched down while monitoring data on a glowing screen.

Mingus was up in the gun turret manning the heavy machine gun. Pervez Anax had wedged himself between two crates. His boots were propped up on a crate as he looked up at Mingus in the turret.

"What do you see out there, Mingus?" Anax asked.

"Dust. Rocks. More dust."

Mingus swiveled the gun around and faced the opposite direction.

"There's nothing to shoot," Anax said to her. "Come down here and play cards with me."

"Later," she said.

The vehicle came to the end of the gravel field and approached a craggy landscape where rock outcroppings and rugged mesas stood above steep ravines. Spade slowed down and maneuvered through the terrain.

"It'll be slow going for a few hours," Spade said.

Capt. Casey had her boots up on the dashboard. She had on the bottom half of her body armor but had removed the top half that covered her torso. Her loose-fitting, brown, sleeveless t-shirt revealed her toned white arms.

The vehicle hit a ditch and bounced, jostling everyone inside.

"Road trips are fun," Capt. Casey said.

Tanaka poked his head up front. His glowing green lenses turned on Spade. "Eyes on the road, Spade," he said.

"There is no road," Spade replied.

Tanaka returned to his spot next to Vomica in front of the monitor.

The vehicle bounced over the uneven ground as it rolled through ravines and around rocky mesas.

"What's your plan after you get Red back?" Capt. Casey asked.

"I don't know," he answered. "What's yours?"

"No plan," she said.

"Do you want to jet out of here?" he asked.

"Not really," she said. "I'm going to stay. But I will understand if you go."

Spade was silent for a while, concentrating on the terrain in front of him.

"I'm not going anywhere," he said. "Not without you." He looked over at her. "And frankly, Mina, I'm upset that you'd understand if I were to go."

"Ditch," she said.

The vehicle hit a ditch and bounced hard.

"Eyes forward, Spade!" Tanaka yelled.

Capt. Casey looked out through the windshield at the rugged, hostile landscape. "I love you, Jace. But I won't hold you back."

"Hold me back?"

Spade steered the vehicle around a particularly rough patch of ground and paid careful attention to the steep ledge they were rolling next to.

"Do you believe in fate, Mina?" he asked.

"Fate? Not really."

"Then why the fatalism?" he asked.

She pondered his question before giving her answer.

"Nothing in my experience leads me to believe that the course of our lives is predetermined," she said. "Events that I have no control over sweep me along and take me places I don't want to go. I bounce from one disaster to the next. I've tried to exert control over my life, but it never works out the way I plan. It's all been pretty random for me."

"But we've had fun," he said. "It's always interesting."

"True."

She looked over at him. Spade was a dashing figure at the wheel of this large armored car. His gloved hand was on the wheel as he steered the vehicle over the alien landscape.

"I've had good times, but there's so much sadness, too," she said. "The galaxy spins around. Events unfold unpredictably. Most of the people and the places I loved have been gone for a long time now. Time marches on with or without me. It gets to me sometimes."

His right hand was on the compartment between their seats. She placed her hand atop his.

"Don't worry about me, though. I'm a big girl." She smiled and turned her gaze back out the windshield.

"I'm worried about you, no doubt about that," he said.

"What about you?" she said. "Do you believe in fate?"

"I'm no philosopher," he said. "But back at The Plunge when we were surfing those waves it got me thinking about how we're all caught in the current of time, and it carries us along like you said. It's always threatening to pull us under. But, if you make the effort, you can ride the wave. If you try, you can get good at it, and ride it on your own terms, and even throw in a little flair. We're still here. All those random events and disasters bounced you all over the galaxy until they brought you to me."

"I wish you would have talked like this the first time we met," she said. "Remember back then? You chased after me, and once you caught me, you dumped me and left me alone. To make matters worse, you abandoned me on a smelly old asteroid. I was stuck there for three years, depressed with a broken heart."

"Can I explain myself?"

"Go ahead."

"The first time I saw you, it was love at first sight."

"Humph!" she exclaimed, incredulously.

"If you recall, Mina, you and Grimes were an item then. And I had a thing for Genie. She was my companion on all those deep space voyages I was taking back then. Well, the four us were a crew and we were zooming across the Inner Galaxy in old Red and we nearly got ourselves killed more times than I can count, and there was all this tension and innuendo and it was driving me nuts. Then Grimes ended up with Genie and I ended up with you, and our crew fell apart. Then when you and I were docked on the Drang Asteroid, I got a tip on the whereabouts of Dr. Zander and I knew by then that you were finished with the Inner Galaxy. But I had to check it out. I knew you wouldn't come with me, so I left. But after I did, when I was drifting out there alone, I knew I had made the biggest mistake of my life."

"You left me to try to steal Genie back from Joe," Capt. Casey said.

"Mina, I'm trying to tell you that you're the only gal for me. Believe me, I mean it."

"You know what's crazy?" she asked. "I think I actually believe you."

"Stay with me. We'll get off this rock and I'll find the place you're looking for. Sun, sea, sand. You and me. Together."

The pale Cextos sun was setting behind a craggy horizon. Its feint rays lit up the thick atmosphere in faded red, green and yellow.

Mingus was snoring loudly in the back. Pervez was snoozing, cuddled up against her large frame. Tanaka and Vomica sat close together in the tight confines of the compartment, staring into a screen propped up on a crate as they played a computer strategy game.

Spade turned on the headlights. The beams shone through the dust and illuminated the rocky ground.

He drove through the night until Capt. Casey saw him struggling not to nod off. She made him switch places and took the wheel.

Capt. Casey drove across the bleak landscape as Spade napped beside her. She kept one eye on the terrain and the other on the sensors that scanned for threats.

Eventually, the sun began to rise. The blackness faded to gray.

"Hey, Jace," she said.

He stirred from sleep.

"Look at that."

The vehicle bounced down a decline and onto a vast expanse that stretched to the hazy horizon. The flat landscape was dominated by monolithic pyramids in the thousands that reached upward to Cextos, which was a flat disk of light rising in the haze behind the dead city of stone.

Tal Taji

Towering stone ruins were silhouetted against the gray haze. The six-wheeled armored vehicle rolled along an ancient, rubble-strewn boulevard toward the lost city.

Capt. Casey drove slowly around the rubble. Tanaka and Vomica had moved forward for a better view out the windshield.

"Pyramid City," Spade said. "I don't have good memories of this place."

"That's not its real name," Tanaka said. "It was called Tal Taji, which means city of rivers in the language they spoke here. The first space drifters that landed here named their colony after this place. Back then, they called their colony New Taji City."

The vehicle entered Tal Taji and rolled between the rough hewn bases of massive pyramids.

"Where are the rivers?" Spade asked.

"They were blasted away when the Craaldans nuked the planet 2,500 years ago," Tanaka said.

"Did they live in these pyramids?" Capt. Casey asked.

"Yes," Vomica interjected. "Each pyramid housed an extended family. Mothers, fathers, children, uncles, aunts, cousins, grandparents. They all lived together in their family pyramid. They would build new levels as the families grew generation after generation. By the time the Craaldans showed up, the pyramids had grown to the height they are now."

"Jace and I were at the top of one of these things," Capt. Casey said as she steered the vehicle through the streets. "It was flat up there, like an observation deck, or a landing pad."

"Not a landing pad," Tanaka said. "They didn't have aircraft here, or even the wheel, for that matter. The tops of the pyramids were used for family celebrations. This was a warlike civilization, and families distinguished themselves through warfare. After a battle, the warriors would drag their prisoners of war to the tops of their pyramids and behead them at sunrise. Then they would barbecue the bodies and gorge themselves on the meat and spend the rest of the day up there debauching themselves. The heads of their slain prisoners would be stuck on pikes on the tops of every pyramid in the city. At sunset, they'd light the heads on fire. Thousands of flaming skulls would light up the night across this city of millions. The celebration was called Night of the Flaming Skulls."

"Thanks for ruining my trip through Pyramid City," Capt. Casey said.

"The population of the planet was about 500 million when the Craaldans arrived," Tanaka continued. "Tal Taji was the biggest city with over 20 million residents. It could field armies of over a million warriors. The armies would march through these boulevards on their way to war. For hundreds of years, the citizens of Tal Taji ravaged their neighbors, killing and enslaving them."

"What was their level of technological development?" Spade asked.

"They never made it out of the stone age," Vomica said. "No bronze, iron or steel. No machines. They fought with spiked clubs and with spears tipped with sharpened stone blades. They didn't have domesticated animals other than a species of large rodent-like creatures that they raised for food."

"Charming," Capt. Casey said.

"This planet had no oceans or significant seas," Vomica continued. "Biop was thickly forested, mostly with conifers, and had many long rivers that were fed by rainfall flowing off the mountains. But the planet was very hot and dry. The rivers emptied into shallow lakes that often dried up in the heat of the sun. Before the Craaldans came, the skies weren't gray like now, but a clear blue."

"When the Craaldans arrived, they set up a camp about 100 miles outside of Tal Taji," Tanaka said. "The city raised an army of six million soldiers and marched on the Craaldan camp. The warriors banged drums and whooped and hollered with great confidence while on the march. The Craaldans had landed three infantry divisions with a total of about 50,000 troopers. When the Tal Taji warriors saw that they had the Craaldans greatly outnumbered, they whooped themselves into a frenzy and sprinted, screaming at the top of their lungs, toward the Craaldan position in a great, thunderous stampede. The Craaldans slaughtered the warriors in a hail of mortar and small arms fire, throwing the Tal Taji warriors into a chaotic panic. Blood and body parts were flying everywhere. The Tal Taji army became a crushing torrent of bodies as the wide-eyed warriors trampled and mashed each other as they retreated back to the city. The Craaldans pursued them and butchered them with their bayonets, killing every last Tal Taji warrior without losing a single trooper."

"Live by the sword, die by the sword," Capt. Casey said.

"The Craaldans spent about six months here killing off the Bioppians in a series of smaller battles that decimated the planet's population," Tanaka said. "They stripped the planet of much of its water and ores and then blasted off with about 5,000 captives. They blew up the planet's moon and extracted a portion of its iron core. Before they left orbit, they bombarded the planet with nukes. This lifeless planet you see now is the Craaldan legacy."

"I wonder if this is what Nebas looks like," Capt. Casey said.

"Yes," Tanaka said. "But without the pyramids."

"Jace," Mingus said through the vehicle's intercom. She was standing in the gun turret. "This is the perfect place for an ambush. I'm feeling vulnerable right now."

"The sensors are showing green," Spade said.

Mingus swiveled around in the turret, swinging her weapon up and down, aiming down alleyways and into pyramid balconies and entranceways.

"We're clear, right, Vomica?" Spade asked.

"Tanaka and I have been monitoring the sensors all night and there's been no movement in the city," she said. "No vehicles have come in or out. Nothing indicates the Craaldans have any presence here. But that doesn't mean we shouldn't be cautious."

The vehicle entered an open stone plaza. At each corner of the plaza stood a 30-foot stone statue of a Tal Taji warrior in full battle dress. The corroded stone warriors wore helmets topped with a row of spikes. Feathered stone plumes were attached to their elbows, shoulders and backs. They held circular shields and spiked clubs and long pikes. Their eyes bulged out of their heads. Their long tongues stuck out from their gaping mouths. Their faces were contorted in horrific scowls.

"They conducted mass sacrifices in this plaza," Tanaka said. "Females, children, the elderly, you name it. On their holy days, they would drag their captives up there on that platform and skin them alive and then cook them on spits and have huge feasts. They'd butcher thousands in a day. The gutters would gush with blood. "

"I've heard enough," Capt. Casey said. "What an awful people."

"Don't be so judgmental, Mina," Vomica said. "They had many good qualities. Other than slavery, they were egalitarian and had no poverty. When they weren't at war, they had plenty of leisure time that they spent with their families. They were very family oriented and respected their elders and placed high value on children and parenthood."

"I'm sorry for being judgmental," Capt. Casey said. "Just because they were murderous cannibals doesn't mean they weren't nice people."

"They also had great music," Vomica said. "Actually, their music is popular in some human communities. There's a deejay on Vacteria who's a descendant of Bioppian runaways. He's pretty awesome."

"Did he work at the Funky Junky?" Capt. Casey asked.

"Roger," Vomica said.

"I remember that guy," Pervez Anax said from the rear compartment.

"Was he the tall guy with red skin, no ears and bugged out eyeballs?" Spade asked.

"That was him," Vomica said.

"He had this long tongue, and right before closing time he would stick it out and light it on fire," Capt. Casey said.

"He never wore a shirt," Mingus said over the intercom. "He had six nipples."

"His name was Steven Manfred and he was the best deejay on Vacteria," Tanaka said. "Rockin' beats."

"Old Steve Manfred," Anax said. "Did I tell you guys about the Vacterian woman I almost married? I met her at the Funky Junky."

Their armored vehicle rolled down the boulevard past row after row of darkened pyramids. They drove for about an hour until they reached the city's outer limits.

The vehicle rolled past ancient rock quarries and then reached the edge of a flat expanse called the Mesolatium Plain.

The vehicle slowed to a stop. Spade and Capt. Casey swapped seats.

"Vomica, give us an intel update," Spade said.

"A formation of Craaldan drones is flying toward Mount Mactus on the opposite side of the planet," Vomica said. "The sensors are detecting no enemy activity in this hemisphere. As you know, we've determined that the Mesolatium Plain is where we will be most vulnerable to a Craaldan attack. We'll be out in the open and easy to see. It's about two hours from here to the Red Wrath if you really punch it."

"Tell me again our odds of being detected," Spade said.

"Best estimate, fifty-fifty," she said.

"Listen up," Spade said. "Strap in. Make sure your body armor is on and your helmet and weapon are at hand. Remember the rehearsals Grimes ran us through the other night and be prepared for anything, copy?"

"Copy that," they said.

"You guys ready?" Spade asked.

"Punch it," Capt. Casey said.

Spade floored the accelerator and the armored car kicked up gravel as it raced forward onto the plain.

Cluster

Spade pushed the armored vehicle to its maximum speed. Its big tires threw up fans of gravel as it ripped across the flat, featureless plain. Visibility through the gray haze was only a mile or two, depending on how the wind was gusting.

"I've been thinking," Spade said.

"Uh oh," Capt. Casey said.

"When we get back to Taji City, I'm going to have a talk with Mayor Magna. I'm going to tell her that as soon as Zephyr Three is completed, we should evacuate the city."

"She's already made her decision," Capt. Casey said. "She wants to stay and fight."

"She's the one who put me on the Zephyr Project," Spade said. "She has misgivings about General Winner's plan."

"The people have decided, Jace. They want to defend their homes."

"Do you think they made the right decision?" he asked.

"Not really."

"It's stupid to throw away so many lives for a dead planet in a fight that can't be won," he said.

"If we evacuate the planet, they're going to come after us, anyway," she said. "It's just delaying the inevitable."

"No," he said.

The car sped past a large section of Escalon Station. The charred chunk of the station's outer wall was half buried in the gravel.

"Something about General Winner doesn't sit right with me," Spade said. "I'm going to talk to the mayor and have her convince her people that the best option is to get out while the going is good. If we have enough lead time, we can make a clean escape. Tanaka mapped out a few solar systems on the galaxy perimeter that look like good places to hide out. We can put the Zephyrs in orbit and build ourselves a ship for the trip to the Calli Sector. We've located some gaseous planets that might have moons that will provide us with raw materials to build a top-of-the-line deep space transport. We'll make it better than Escalon."

"The people love General Winner," she said. "They want to follow him. They believe in him."

"That last indirect fire attack spooked them," he said. "It woke them up to reality. If Lourdes explains to them that evacuation is the best option, they will follow her."

"I don't know, Jace."

"Please back me on this."

He reached over and squeezed her gloved hand.

She looked at him and held her gaze. The bangs of her cropped black hair fell over her dark eyes.

He loved the smoothness of her fair skin. Her cheeks were rosy from the stuffy heat in the vehicle cabin.

It had taken him a while to figure it out, but she was the girl of his dreams. He had been attracted to her the first moment he saw her. But the realization that he needed her came only after separation. His biggest fear now was losing her again. As she sat in the passenger seat looking at him, he worried about the wheels that were turning behind her dark eyes.

"I've got your back, Jace," she said. "Always."

"I have a visual on the Red Wrath," Tanaka said. "A mile and half out, at your 12 o'clock."

"I see her on the scanner," Spade said.

A sudden crush of extreme force flipped the vehicle into the air. The ground erupted in a giant bulging geyser of dirt. The vehicle flipped around and around and crashed to the ground and rolled violently. The chaotic force of the impact jarred them with bone-crushing power.

Spade wasn't sure how much time had elapsed when he came to. His head throbbed acutely. He felt a sharp pain in his left temple and another in his left wrist. A powerful pressure contracted on his legs and chest, rendering him immobile. Warm blood flowed from his temple and trickled off his forehead.

He began to collect his bearings. The vehicle was on its right side. He was pinned behind the steering wheel. His seatbelt suspended him in his seat. His body weight crushed against the straps as he hung above Capt. Casey, who was still in the passenger seat which was now below him. She was unconscious in her seat. Her head rested against the door peacefully.

The outside air was flowing into the cabin. Each inhalation burned his lungs.

"Mina," he said.

She did not stir.

His helmet was by her feet, out of reach. He struggled to free his right arm and then pulled a knife from a sheath strapped to his leg. He cut through the straps that pinned him to his seat. He pushed against the top of the car to keep from falling onto Capt. Casey as he lowered himself down to her. Every movement caused his wrist to burn with pain.

Capt. Casey's helmet was still on its mount on the floor between the two seats. He lifted her head and slid on her helmet and started up the oxygen flow.

He picked up his helmet and put it on and activated his oxygen flow.

"Mina, do you copy?" he said into the helmet communicator.

She coughed.

"Anyone else copy?" he said. "Report in."

"Tanaka copies."

"Vomica's here."

"Anax is up."

"Mingus?" Spade asked.

"She's unconscious," Anax said.

"Get her helmet on," Spade said. "Pronto."

It was claustrophobic in the confined space of the cluttered car, and every movement was now difficult. Spade struggled to get a proper angle to cut away the straps that held Capt. Casey to her seat.

"That was a landmine," Tanaka said. "It had a jammer. That's why we didn't pick it up on the sensors. They knew we were coming."

"I'm picking up movement on the scanner," Vomica said.

"A Craaldan drone is approaching at our three o'clock!" Tanaka said. "Three miles out! It's coming in fast!"

"Get out of the car now!" Spade said. "Move!"

Spade tugged at Capt. Casey and attempted to pull her up from her seat.

"The rear hatch is jammed," Anax said. "We'll have to go out the front."

"That drone just landed, 500 yards out!" Tanaka said. "It set down in a depression at our three o'clock!"

"Patch me the feed," Spade said.

Spade watched an infrared video feed on his helmet display. Five Craaldan troopers were moving through the haze. The troopers dropped down in the prone on the gravel with their weapons pointed toward the car.

"They're getting a bead on us," Spade said. "We need to get out of here."

"They could have hit us from the air," Vomica said. "Why aren't they shooting?"

Spade pulled Capt. Casey up from her seat. They stood on the car door, which was pressed against the gravel.

Spade tried to open the driver's side door above him but the latch was jammed. He grunted as he struggled with it and pushed with all his might against it.

Tanaka clambered up to the front cabin, moving around them like a spider in the confined space. He wedged his back against the seat and kicked the latch with his boot. He, Spade and Capt. Casey then pushed the heavy door upward.

Tanaka climbed out. Spade boosted Capt. Casey up and out.

He continued monitoring the feed, but now he could no longer see the Craaldans through the haze.

"Move, Vomica!"

He helped her as she clambered up and out the door.

"Let's move, Perv!" he said.

The air in the cabin was now thick with gray dust. Anax tugged Mingus' huge form through the jumble of gear that cluttered the rear cabin. When he reached the front compartment, he tried to pull Mingus through, but her big body wedged between the seats and gear.

"You climb out," Spade said. "I'll lift her up and you pull her out. Tracking?"

"Roger that."

Anax climbed out and stood over the door atop the capsized armored car. Spade pulled and tugged and grunted trying to pull giant Mingus through the tight space, but there wasn't enough room.

He pulled his knife from its sheath and desperately hacked away at the passenger seat. He created enough space to tug her limp form through.

"Grab her before she crushes me down here," Spade said.

"Jupiter's Ghost, she's heavy!" Anax said.

Spade pushed her from behind while Anax flexed and pulled using all the strength in his arms and legs. Anax grunted and stood erect on the side of the car as he pulled her up from the door.

In an instant, Anax's head exploded in a pink mist. A sniper round hit its mark. His headless body fell limp. The entire weight of Mingus's huge armored form fell atop Spade, crushing him downward onto the door beneath him.

Prisoner of war

"Pervez!" Capt. Casey screamed.

Capt. Casey, Tanaka and Vomica fired rapid bursts from their weapons into the haze. The red tracer rounds streaked into the gray.

"Hold your fire!" Spade said. "You'll give up your positions."

He struggled desperately to get free from under the crushing weight of Mingus' body until he found himself in the rear compartment of the car.

A rocket whizzed over the gravel from the three o'clock and struck the front of the car with a clang. It exploded with a ba-crumph.

The force of the blast smashed Spade hard and knocked him forcefully against the inner wall of the car. Shrapnel ripped through his armor.

The rocket had detonated in the engine block and had ripped open the bottom of the car.

He lay with his back against the ceiling of the wrecked, overturned car. Hot, sticky blood flowed beneath his flight suit.

He was still receiving visual feeds from the car's sensors. The cameras had been mounted on poles, but now one of the cameras was lying on the ground, while the other stuck out at an odd angle from the gun turret. He could see Capt. Casey, Tanaka and Vomica on the ground in the prone with their weapons pointed toward the Craaldans' last known positions. They were spaced apart in a semicircle at the vehicle's nine o'clock. They had no cover, other than a few melon-sized rocks that they did their best to hide behind.

Spade could see the five Craaldan soldiers moving in through the haze. They were bounding. One of them hopped to his feet, ran 20 yards, and dropped back down. Then the next one ran while the others covered him.

"Three o'clock," Spade said. "Bounding."

"He's up!" Tanaka said. "I see him!"

"Jace, get out of there!" Capt. Casey said.

"I can't," he said. "I'm trapped."

Tanaka fired a burst at a running Craaldan, who immediately dropped and took cover in the dirt.

The Craaldans returned fire. A barrage of molten metal exploded from their high-powered weapons. The storm of rounds ripped the armored car apart in an explosion of metal and glass. Grenades thump-thumped, throwing off shrapnel-laced, bone-crushing shockwaves.

The Craaldan barrage ceased. Spade lay still in the smoldering car. It was now open to the sky. His helmet was cracked. His armor was punctured in several places. He was bleeding badly and having difficulty breathing. He worried that he was bleeding out.

"Anybody copy?" he rasped.

He pulled himself up over the backside of the car and looked out at the plain. He saw no sign of his friends.

He looked over his shoulder through the haze. An armored Craaldan trooper strode over the gravel toward him. The soldier was 10 feet tall in his black mechanized armor. He had a yellow faceplate and yellow coloring at the joints and carried a CX-649 weapons system, which he was pointing at Spade's back. The trooper dropped the muzzle and slung his weapon over his shoulder. He popped a long bayonet from his fist. It extended with a zing.

Spade struggled to climb over the side of the car but he was too weak. Searing pain shot from his wrist with every movement. His legs were unresponsive. Sticky blood ran over his eyes. The Bioppian air was leaking into his helmet. It burned in his nostrils and lungs. Waves of white pain whipped up his spine as he struggled to climb out of the car.

"Get down, Jace!"

Capt. Casey sprinted out of the haze with her weapon at the ready. She fired a burst at the approaching Craaldan, who dove for the dirt.

Capt. Casey slid on her haunches in the gravel and came to a stop with her back against the wrecked undercarriage of the car. She stood and popped off another burst before ducking back down. She grabbed Spade by the back of his shoulders and pulled him over the side of the car and down to the dirt.

The two of them had their backs against the wreckage of the vehicle. Spade was without his weapon. He could hear Capt. Casey's rapid breathing over the radio.

On the video feed, he could see Craaldan silhouettes moving in through the haze, quickly but cautiously. Two had their bayonets extended. The three others were covering them with their weapons at the ready.

"Do you see them?" Spade rasped.

"Roger," Capt. Casey said. "They're going to skewer us."

The Craaldan troopers were only a few yards away now.

"Jace," she said.

"Yeah?"

"I love you."

Three AAV-64 aerial attack vehicles zoomed in low and made a pass over the wrecked armored car. Two of the gray hornet-like aircraft screamed away while the third swung around and hovered several hundred yards away. The aircraft turned its nose toward the armored car. Its powerful jet engines emitted a deafening whine as they blasted exhaust downward into the gravel. The aircraft's chain gun swiveled left and right under its nose. The gun fired, chewing up the gravel around the car like a band saw cutting through plywood.

One of the Craaldan troopers stood up and took aim with his CX-649 as the chain gun rounds ripped past him across the gravel. The trooper fired a burst, which hit the AAV-64 square in the cockpit. The canopy shattered. The aircraft drifted to the right and then quickly lost altitude. Gravity took hold and the aircraft slammed sideways into the ground with a crunch. It exploded with a clap.

The two other AAV-64s made another high-speed pass, tearing up the gravel with their chain guns as they screamed past overhead.

A big Craaldan trooper vaulted over the side of the armored car and stood over Capt. Casey and Spade. The huge armored soldier looked down at them from behind his yellow faceplate. His long bayonet was unsheathed.

Capt. Casey looked up through her dented faceplate at the towering armored alien.

"Zeth?" she asked.

She raised her weapon, but with a flick of his bayonet, the Craaldan sliced it in two.

The big trooper looked over his shoulder at the fast approaching AAV-64s. Both aircraft fired salvos of rockets from the pods that extended from their underbellies.

The explosions sprayed rocks and gravel and smoke. A rocket impacted close to the armored car. The force of the blast heaved the wreckage into the air, tossing Spade upward. He hit the gravel hard, landing flat on his face.

He was stunned for a moment. He tried to move but he was paralyzed. He blinked his eyes and tried to focus. Lying in the dirt a few yards away was Pervez Anax's headless body. White phosphorous sparked and burned on the scorched armor on Anax's back.

The Craaldans were retreating back to their aerial drone. An AAV-64 hovered several hundred yards away. It opened up with its chain gun and hit one of the running Craaldans, cutting him in half.

A Craaldan soldier turned and faced the hovering aircraft. The soldier was their gunner and was armed with a CX-1049, which was a larger version of the weapon his fellow riflemen carried. A rocket launcher flipped open from the side of his big gun.

The Craaldan pulled the trigger and a rocket corkscrewed upward and struck the AAV-64 in the belly. The explosion broke the hovering aircraft in two. The two separating pieces fell toward the ground.

The canopy blew off the front of the falling aircraft and the pilot and his gunner ejected. They rocketed upwards until their seats fell away and their parachutes opened. As they drifted downward, the Craaldans took aim and opened up on them. The Craaldan rounds flayed the bodies of the two humans into chunks of flying meat. Their parachutes gusted away in the wind.

Spade saw a Craaldan stand up from the smoldering wreckage of the armored car. The big trooper kicked away debris and then trotted off over the gravel. He was carrying Capt. Casey's limp form under his arm.

"Mina!" Spade yelled through gritted teeth.

He pulled himself to his feet and chased after them, limping in agony but running as hard as he could. He stumbled and fell but got up and pursued them with an intensity of purpose. He scooped up his weapon from the dirt without breaking his run.

He was out on the open ground now but the big Craaldan was pulling away. Spade dropped to a knee, took aim and fired off a shot. His round hit its mark and knocked the Craaldan flat.

A barrage of rounds were fired back at him. Spade hit the dirt and took what cover he could behind stones.

The lone surviving AAV-64 made another pass and swung around, firing its chain gun. Spade stood and ran toward the fallen Craaldan.

About two hundred yards to his right, an AUV-60 aerial utility vehicle came in low and touched down. A squad of soldiers in white and blue armor jumped out and ran toward the drone as their AUV-60 lifted off and turned and flew away low to ground.

The Craaldans fired at the approaching human soldiers, hitting one and knocking him down. The human soldiers dropped to the dirt.

Spade sprinted across the gravel with his weapon at the ready. He was expecting to see Capt. Casey and the Craaldan he had shot, but he didn't come upon them.

"Mina!" he yelled as he ran.

The gravel crunched under his boots as he ran through the gray haze. He saw the black Craaldan drone parked in a depression. Its rear door raised and clamped shut and the aircraft lifted off.

It hovered upward and leaned forward and then blasted away.

Spade ran after it. He stopped and fired his weapon but the aircraft was gone. There was only dust.

Thick dust clouds gusted over the plain. In front of him, a column of oily black smoke billowed upward from the shattered shell of an AAV-64.

Spade dropped his weapon. Intense pain seized his nerves. His lungs burned. Blood flowed thickly from his nose and pooled inside his helmet. He felt weak-kneed and lightheaded. His field of vision narrowed and the world faded to white. He leaned over and put his hands on his knees to keep from falling over.

"Mina," he said.

Ate up

Spade stared at the cracks in the ceiling. He was on his back on a gurney in a plain room with tan walls.

He was shirtless. He lay still not knowing how he got here or how long he had been here.

A bandage was wrapped tightly around his head, and another around his wrist. A type of organic epoxy had hardened over the numerous gashes, cuts and puncture wounds that covered his torso. A long red gash traced over his forehead above his right eye socket, and another on his cheek beneath his left eye.

He expected to see glowing red lenses appear at any moment, until he remembered that Dr. Ebos was no more.

"Mina," he rasped.

He sensed a presence in the room. He propped himself up on his elbows and saw the spiky, platinum hair and pale blue eyes of his friend Joe Grimes.

Grimes sat in a chair with its back leaned against the wall. Grimes watched him. "Two times I've saved you now."

"Seven left."

"Cats have nine lives. Dogs have one."

"How long have I been here?" Spade asked.

"Thirty-six hours," Grimes replied. "The medics spent the first eight hours picking shrapnel out of your carcass. They pulled an unexploded bullet from your hip and another bullet fragment from your ribs. They kept filling you up with plasma but it just leaked out onto the floor, like refilling a bucket that's full of holes. Messy."

Spade sat up and turned and put his bare feet on the warm floor.

"I always thought you were a cream puff," Grimes said, "but I must admit, you can take a bullet."

"It's not the first time," Spade said.

Spade stood and walked to the mirror and looked at his battered face. He rubbed his blackened, bloodshot eyes. Grimes watched him closely from his chair.

"Tell me what happened," Spade said.

"I had one of my guys watching you by satellite," Grimes explained. "He saw when you hit that landmine. We picked up the track of an incoming drone so I scrambled three AAV-64s and loaded up a QRF squad into an AUV-60. One of the 64s was shot down right away with both crew members killed. A second 64 took out a Craaldan heavy infantryman before he was shot down—both crew members killed. One of my riflemen was shot and killed right after we exited our 60. We started laying down grazing fire. Genie sniped another Craaldan trooper before they retreated to their drone and bugged out. We found you half dead in the dirt and medevacked you out."

Spade tried to bring himself to ask about Mina but couldn't find the words.

"Tanaka and Vomica are fine," Grimes said. "The concussion from a grenade had knocked them out cold. They were unconscious when we found them. Mingus was shot full of shrapnel like yourself and suffered broken bones, but she is strong and will make a full recovery. Anax is dead."

Spade's hands were on the sink as he looked vacantly into the mirror. He closed his eyes.

"We couldn't find Mina. I had my guys form a line and we walked up and down the entire grid square, turning over every rock and searching through every dirt pile. We were out there for hours. I had the scanners going. We used satellite, infrared, radar, lasers, everything. General Winner was livid. He ordered us back in and chewed me out, blaming me for the whole fiasco."

"They took her," Spade said.

He grabbed the shirt that hung from the wall and put it on.

"Where are you going?" Grimes asked.

"I don't know," Spade said. "Somewhere. Anywhere."

Spade searched for his boots but they were nowhere to be found. "I need to talk to the mayor."

"She's not the mayor anymore," Grimes said.

"What?"

"While you were out, she made a citywide announcement stating that because of the planetary emergency it was imperative to have a streamlined command structure. She turned over the city to General Winner. Elections will be held after the threat has passed."

"Martial law?"

"You got it."

"Where is she? I need to talk to her."

"She's usually at the Mayor's Cell," Grimes said.

Spade walked barefoot to the door. Grimes stood from his chair.

"Hey, Spade," Grimes said. "I've got one bit of good news for you. We recovered the Red Wrath. It took four ACV-47s to lift it and haul it in. General Winner nearly blew his top when he found out I sent the 47s out there."

"Where is she?"

"Maintenance Hangar 4," Grimes said.

"Thanks, Grimes," Spade said. "I owe you one."

"You owe me more than one," he said.

Spade reached for the door.

"Hold on," Grimes said. "I got your boots and flight suit from your CHU."

Grimes tossed him a bag.

Spade dressed and they left the room. They walked down a narrow hallway. Grimes led him into a room where Mingus was propped up in a hospital bed eating a meal.

"Jace!"

Spade walked up to her and took her big hand. "You look good," he said.

"You look like hell," she said.

"You should stop hanging out with me," he said. "I'm trouble."

"You are," she said. "But don't beat yourself up about it. We chose to go out there with you. Pervez chose. And Mina."

She patted his hand. "I'll be out of this bed in a day or two," she said. "I'll be here if you need me."

"What are you eating?" Grimes asked. "The smell. I'm dry heaving inside."

"Biop slop," she said. "Hospital Biop slop, so it's even tastier."

Spade and Grimes left the clinic. They walked through the city's narrow, dusty corridors. The few people who were out and about were armed and wearing armor. Spade and Grimes entered a station and boarded a tram to the Mayor's Cell.

The Mayor's Cell was empty. It seemed abandoned. They walked down a dark hallway toward the mayor's office.

They heard sobbing.

They entered the office waiting area. Vice Mayor Malva Fung was seated behind the receptionist desk with her face held in her hands. She was in body armor. Her long, tawny hair was a tangled mess. It covered her face and shoulders as she sobbed. She inhaled deeply before sobbing again.

"Malva?" Grimes asked.

She looked up. Her eyes were red. She was a wreck.

"Oh, Sergeant First Class Grimes," she said. She stood up from the desk. "Sergeant First Class Grimes!"

She let out another sob.

"What's wrong?" Grimes asked.

"Lourdes is dead. Oh, it's awful. Lourdes is dead."

She bawled uncontrollably and nearly fell to the floor, catching herself on the desk.

Spade grabbed hold of her and held her. The vice mayor buried her face in his chest as she cried.

"What are you saying?" Grimes asked, with deep concern. "Tell us what you are saying."

Malva sobbed on Spade's chest. "Lourdes wasn't herself anymore after she gave up the mayor's seat. She was so nervous and fidgety and couldn't concentrate on anything. I should have seen it. I knew she was under pressure. I should have done something. But I never would have imagined she would do something this drastic."

Malva's hands were on Spade's shoulders. She pressed her face in his chest as she cried.

"What did she do?" Spade asked.

"She jumped off the roof of the Mayor's Cell," Malva said. "Oh, Lourdes. Oh, Lourdes."

"Impossible," Grimes said.

"She died from a fall?" Spade asked.

Malva nodded her head, still pressed against Spade's chest.

"Were there any witnesses?" Spade asked.

"I left her alone in her office last night. I was so worried about her when I woke up this morning. I went to her villa but she wasn't there. I came here and searched everywhere. I was in such a panic. We made citywide announcements and I organized a search party. Then a Heliac Ranger found her outside. She had walked out onto the roof without any outerwear, not even a mask. She jumped and fell three-stories onto the courtyard."

"How do you know she jumped?" Spade asked.

"There is surveillance video," she said. "Oh, Lourdes."

"You saw the video?" Spade asked.

"I couldn't watch. It's too awful. Oh, Lourdes. How could you?"

"Listen to me," Spade said. "Where is the video?"

"At the TOC," Malva said between deep inhalations. "General Winner has it."

Spade stepped back. He held her shoulders and then swept the hair from her wet face and looked her in the eyes. "Are you going to be OK?" he asked.

"No," she sobbed.

"Stay with her, Grimes," Spade said. He placed the vice mayor into Grimes' arms.

"What is happening to us, Sergeant Grimes?" she asked. She buried her head in Grimes' chest. "Our whole world is falling apart."

"Take her to Ramone," Spade said. "Don't leave her alone, not for a second."

"Where are you going?" Grimes asked.

"To the TOC."

Confrontational

Spade walked into the guard shack in front of the TOC and was stopped by a soldier. The big armored Megalan insisted that Spade was not authorized for entry.

Spade's armor had been destroyed so he was attired in Taji City outwear as he stood in the courtyard arguing with the guard to no avail, until finally giving up and shoving the big man to the ground. Spade walked past the astonished guard and entered the TOC and walked straight to Gen. Winner's office passing LT Horgas without saying a word.

"Captain Spade!" she said as he walked past her desk. "You do not have an appointment!"

Gen. Winner was at his desk talking into a microphone while looking at maps on a computer monitor.

"We need to talk," Spade said.

Winner looked up from his screen at Spade who stood in front of his desk. Winner's eyes lingered on the bandage wrapped around Spade's head and on the bruises and cuts on his face. Spade stood in the heavy boots, khaki canvas overalls and air filter backpack that Taji residents wore when venturing into the atmosphere. Spade's air mask dangled from his hand.

"Stand by, Colonel Ripper," Winner said into his microphone. "I have an unexpected visitor. I will contact you in five mikes."

"Roger that, General."

Winner turned in his chair. His piercing blue eyes gave Spade the once over.

"You look terrible."

"I'm not buying this suicide line, Jack," Spade said.

"Stand down, Spade," Winner said.

"Mark my words. I am going to get to the bottom of this."

Winner stood up from his chair. His intense blue eyes were locked onto Spade's.

"You are emotional," Winner said. "I understand. None of us thought Lourdes would do something this extreme. Her action has complicated an already difficult situation. But in war, we must expect the unexpected and react accordingly, and drive on. Right now, you need to get a grip on yourself."

"Two deaths from falls." Spade leaned in close. "I ain't buying it, Jack."

"There is video of her death. I don't have time for this. Lieutenant Horgas. Call security."

"Show me the video."

"Fine."

Winner tapped at his keyboard and turned his monitor to Spade. The screen showed grainy video from the roof of the Mayor's Cell. Beyond the flat roof stretched the city skyline. The mishmash of water towers, blast walls, radio antennae, DFACs, hangars, CHUs and flat-roofed buildings extended to the city's outer walls. The sky beyond the roof was the usual hazy gray. In the distance, an enormous wall of dust was rolling in across the plain.

"This feed is from a weather camera," Winner said. "That's the dust storm that hit us last night."

On the screen, a door to an enclosed stairwell swung open. A woman in white stepped out from the stairwell onto the roof. Her face and the bare skin of her shoulders and arms were exposed to the corrosive air. But she remained calm. Her back was to the camera as she walked across the roof. Her long black hair was braided tightly down her back. The city skyline stretched out in front of her. She came to the roof's edge and stood for a moment. Then she fell forward and disappeared beneath the ledge.

Winner's eyes were moist as he closed the video. Spade held his chin tightly in his hand.

Three soldiers entered the doorway and stood behind Spade. Winner waved them off with a nod of his head.

Winner sat down in his chair and opened a map on his monitor.

"You have been reassigned as a crew chief for an AUV-60," Winner said. "Report to your platoon sergeant. That is all."

"Negative on that," Spade said and turned to leave. "I will be in Zephyr Crater."

"Darn it, Spade." Winner again stood from his chair. "You destroyed the vehicle I released to you. Seven killed and two aircraft lost because of your selfish desire to recover your own crashed ship. Look at yourself. You are a walking train wreck. You got Mina killed, for goodness sakes!"

Spade stared at Winner without emotion. His face was blank. "She's not dead."

"Get real," Winner said. "You took her out there and let those sadistic torturers take her. I hope for her sake she died before they could rip her apart."

"You bastard."

"I will lock you up and throw away the key if I so much as hear another word out of you. I should have you hanged."

Winner sat down and returned his gaze to his monitor. "I canceled the Zephyr Project. I need every warm body in this city locked and loaded and prepared for battle. I have wasted enough time with you. Report to your platoon sergeant or I will have you arrested. Dismissed."

Spade stood still for a moment. The three soldiers behind him moved into the room.

"Colonel Ripper, do you copy? Back brief me on the combat protocols for airfield defense. Start from the top."

One of the soldiers put his hand on Spade's shoulder. Spade turned and pushed past them and exited the office.

He walked brusquely out of the guard shack past the guard. Spade was in a daze as he walked beside a blast wall on a gravel road. The sun had set and the road was eerie in the twilight. Streetlamps dimmed with each gust of dusty wind.

Spade walked into a domed concrete entryway that led into a narrow corridor. He twisted open a door and entered a metal decompression room that flushed out the Bioppian air. He took off his mask and walked down narrow passageways until he reached the morgue.

He entered a room full of metal gurneys. They were empty except for one at the far end. A nude male corpse lay on the gurney. The portly, bearded coroner stood over it.

The coroner looked up from the body as Spade walked to him. "Captain Spade. Can I help you?"

"Where is the mayor?" he asked.

"She's dead, sir," he said, somewhat perplexed.

"Where is her body?"

"It was cremated two hours ago. I've cremated all the bodies that arrived this week, except this one. He is an AAV-64 pilot who was killed on the Mesolatium Plain. He is now ready for the crematorium."

"Why did you cremate the mayor?" Spade demanded, angrily.

"I have orders to conduct autopsies on the deceased and then remove the bodies to the crematorium. We must take the necessary sanitary measures because of the limited resources we have available. I am under direct orders to cremate the corpses."

"Where is Dr. Ebos?"

"I had to take the necessary sanitary measures. It was a direct order. I am sorry, Captain Spade."

Spade grabbed the little man by the collar and shoved him against the wall. "I told you not to cremate him!"

The coroner's eyes were wide. He was terrified.

Spade released him. He turned and walked out of the building. He walked through corridors until he reached a tram station. He rode a tram across town.

He exited at a hangar and asked around until he found his platoon sergeant. The platoon sergeant was a small Taji City male named Sgt. Lepros.

Spade walked up to the small man. Spade towered over him.

"Captain Spade," the sergeant said. "I mean Specialist Spade. My commander told me your rank is now specialist."

Spade studied the small bearded man who was wearing beat up Heliac armor. Spade got the feeling this sergeant had never supervised so much as a cleaning crew, let alone a platoon in a combat aviation company.

"Welcome to third platoon," Sgt. Lepros said. "We're hoping to use your flight skills and combat experience to our benefit."

"I don't know if you've noticed," Spade said, "but I'm a little banged up. Beat down. Tired. I need sleep."

"Roger. You have reported in and I am relieved on that number. Get some rest and report back tomorrow at 0600. Soldier care, hooah."

Spade smiled halfheartedly at the little man. "Thanks, Sarge."

"Thank you, Captain—" The sergeant caught himself. "Thanks, Specialist Spade."

Old Red

Spade sat in the pilot's chair in the Red Wrath. His boots were up on the control panel. He slowly twirled a cigar through his fingers.

"May I come in?" Grimes said.

"Be my guest."

Grimes entered the cockpit and sat in the chair next to Spade.

"Old Red," Grimes said. "You got us out of a scrape or two." He traced his hand over the control panel. "I've missed this old warhorse."

Spade's eyes stared out into the hangar but didn't seem to focus on anything.

Grimes leaned back in his seat and put his boots up. "When the four of us were riding Red across the galaxy, I remember sitting in this chair and coming to the conclusion that I was done with the human species."

Spade ran the cigar under his nose. "Genie can have that effect on a man," he said.

"No, that's not it," Grimes said. "We humans are always quarrelling and fighting with each other even when our enemies are bearing down on us. I was through with dealing with petty human conflict and backstabbing and human weakness. It had worn me down."

"It ain't easy being human," Spade said.

"I was in love with Mina but she was in love with you," Grimes said.

Spade's gaze fell. He sat slumped in his seat with vacant eyes.

"I saw the connection you two had and there was nothing I could do about it," Grimes said. "It was hard for a man like me to let her go, especially to you of all people."

"Is that why you gave up on humanity?" Spade asked.

"No," he answered. "After Mina and I broke up, I sat here in this chair, looking out into the black, and I contemplated the course of my life. I went over my earliest memories, which are of training to fight. I loved it right from the start. I have always loved the soldier's life. As a young man, I remember itching for war. When war finally came, I was ready, and I wanted it. But it was horrific, and the fall of Heliac traumatized those of us who survived. Early on in the fighting, I realized that the human soldier could never measure up to a Craaldan trooper. The Craaldans are bigger, stronger, faster, with better weapons. They have better training, better tactics, more experience, and there's more of them. They follow orders. They don't kill their own. We humans could barely stop bickering with each other long enough to defend ourselves, so what made us think we could beat them? It had been pointless to try."

"Yet here you are, ready to try again," Spade said.

Grimes was silent for a long moment.

"Maybe General Winner can lead us to victory for once," he said.

"And then what?" Spade asked.

"Then I can leave this place with peace of mind."

"In war he seeks peace," Spade said.

"The Craaldans are ruthless and cruel, but when it comes to military leadership, they are second to none. Good leadership is rare in our species. I feel like Winner might just have it in him. We will see."

"Lourdes was a leader," Spade said. "She was one of the good ones."

"She was a small town mayor who cracked under pressure," Grimes said. "It's a shame. She didn't seem the type."

"It was out of character," Spade said.

The two men sat silently. Spade thought about lighting his cigar, but decided against it. He put it away in one of his pockets.

"What's your plan, Spade?" Grimes asked.

"Red and I are going to get Mina back."

"The odds are she's dead," Grimes said.

Spade stared forward with an unfocused gaze.

"How will you do it?" Grimes asked.

"I'll fly in there with guns blazing, park, walk into their camp, and then I'm going to drag her out of there."

"Their sensors will track you as soon as you lift off from Taji City," Grimes said. "They'll hit you with laser cannons and missiles long before you reach Mount Mactus. You'll be dead before you hit the ground."

"You forget. I ain't the dying type."

"Do you want to hear my plan?" Grimes asked.

"I would love to."

"Genie has equipped our QRF aircraft with electronic countermeasures that can deceive Craaldan detection systems," Grimes said. "We fly in there undetected and three AUV-60s drop three air assault squads right in the middle of their camp. We hit them hard and fast and grab Mina and bug out of there. Their drones will try to give chase so we orbit an air weapons team to stall them while we make our escape."

"I've been studying the aerial shots of their camp," Spade said. "It's basically a tactical assembly area in a crater on the top of Mount Mactus. They've been preparing their attack, but not expecting us to attack them. They've got aerial defenses but otherwise the camp is unguarded."

"It would be stupid for us to attack them," Grimes said. "They know we're stupid, but they don't think we're that stupid."

Spade pulled up a visual display on the console. It depicted a flat crater at the top of an enormous rock mountain that dominated a rock-covered plain. In the center of the crater was an airfield where drones were parked in protective stalls. The remainder of the crater was filled with several hundred clamshell tents.

"There's the command post," Grimes said. "They took part of the bridge from their destroyer and set it into the rock face. Interesting. Things have changed since I last looked at the visuals. The main body has departed."

"The main body left 20 minutes ago," Spade said.

"You're kidding," Grimes said.

"I've alerted Vomica and Tanaka. They are trying to locate it."

"That means the attack on the city is imminent," Grimes said.

"It's coming," Spade said.

"We've got some time," Grimes said. "It'll take them a while to assemble at their rally point. This development actually improves our chances of conducting a successful raid on their command and control center."

"The trick is finding Mina," Spade said.

"If we can capture the command post, Genie can plug into their computers and see where they're holding her," Grimes said.

"OK," Spade said. He stood from his chair. "Get your team. Let's go."

"Slow down," Grimes said. "My guys are cleaning their weapons as we speak. We'll conduct a final mission rehearsal at 2100 hours. Then I want them to rest up. Mission start time is 0400."

"Do they know what they're getting into?" Spade asked. "We might lose men."

"They're mostly Rangers, so yeah. They're all itching to raid the Craaldans. It beats sitting around here waiting for them to come kill us."

"Does Winner know about this?" Spade asked.

"Negative. He would never approve it. He's going to blow his top when he finds out about it. He might have us hanged if we make it back alive."

Spade sat back down in his chair. "Do you trust Jack Winner?" he asked.

"I've known a lot of Rangers in my day. I'd rank him up there with Lieutenant Colonel Greg Skyles. Winner is squared away, no nonsense, and totally focused on victory. From what I can tell, achieving victory in this battle has been the primary motivation for his every waking action since I met him. I trust him to competently lead the defense of this city."

Grimes paused. "What's strange is he reminds me of you in some ways."

"How so?"

"That look he gives when he wants me to do something for him. The way he walks. I don't know."

"He killed the Zephyr Project," Spade said.

"He felt it was sucking up resources. But I've got Genie supervising a clandestine work crew. Zephyr Three is almost complete, so our backs are covered if things go bad."

"Grimes, I'm shocked. You really are one squared away soldier."

"If I was squared away, I wouldn't be leading a raid into an enemy camp in defiance of a general officer."

"You're taking the initiative," Spade said. "We in the officer corps like that in a soldier."

"The officer corps?"

Grimes stood from his chair and turned to leave. He slapped Spade on the shoulder.

"You're junior enlisted now, Specialist Spade."

Part III

Torture table

The room was nothing more than a chamber carved into rock. A metal table stood in its center.

Sweat ran down Capt. Casey's brow. The room was dimly lit and uncomfortably hot. She stood against the back wall with her arms wrapped around her chest.

She was unarmed. Her black hair was slick with sweat. Her black coveralls were tattered and torn. She was black and blue and disoriented.

She had trouble focusing her eyes in this dungeon of a room. She couldn't figure out where the dim light was coming from. There didn't seem to be any light fixtures in the rock. She didn't see windows or a door, either.

She shuffled away from the wall and toward the table. As she got closer, she noticed wrist and ankle clamps set at its ends. The dirt floor around the table was dark and wet.

The table had been wiped down, but not well. It was smeared with blood. The pungent stench of rotting blood stung her nostrils. She put her hand over her mouth and nose and stepped away from the table.

She stood for a moment not knowing what to do. The dimness played tricks on her eyes. She thought she saw faces in the rock. The faces shifted and changed and grew larger and smaller. She rubbed her hands over her eyes.

She shuffled to the wall and placed her hand on the warm rock. She walked along the wall, searching in the dimness for a window or door.

As she walked, her shins hit something made of metal. She strained her eyes to focus. It looked like a bench. She reached down and felt it with her hands. It was a long cot made of metal.

A Craaldan soldier sleeps here, she thought. Her heart began to pound.

"Is anyone there?" she asked.

Her voice sounded muffled in the stuffy heat. She stood still for a long while; then shuffled along the wall searching with her hands for a door or window. She bumped into a weapons rack. Her hands fumbled over its sharp edges as she searched for a weapon, but it was empty.

Her hand found a nook carved into the wall. There were several of them. She peered into one of the crevices.

A face!

She jumped back with a gasp. Her heart raced beneath her chest.

She squinted, trying to focus as she looked into the nook, wondering if her eyes were deceiving her. She leaned forward peering into the dark cranny in the wall. A wave of horror jolted her as she recognized the face of Lt. Col. Greg Skyles. His decapitated head sat inside the nook like a knickknack on a fireplace mantle.

In the next nook was the head of Tarvey Rigo.

"Oh, Tarvey!" she cried.

She saw the faces of Jober Mope and Leonard Brute and recognized several of Skyles' Rangers, as well as a few others she had known on Escalon. She shuffled past them. One nook remained empty.

She was breathing rapidly as she traced her hand against the wall, walking around the room until once again her shins struck the cot.

She stood for a long moment in the dimness and the heat. The sweat dripped down her brow. It trickled down the center of her back.

She sat down on the edge of the cot and nervously twisted the ring on her finger. It twisted around on her slippery sweat. She held her face in her hands and cried for what seemed an eternity.

A door swung open casting a red dusty glow into the room. A giant bipedal form stood in the doorway. It stepped into the room. The door shut with a forceful thud.

Capt. Casey's heartbeat raced in panic. Blood pulsed in her temples and her breathing quickened. She could see him now. He was a Craaldan.

He was shirtless. His skin had the look of rough granite. Muscles ribbed his torso like steel cables. His gray skin was tight on his fearsome face. His large, yellow eyes stared down at her with clinical focus.

She could not bear the fierceness of his skeletal countenance or the predatory cruelty in his eyes. She looked away.

He walked toward her. She stood from the cot and backed against the wall, stumbling and pressing her hands against the rock.

"Stop right there," she said.

He took a few more steps and stopped and stood in the dim light looking down at her as she pressed herself against the wall.

"I'm warning you," she said.

"I know not to take your warnings lightly, Captain Mina Casey," he said in his gravelly and sulfurous voice.

"Lieutenant Zeth? Is that you?"

"I am Major Zeth now," he answered.

"Wow, they'll promote anybody these days," she said.

"The trouble your species has caused the Craaldan has been more damaging than expected," he said. "Suddenly, my expertise in anthropology has become valuable to my command."

"Congratulations," she said. "Good for you, Zeth."

The giant Craaldan pulled a blade from a strap on his thigh. It was thin like a razor. "Humanity is in its twilight hour," he said. He held up the blade and examined it in the dim light. "Your extinction is assured. In this, I have played no small part."

"That's great, Zeth. Will you get a medal?"

He reached out his hand. It was long and knobby. His elongated fingers were tipped with black fingernails that were sharp as claws.

"Come," he said.

"No," she said. She was pressed firmly against the rock. She tried to look at his face but the heat of his gaze penetrated her skin and struck fear in her heart. She looked away. "I don't want to be tortured."

"Fear and pain." His yellow eyes burned into her body. "The human nervous system reacts with great intensity to fear and to pain. The fear of death is strong in your species." Zeth turned over his blade in the dim light. "Curious."

She knew of their cruelty. She had seen the results of their sadism. Their game was to increase the pain in their victims until death could be held back no longer. They clinically picked their victims apart to inflict maximum agony and horror.

"I accept that I'm going to die," Capt. Casey said. "But not like this. Zeth, please. I ask you. Kill me quick."

"A plea for mercy excites the cruelty in my nature." His eyes were afire. "Come."

Tears welled in her eyes.

He beckoned her with his fingers.

She took his bony hand and he led her to the torture table.

Air assault

Three AUV-60s lifted off from the runway in the darkness of night. They climbed vertically before their noses dipped and they jetted forward.

"Demon Flight 7, this is Taji Tower. You were not cleared for takeoff. Over."

"Copy that, Taji Tower."

"Demon Flight 7. What is the nature of your flight?"

"Mission top secret," the pilot in command said. "Destination unknown."

"Demon 7. Seriously?"

"Roger that."

The AUV-60s gained altitude until joining up with a pair of AAV-64s. The larger AUV-60s trailed the fast-flying attack aircraft as the formation rocketed through the thick atmosphere. The pilots in the trailing aircraft could see the white hot blasts from the engines in front of them; but otherwise, visibility was zero in the opaque blackness of the Bioppian night.

Genie sat in a sling on the inside wall of the lead AUV-60. She wore a black, form-fitting combat suit and a cap with the visor pulled low over her iridescent eyes. She checked her weapon.

The other soldiers in the aircraft were suited up in full battle rattle. They had on their body armor and helmets with the black faceplates clamped shut.

"She's going into battle," Spade said over his helmet radio, "and she's sexy as all get out."

"That's my girl," Grimes said. "It's why I love her."

"Is that why, Joe?" she asked. Her mouth didn't move. She had transmitted her voice over the radio net.

"That's one of the many reasons I love you, sweetheart," Grimes said.

"Have I told you that I'm thinking of swapping out this body for a new one?" she asked. "I'd like one that resembles the Tetrailani from my home world. It would be a natural fit for me."

"Like with tentacles and claws and dozens of eyes?" Grimes asked.

"Yes. Would you still love me then?"

"Would you still be a master sniper and Level 30 combatives qualified?"

"Of course."

"It would take some getting used to. But I'd still love you, babe."

She pulled a cleaning rod through the barrel of her weapon and then looked down the muzzle.

"You're just testing me. Right, babe? You're not really switching to a Tetrailani body."

"Who knows?"

Grimes was silent behind his faceplate.

Genie looked up from her weapon and smiled at Spade. She winked at him.

Spade checked his weapon one more time. He had test fired it and cleaned it before they had loaded up onto the AUV-60. The new rounds Gen. Winner had supplied them with might just give them the edge they needed, he thought. He checked his magazines and then rechecked his weapon, then checked it again.

"We will find her, Captain Spade," Genie said.

"I know we will," Spade said. "We have you."

Their aircraft banked sharply. The three AUV-60s dropped altitude with gut-wrenching speed. The two AAV-64s banked and pulled away.

The AUV-60s dropped low and then skimmed the rocky ground.

"Touchdown in 10 mikes," the pilot said over the radio.

"Demon 7, we're getting close," Grimes said. "Conduct pre-combat checks. Check your battle buddy. When we hit the ground, stay focused. Stay tactical. By the numbers. Roger?"

"Hooah!"

The doors on the sides of the aircraft slid open. Hot air blasted inside as the aircraft shot over the surface of the planet.

Spade could see the rocky ground in the twilight. Their aircraft was jetting over a landscape of rolling hills covered with jagged boulders. In the distance, a volcano spewed magma, which glowed red through the grainy atmosphere.

Grimes pointed forward. An enormous conical mountain ascended high into the upper atmosphere. The silhouette of the massive terrain feature dominated the view.

"Mount Mactus," Grimes said.

"They haven't detected our approach," Spade said. "Nice work, Genie. Your countermeasures worked like a charm."

"Did you have any doubt, Captain Spade?"

"I must admit, I did. But then, I'm a slow learner."

The three aircraft reached the base of the mountain and zoomed low against the rocky incline. The aircraft ascended to the summit and then dropped over the crater ridge.

Anti-aircraft missiles launched from the airfield under blasts of fire. Pods on the sides of the AUV-60s fired off explosive flares that popped and streamed in great fiery arcs. The missiles veered in confused zig-zags as they chased the flares.

Laser cannons at one edge of the airfield swung around and pointed their barrels at the inbound human aircraft. The cannons fired.

Counter-lasers on the pods fired back instantaneously, intercepting the fires from the ground cannons. Kinetic waves from the impacts rocked the AUV-60s with a sudden and powerful turbulence.

"Hold on," the pilot said over the radio. "It's gonna be a hard landing."

Spade could see the crater floor quickly rushing up at him from his vantage point inside the AUV-60. The aircraft hit the ground with a tremendous thud.

"Go! Go! Go!" Grimes said.

Spade jumped out of the aircraft and ran forward with his weapon at the ready. He was on point for first squad. The squad was in a full run as it assembled behind him in a squad wedge formation, with Grimes at its center.

Second and third squads hit the ground running as the AUV-60s lifted off behind them. The heavy machine guns on the sides of the aircraft opened up with flashes and head-rattling roars. Their rounds ripped through clamshell tents, parked drones and anti-aircraft laser cannons with explosive force.

A burst of enemy fire hit the rifleman running at Spade's rear right. The rifleman ripped apart in an explosion of armor and guts.

Spade sighted the Craaldan trooper who had fired the burst. The huge Craaldan was clad in black and yellow mech armor and was running on the airfield toward them.

Spade fired one shot from a sprint. His round struck center mass, knocking the Craaldan to his back.

"Nice shot!" Grimes said. He fired a double tap into the downed soldier as they sprinted past.

Pop! Pop!

The big Megalan grenadier at Spade's rear left fired off grenades to the left, front and right. The concussive blasts provided cover as they sprinted across the rocky ground to the command and control center, which was positioned against the crater wall.

Spade reached the main door. It was a large slab of metal set into a salvaged section of the wrecked Craaldan destroyer. The Craaldans had converted a scorched section of their ship into their command post.

Spade and five members from the lead squad stacked against the wall beside the door. The three remaining members took cover. They scanned the area with their weapons, providing rear security for the stacked squad members on the door.

"Second squad!" Grimes said. "Cover us! Three-sixty security. Shoot anything that moves."

Genie stepped to the front of the stack and delivered a lightning kick to the huge door. It fell forward and landed in a thud of dust.

"Fire in the hole!" Spade yelled.

He tossed a grenade inside and ducked. A powerful blast spewed fire, dust and metal out of the doorway.

"Go! Go! Go!" Grimes yelled.

Spade was on point. He inhaled deeply and ducked through the doorway.

Fatal funnel

Spade broke left with his muzzle pointed forward into the dust. He entered the room, scanning his sector of fire just as they had rehearsed back at the hangar. He could see nothing through the darkness and dust. He switched on his infrared but picked up nothing more than glowing white heat signatures from the grenade blast.

His fellow squad members moved in quickly behind him to their assigned positions in the room.

Pop! Pop! Pop!

The Ranger behind Spade scored direct hits on a stunned, half-armored Craaldan who was rising from his back on the floor. The Craaldan spasmed and went still.

An explosion of molten metal spewed from the right side of the room and hit the Megalan grenadier, who blew apart in chunks of metal and meat. The source of the fire was an armored Craaldan who was squatted down behind a bulkhead. The squad returned fire. Grimes walked up to the Craaldan firing steady bursts until the enemy trooper jumped out and was cut down by the combined fires from the squad.

"Room clear!" Grimes said. "Head count."

"One," Spade said.

"Two," the Ranger behind Spade said.

"Three," Genie said.

"Four's down," Grimes said. "I'm five. Stack right."

Spade, the Ranger and Genie stacked against the wall next to a sealed doorway while Grimes covered the door with his weapon.

Behind them outside the main door, a firefight had broken out. Second squad was shooting it out with approaching Craaldan infantry. Drones were taking off from the airfield.

"What are we doing, Grimes?" Spade asked.

"We're in the decompression chamber," Grimes said. "When we get through this door, we'll be inside. Take down the door, Genie."

Genie walked up to the door and delivered a swift kick and ducked back behind the wall. The door whipped open. The dusty air from outside streamed into the newly opened doorway. Then a torrent of molten metal steamed out of the doorway, grazing Grimes who dove and rolled out of the funnel of fire.

"Cover the doorway!" Grimes yelled. "Don't let them through!"

The fire ceased. A grenade bounced and rolled into the decompression chamber.

"Grenade!" Spade yelled.

Genie moved like quicksilver. She picked up the grenade and tossed it back through the doorway and it exploded immediately. The concussion knocked Genie down with tremendous force. She somersaulted backward across the room until she hit the back wall.

A huge armored Craaldan rushed through the doorway with both bayonets drawn from his fists. The Craaldan punched his bayonet at Grimes who was on the floor. Genie darted forward and deflected the stab with her hand, allowing Grimes to roll out of the way.

A second Craaldan came through the door and both Spade and the Ranger behind him fired and lit him up. The Craaldan spun around and crashed against the wall.

Genie swung around onto the back of the first Craaldan. She whipped her rifle over his head and pulled it against his throat with both hands. She arched her back and strained and ripped off his helmet. The big Craaldan spun around helmetless, clawing with his bayonets at Genie on his back.

Grimes stood and pointed his weapon and fired a shot.

Pop!

The Craaldan fell to his knees and let out a roar. Genie jumped to the ground.

Pop! Pop! Pop!

The big trooper fell forward with a thud.

"Go! Go! Go!" Grimes said.

Spade ducked into the next room and broke left and covered his sector of fire. The Ranger behind him entered the doorway and was immediately hit by a burst of rounds. He was ripped to shreds. Spade turned and saw the shooter.

The big Craaldan turned his weapon at Spade.

Spade fired and hit him in the faceplate. Genie entered the room and ducked as a stream of molten metal spewed over her head. Spade turned and sighted the second firer and hit him center mass with a three-round burst. Grimes rushed into the room firing off shots at the two downed Craaldans.

The dust and smoke in the room were as thick as liquid.

"Room clear!" Grimes yelled. "Eyes on the next doorway! Accountability!"

"One."

"Two's down," Grimes said.

"Three," Genie said.

"Four's down. I'm five," Grimes said. "This looks like a foyer. That looks like a security desk for screening visitors."

Grimes took a knee and looked at the dead Ranger in the doorway. The Ranger's faceplate was cracked open. His face was set in grisly death smile. The lower half of his body had been completely ripped away.

"I don't remember that Ranger's name," Spade said.

"Sergeant Fred Mackler," Grimes said. "A good man. The Megalan grenadier was named Private First Class Melissa Kang. She was a quick study and strong as an ox."

"We can't clear rooms like this much longer," Spade said.

"I only need a computer," Genie said.

The door next to the guard desk swung open.

"Get down!" Grimes said.

Molten metal streamed through the doorway, lighting up the room with staccato flashes.

"Fire in the hole!" Spade yelled, and tossed a grenade into the adjacent room. The sudden blast hit him with a wallop and jarred his bones.

Genie sprinted in front of the doorway and vaulted over the security desk as a hail of fire streamed through the doorway, tearing through the back wall of the room.

"Fire in the hole!" Spade said. He cooked the grenade for a moment and tossed it toward the doorway. A round struck it and set it off early and the blast walloped him hard.

He was disoriented. A piercing ring filled his skull. It felt as if someone had just cracked him over the head with a stone.

A Craaldan grenade bounced through the doorway. Grimes ran and dove and slid and scooped it up and tossed it back. It exploded just inside the doorway. Grimes vanished in a blast of dust and fire.

Spade rose to his feet and aimed his weapon at the door. A Craaldan rushed through and Spade lit him up. A second rushed through and Spade plugged him full of holes.

"Grimes! Answer me!" Spade yelled.

"I'm OK," Grimes said. "Got my bell rung. Get down. Genie, where are you?"

"I have interfaced with the computer at the security desk," Genie said. "I've hacked into the command center's main computer. I have located Mina. The eight digit grid coordinates are: one, seven, six, six, niner, niner, eight, six. I am patching you a visual of the map, Captain Spade. It appears Mina is in a complex of holding cells that are carved into the crater wall."

"Got it," Spade said.

A torrent of fire blasted through the doorway. A support column collapsed and sections of the ceiling started to cave in. The intensity of fire through the doorway increased.

Genie jumped up on the desk and cartwheeled in the air over the steam of molten rounds. She landed on her feet in a crouch on the other side of the doorway. In a smooth motion, she pulled a grenade from her belt, armed it and tossed into the adjacent room.

"Frag out," she said, and ducked.

The grenade exploded with tremendous whump.

"Let's get Mina," she said.

"Roger that," Spade said. He sprinted out of the room through the decompression chamber and out of the command center. Grimes and Genie followed, firing their weapons behind them as they backed out of the building.

An intense firefight was raging outside as second squad and the three remaining soldiers from first squad blasted away at Craaldan infantrymen who were picking them off one by one. The humans were in dug in positions but were exposed to the accurate Craaldan fire.

Spade sprinted past his compatriots and out onto the open ground. The Craaldans shifted fire and sprayed bursts from their weapons at him as he ran.

Dehumanization

"Get down, Captain Spade!" Genie yelled.

"Take cover, you fool!" yelled Grimes.

Spade ran over the flat ground following the most direct route to the grid coordinates on the map shown on his visual display.

Two Craaldan troopers fired on him from behind a berm. Their rounds tore up the rocky ground around him as he ran.

"Suppressive fire!" Grimes ordered. "On that berm!"

The human squad laid down a base of fire, throwing up explosions of dirt and rock on the berm. The Craaldan troopers ducked for cover behind it.

A black drone zeroed in on Spade, dropping down toward him through the dust clouds. But an AAV-64 pulled in behind it and scored direct hits with its chain gun. The raptor-like drone crunched into the crater floor in a fiery explosion of metal and rock. The AAV-64 nearly scraped the rocky surface as it pulled up vertically and blasted away.

Spade dove and rolled for cover behind a boulder. Craaldan heavy infantry troopers were exchanging fire with the human squad in the distance. The firefight raged on without him.

He spotted a large door set into the rock of the crater wall. The grid coordinates Genie had given him led to a point somewhere beyond the door.

Spade ducked down and ran to it. He turned its large metal wheel with both hands, and with great effort, he pulled it open. He stepped into a decompression chamber and pulled the door shut behind him.

The Bioppian air flushed out of the chamber, which refilled with breathable oxygen. Spade pushed a button on the wall and the inner door whushed open to a dark and cavernous corridor. He took a knee against the wall and looked down the long cavern, scanning for movement with his weapon. The coordinates on the map displayed by his internal computer marked a point midway down the corridor.

He peered down the cavern, which was nothing more than a hollowed out chasm in the rock, dimly illuminated by a red glow.

"Mina!" he yelled over his external speaker.

Each side of the cavern was lined with empty cells enclosed by metal bars. Spade switched on the light attached to the end of the barrel of his weapon. He walked slowly, scanning each cell, approaching the point marked on the map. The beam of white light cut through the dusty air like a laser.

The grid coordinates led to a cell. He walked up to it and looked inside.

"Mina?"

He shone his light on the dirt floor and walls, but the cell was barren.

He pulled off his helmet.

"Mina, are you there?"

The air was stifling hot. He wiped the sweat off his brow.

"Where are you?"

He continued walking down the cavern, shining his light left and right into each of the empty cells. At the end of the cavern was a large metal door. He put on his helmet and held his weapon at the ready. He pushed the heavy door with his shoulder and it slowly swung open.

He stepped inside scanning the dark room quickly with his weapon. A metal table stood at the center of the room. Several grimacing heads sat inside crannies in the wall. A weapons rack and a cot were set against the far wall.

Something was on the cot—an inert lump. It was hard to tell in the dim light. He switched on his infrared and the lump glowed yellow.

Spade walked over to the cot with his weapon at the ready.

"Mina?"

He reached down with his hand and pulled back a blanket. Her face was serene and beautiful as she slept peacefully.

He removed his helmet and kneeled beside her. He placed his armored hand on her shoulder.

"Mina."

Her eyes opened wide. Reflexively, she cracked him in the mouth with her elbow. He fell back on his haunches. She sprung off the cot, kicked him in the chest and ripped his weapon from his hands. She flipped the weapon around and pointed the muzzle between his eyes. Her dark eyes were ablaze.

"Sweetheart. That's no way to treat your hero."

She was breathing rapidly. She looked down at him with wild eyes. His head was still bandaged and his face was cut and bruised.

"It's me, Mina. Your man, Jace."

He slowly pushed the muzzle away from his face with the palm of his hand. He climbed to his feet and faced her.

She stood before him with his weapon dangling at her side. She was wearing the baggy, orange jumpsuit of a Craaldan slave.

"Mina, are you OK?"

"No."

He stepped forward and put his arms around her. She stood straight with her arms at her sides as he held her.

"I'm not OK."

"We need to get out of here," he said.

He kneeled down and removed the assault pack from his back and took out rubber boots and a canvas outerwear suit with an air tank and air mask. "Put these on."

She didn't move. He looked up at her. In the dim light, he could see tears carving channels through the dirt smeared on her cheeks.

"You shouldn't have come," she said.

"We don't have much time."

He stood and helped her out of her jumpsuit and into the heavy canvas protective overalls. He helped her put on her boots and placed the air tank on her back and pulled the mask over her face.

"Inhale," he said. "How does it feel?"

She gave him a thumbs up under the heavy glove on her hand. He put on his helmet and grabbed her hand and pulled her behind him.

"Do you copy, Mina?" he asked. "Mina, do you hear me?"

"Roger."

"Stay close," he said. "Things are about to get hazardous."

He pulled her through the decompression chamber and then out the heavy door. He pulled her down behind a boulder.

The firefight was still raging in front of the command center, but the rate of fire from the humans had diminished. It had intensified from the Craaldan side.

"Grimes, do you copy?" Spade said. "Grimes. I have Mina. I say again, I have Mina."

"Roger that," Grimes said. "Second squad, break contact, break contact! Fall back to the pick-up zone! Go, go, go! We're coming in hot, third squad! Cover us! We're going to need some air support down here! You hear that air weapons team? Demon 7, we need those 60s five mikes ago!"

The soldiers of second squad dashed out from their positions and sprinted across the open ground. Craaldan soldiers popped up from behind several berms. Spade zoomed in with his optics and sighted a Craaldan lieutenant who appeared to be giving orders.

Spade took aim and shot the lieutenant through the top of his helmet. Spade adjusted his weapon and fired on what appeared to be a platoon sergeant, and struck the big Craaldan in the side of the neck. The round tore out the other side and the sergeant went down hard.

The Craaldan troopers on the berm shifted fire and rounds exploded against the boulder. Spade pulled Capt. Casey closer to him and hunkered down as the Craaldan rounds cut the big rock to shards.

The two AAV-64s zoomed down and strafed the Craaldan position before streaking skyward into the gray haze.

Spade lifted Mina to her feet and pulled her by the hand as they sprinted to the flat ground beyond the airfield. She struggled to run in the awkward canvas suit.

The remains of second squad were sprinting off to their right.

Spade spotted Genie. Genie sprinted several yards, stopped and turned and fired a burst from her weapon. She tossed grenades and then darted forward again.

Three AUV-60s appeared on the ridgeline and then dropped toward the crater floor.

"Where are you, Spade?" Grimes called out. "No time to take a rest!"

"At your six, one hundred meters," Spade said.

The AUV-60s touched down on the flat ground. Third squad was dug in and laying down a heavy base of fire as first and second squads piled inside their aircraft.

The heavy machine guns on the sides of the aircraft exploded to life, unleashing a curtain of fire that swept the airfield like metallic lightning. The soldiers of third squad abandoned their positions and piled into their aircraft.

"Come on, Spade!" Grimes yelled. "Double time!"

Spade ran up to the trail AUV-60 and lifted Capt. Casey inside as a powerful backwash from the engines whipped up a tornado of dust. He dove in after her.

"Go, go, go!" Grimes yelled to the pilots.

The three aircraft lifted off as the AAV-64s strafed the airfield. After the attack aircraft made their pass, Spade sighted a Craaldan trooper below who stepped out from behind a berm. He was holding a CX-1049 and aiming it skyward. A missile launcher flipped out from the side of the Craaldan's big weapon.

"Manpad at your nine!" Spade yelled over the net. Spade took aim with his weapon and popped off a shot, but not before the Craaldan fired a rocket. The rocket zipped off the rocket launcher and corkscrewed skyward toward the lead AUV-60.

The lead aircraft fired off flares, but it was too late. The rocket struck it in its belly and it ripped apart in an expanding ball of flame.

The two surviving AUV-60s cleared the crater's ridgeline and jetted upward through the haze. The two AAV-64s pulled in behind them.

"Nuke it," Grimes said.

"Roger that," the pilot said.

A missile shot off a pod on the belly of the AUV-60 and then streaked around toward the crater. It rocketed down below the ridgeline and then detonated.

A shockwave hit their aircraft and spun it around end to end. The doors were still open and the soldiers inside held on for dear life as red warning lights flashed and an alarm blared.

The pilot recovered from the spin and resumed his climb. Through the open door, Spade could see the burning fires of a nuclear mushroom cloud that was rising above Mount Mactus.

General Monmath

The boiling mushroom cloud expanded above the massive mountain. The gigantic cloud glowed red, blue and yellow as it billowed in the haze. Lightning flashed and spiderwebbed over the radioactive plume of fire.

"Second squad, give me a status report," Grimes said.

"Second squad had four killed in action, two missing," the squad leader said over the net. "Private Margos has a sucking chest wound, but he'll live."

"Copy," Grimes said. He looked at what was left of first squad in his aircraft. Genie, Spade, himself and a soldier named Private First Class Coper had survived.

All of third squad, two pilots and two crew chiefs had perished when their AUV-60 was destroyed over the crater. The AAV-64s had both made it out.

To Grimes' great relief, Capt. Casey was rescued alive.

Capt. Casey sat on the floor of the aircraft with her knees pulled to her chest as she leaned against Spade who had his arm around her. He was in his battered armor and she was wearing her heavy canvas outerwear and an air mask. Her eyes were closed.

"It's good to see you, Mina," Grimes said.

She opened her eyes and looked at him for a moment through her mask with her head still leaned on Spade's shoulder. "You shouldn't have agreed to this, Joe. My life was not worth theirs."

"They volunteered for this mission, Mina," he said.

"Nobody should have died because of me."

Grimes looked away. "They were good soldiers. I hope you can understand. Good people."

"Don't tell me that," Capt. Casey said.

"Mina, they were willing to die if it meant saving you," Genie said. "We all were. But nobody died because of you."

"It's strange that I am in this situation again," Grimes said. "I am drawn to war, like a moth to the flame. But I hate it more than anything to see a soldier die."

Capt. Casey gazed at him for a moment and then closed her eyes. Grimes stared out the open door into the gray.

"I know war is wrong, but why does the thought of it still appeal to me? Is it the physicality, the camaraderie, the high stakes of this dangerous game, the life-or-death finality of it? There are many men like me, fascinated by war, seduced by grandiose notions of heroism. I watched thousands of them chase that fascination into early graves. I am now reminded again how I came to hate war. In many ways, Mina, you have been an inspiration to me. What I love about you is that all you've ever wanted in this universe is a simple life. My wish is that some day you will find it. It took me a while to figure out what you have always known—that there are no heroes in war, only the living and the dead."

"Enough philosophizing," Spade said. "And no more talk about dying. Our mission here is survival. When we get back to Taji City, I'm putting an end to this misadventure. We need to get everyone on the Zephyrs. We can still get off this rock while the going is good."

"General Winner will not allow it," Grimes said. "He will not retreat."

"There's no sense running, Jace," Capt. Casey said, without opening her eyes. "Their reinforcements will be here soon. We can't outrun them in those rickety Zephyrs."

"What reinforcements?" Spade asked.

"The 29th Expeditionary Fleet," she said. "General Monmath is coming."

"What?" Grimes asked. "That can't be. How do you know this?"

"General Monmath will be here any moment," she said.

Grimes was perplexed and alarmed. He had personal experience with General Monmath. The general had destroyed his home world of Jing and had massacred nine regiments of

Heliac Rangers. Legend had it that the general's expeditionary troopers had perfected the science of human torture through extensive practice on Ranger captives.

"Monmath is a destroyer of worlds," Grimes said. "Why would the Craaldan Empire send him to a tiny human outpost at the edge of the galaxy? He has bigger fish to fry."

"He destroyed Paltros and killed every last human there," Capt. Casey said. "He will retrieve his shipwrecked comrades here, and then he will attack Meglos."

"He destroyed Paltros?" Spade asked.

"Yes," she answered. "Meglos is now the last human-occupied planet in the galaxy. Once it is destroyed, there will only be a few scattered human outposts left. Craaldan kill teams are already going after them. Monmath has been tasked to hastily complete our extinction before he returns to the Inner Galaxy to rejoin the war against the Diocon Empire."

"Paltros wasn't my favorite planet, but at least it was one of ours," Grimes said. "I can't believe it's gone."

"The population of Paltros was 30 million," Genie said. "There are five million humans on Meglos and perhaps three million space drifters spread across this sector of the Outer Galaxy."

"There are not many of us left," Grimes said. "And there are hundreds of billions of Craaldans."

"The Craaldans are a cancer," Capt. Casey said. "They have been metastasizing across the galaxy for millennia, destroying everything they touch, wrecking civilizations and burning whole ecosystems to extinction. They are fully aware of what they have become. They have embraced what they have become."

"You're scaring me, Mina," Spade said.

"The Craaldan knows that the path he follows will eventually lead to his own destruction," she said. "Regardless, he presses forward relentlessly."

Their aircraft rapidly dropped altitude as it approached Taji City. Flashes of light illuminated the haze. Heavy booms rolled across the sky like thunder. The two AUV-60s circled over the city and descended to the airfield. Streams of light shot upward and arced out of the city to the north and the east.

Gen. Winner's C-NAM aerial defense system was firing frantically. Frenetic streams of fire burst from large cannons mounted inside rapidly swiveling domes. The C-NAM counter fire batteries were knocking down missiles, artillery shells and mortar rounds. The C-NAM fire was also keeping the Craaldan drones at bay.

"They're still trying to sneak one in on us," Spade said.

"They're not trying to sneak one in," Grimes said. "It's a full bombardment. General Winner's C-NAM system is protecting the city from annihilation. You better thank your lucky stars it's there. If that C-NAM goes down, we're done for."

"Thank you, lucky stars, for General Winner," Spade said.

Their AUV-60 touched down on the tarmac. They jumped out and ran to the hangars with their heads down. The roar of the C-NAM was ground-shaking and deafening.

A powerful boom rocked the city. A shockwave followed by a wave of dust swept over them. In the distance beyond the city walls, a nuclear mushroom cloud expanded above the horizon.

"That's one of ours," Spade said. "I hope it hit its target."

"Doubtful," Grimes said. "Their air defenses are better than ours. The nuke went off course and detonated."

They entered an empty hangar and removed their helmets. An alarm wailed hauntingly. Every few moments came the urgent announcement: "Incoming! Incoming! Incoming!"

Grimes gathered the remainder of his QRF platoon. They stood around him in the hangar like a sports team listening to a coach. Their faces were covered in dirt and sweat. They weren't even a full squad now.

"OK, Demons," Grimes said. "Our rescue mission was completed, but at greater cost than I had hoped. I'm proud of you, but our war has only just begun. The battle of Taji City is about to commence. Our mission now is to defend the C-

NAM. We're going to hook up with fourth squad on the east perimeter and make sure the enemy does not get its hands on our air defenses. Roger? Stay close. Follow me."

Grimes turned and jogged off as his squad members put their helmets on and trotted after him. Genie trotted off but stopped and turned and faced Spade and Capt. Casey.

"Are you coming?" she asked.

"Negative," Spade said.

"I see," Genie said. "In the case of a retreat, I will lead the humans to the Zephyrs," she said. "But we will be vulnerable with the Craaldans at our backs. We will need cover."

"I'll cover you, Genie," Spade said.

"Thank you, Captain Spade." She turned and trotted away.

Maltreatment

Capt. Casey jogged behind Spade through the empty corridors of the city. The mournful wail of an alarm rose and fell as they ran past stores and eating establishments that were locked up with the grates pulled down over their doorways.

"Incoming! Incoming! Incoming!"

The walls vibrated. The cement floor rumbled and rolled. Dust fell from the ceiling. The overhead lights flickered.

"All hands, report to battle stations. Report to battle stations. Incoming! Incoming! Incoming!"

Capt. Casey stopped running. She put her hands on her knees and bent over to catch her breath.

"Are you OK?" Spade asked.

"It's hard to keep up in this suit," she said. "It's like wearing a sleeping bag, and having potato sacks on my feet."

"We'll go to your CHU," he said. "There's armor there you can wear."

They entered a tram station but it was dark. The trams weren't running.

"We'll have to head outside," Spade said. "That's the shortest route back."

They entered a dark tunnel and pushed open a hatch and stepped outside into the thick Bioppian atmosphere. The air glowed with an orange hue. The skies on the horizon beyond the city skyline were a deep red. They trudged over a gravel road between blast walls.

An abandoned six-wheeled utility vehicle was parked in front of an empty metal building. Spade climbed inside and started it up.

"Get in."

They sped over the gravel between blast walls and past blockish cement buildings and water towers until they reached a residential area where containerized housing units were stacked in pods behind walls.

Spade skid the vehicle in the gravel and stopped in front of Pod 33. They jumped out and ducked into the pod, which was full of CHUs lined up in rows. Spade opened a hatch and they entered a small metal decompression chamber that flushed out the dusty air. They entered a narrow tube walkway and ducked left and right and then climbed up a metal ladder to Capt. Casey's CHU.

"I don't have my keys," she said.

"Step back," Spade said.

He adjusted the setting on his weapon and then fired a round into the doorknob. It exploded in sparks and he pushed the door open.

"Home sweet home," he said.

The metal blinds were open. The window looked out at the dusty plain beyond the city walls. A nuclear mushroom cloud expanded on the horizon. A distant mountain range of jagged peaks was silhouetted against the roiling light. Biop's usual dusty gray atmosphere was now aglow in a burnt brown and orange hue.

Capt. Casey sat on her bed and leaned her head back and caught her breath.

Spade dug through a metal crate. "Here's the armor and an M-929. Get out of that potato sack."

"Does it make me look fat?"

He turned and looked at her as she sat on the bed wearing the brown canvas outerwear. "Mina, you are the only gal on this planet who makes Bioppian outdoor fashion look sexy."

"I don't know. Genie looks good in just about anything."

Spade kneeled down in front of her. He wiped the sweat from his brow with the back of his hand.

"You look awful," she said.

"It's been one of those days," he said. He still had a bandage around his head. His face was black and blue and peppered with cuts. A long gash was healing on his forehead above his right eye, and another across his cheek below his left.

He helped her remove her large Bioppian boots. She stood up and he removed the air tank from her back. He unzipped the suit.

It fell down around her ankles. She stepped out of it.

Spade sat on the bed and looked at her nude form as she stood with her back to him. From her neck down her back and down the back of her legs, she was striped with ghastly welts. Her skin was marred with puncture wounds, and splotched with deep purple contusions.

She walked across the room to a wall locker and opened it. She put on panties and a loose-fitting brown t-shirt. She turned and faced him.

"I should have never let them take you," he said.

"Don't let it happen again, OK?"

She stood for a moment looking uncertain. He got up and took the armor out of the crate and held it for her, waiting for her to slide her arms in. But she didn't. She turned and sat down on the bed.

"Mina, we should hurry," he said. "We have to tell Winner that Monmath is coming and that it's pointless to defend the city. We have to tell him to give the order to board the Zephyrs."

"I haven't minded living here," she said. "This CHU isn't much, but it's comfortable." She patted the bed with her hand. "Won't you stay with me awhile?"

He stood in the center of the small room holding her armor, watching her.

She leaned over and looked at the little aquarium on her desk where a tiny glowing creature swam in the clear water. "Hi, Gary. Did I tell you his name is Gary?"

Spade sat down on the bed next to her. "I thought his name was Bob."

"Bob died. This is Gary."

"Oh."

She looked into the aquarium for a while. She sat up on the bed and then rubbed her eyes with her fingers.

"Are you OK?" he asked.

"I can't do this anymore, Jace," she said.

"You can, if you try," he said.

She sniffled. "I don't want to try."

"I need you to," he said.

"All these troubles," she said. "All this pain. It won't end. I want it to end. Just leave me here. Leave me here, would you?"

"No. Your soul is not meant for this dusty old rock in the middle of nowhere. We're going to make it out of here."

"My heart is broken," she said. "My soul is tired."

"Troubles come and they will pass. In your heart, you know that."

She started to cry.

"Your star is out there somewhere, waiting for you. You'll find it and find yourself and your dreams. We'll find them together. Don't give up, Mina. Follow your heart and nothing else."

Tears rolled down her cheeks. "I knew it was going to hurt. It hurt so much, Jace. I didn't want to survive."

"But you did. You survived."

She cried next to him on the bed. He put his arm around her and held her.

"Your tired old soul loves life too much," he said. "It won't let go."

He held her for awhile. The walls of the CHU rumbled every few moments from distant explosions. Dust settled downward from the ceiling and filtered across the light. Outside the window, the sky above the horizon was a fiery red.

"You won't let me go," she said.

"Never," he said. "I'm your man. Always."

He stood and pulled her to her feet. He held up her body armor and she slid her arms inside. He helped her into the armored suit and buckled her boots as she sat on the bed.

He wiped the tears from her face with his gloved thumb. "Never forget that I love you," he said. "Stay close and we'll get through this. Copy?"

Spade slid her helmet onto her head. "Copy that," she said.

He stood and put on his helmet. She stood and picked up her weapon.

"Stay sharp. Stay tactical," he said. "Follow me."

"OK. Lead the way."

Dragon fire

The C-NAM system spewed streams of fire over the skyline. The fires swept back and forth, arcing over the city in frenetic bursts of electric white. Missiles shot straight up and then veered in every which direction. Pulse cannons flashed beams of kinetic light.

The loudness of the C-NAM was overpowering. It hammered their eardrums and rattled their teeth and skulls inside their helmets as their six-wheeled vehicle raced over abandoned gravel streets.

"The C-NAM is stopping the bombardment and their drones," Spade said over the roar. "It's as good as anything I've seen."

"I wonder how much longer it can hold up," Capt. Casey said.

"Not long enough to protect us from General Monmath," Spade said. "But hopefully it will buy us enough time to get everyone to the Zephyrs."

They sped past other vehicles that zipped between the blast walls. Troops in white and blue Heliac armor were moving with urgency in small formations. Two AAV-64s flew low over the city beneath the C-NAM's curtain of fire.

Spade slowed on the gravel road. Vehicles were parked on the roadway. A complex of large, clamshell tents was set around a long, one-story cement building. The building's roof was thick with satellite dishes and antennae. Armored troops moved between the tents or from the main building, running with their heads down across the gravel.

Spade parked his vehicle against a blast wall. He and Capt. Casey trotted to the cement building and ducked into a low, unguarded door. They walked through a series of plastic tarps as fans sucked the dust and toxic gases from the air.

Once inside, Spade and Capt. Casey removed their helmets and looked up and down the dusty hallways.

"Hey, soldier," Capt. Casey said to an armored Megalan man who was lumbering toward them. "Where's the general?"

"Over there." The big man pointed down the hallway and lumbered away in haste.

Spade and Capt. Casey walked down the hallway until they came to a doorway that opened to a dimly lighted operations room that was filled with screens that were aglow in the dark. Soldiers stood in the greenish light looking into the screens as they talked into radios and typed on keyboards. At least 50 people were in here monitoring the screens. Their faces had looks of seriousness and intense concentration as they talked with urgency into their radios.

"There," Capt. Casey said.

Gen. Winner paced in front of a large monitor as several soldiers stood around him, watching the wall-sized screen with alarm.

Winner was in his gleaming blue armor. His blonde mustache was well-groomed, but now thick on his upper lip. His blue eyes were intense as he glanced up at the screen while pacing in front of it.

The screen depicted the overhead view of a stark landscape of serrated hills and snake-like gullies carved into rock. Static intermittently interrupted the black-and-white video feed.

"Dragonmaster 7, this is Warfighter 6," Winner said. "I need your insertion team to fight its way through and get that package onto the target. You are almost under their air defenses. Do you hear me, Dragonmaster 7?"

On the screen the black silhouettes of predatory drones circled above a ravine. The drones fired molten metal from their noses. Streams of glowing light from the drones terminated in explosions in the ravine that briefly whited out the screen.

"Sir, they've got a fix on the insertion team," a bearded Taji man said from his seat behind a monitor. "I'm tracking three Craaldan infantry squads converging on Dragonmaster's last known position."

"We've lost him, sir," a female Heliac master sergeant said as she held her finger to the radio at her ear.

"Dragonmaster 7," Winner said. "Do you copy? Talk to me, Dragonmaster."

The image on the screen distorted and flashed until all that was depicted was static snow.

"The signal is dead, sir," the master sergeant said. "They took out our satellite."

"Darn it." Winner, in his blue armor, paced in front of the screen, deep in thought. He stared downward as he walked.

"There's no way we can detonate the nuke from here?" he asked.

"Negative, sir. They are jamming our signal now."

"That was our last chance to block their approach," he said. "Get Griffin 6 on the net and tell him that Operation Dragon Fire was a no go. Griffin knows what to do. We're not where we want to be, but it's not like we haven't rehearsed for this scenario."

"Roger, sir."

"I will be on the wall," Winner said. The tall general put on his helmet and clamped the faceplate shut. He grabbed his weapon from a rack and walked across the operations room toward a doorway.

"General Winner!" Spade bellowed from across the room.

Everyone turned from their screens and looked up at Spade.

The general didn't stop as he pushed through the doorway. His aide-de-camp, LT Horgas, followed after him.

Spade put on his helmet and followed Winner out the doorway. He pushed through hanging plastic tarps and emerged into the glowing atmosphere. The sky above was afire with color—orange, red and yellow. Streaks of blue fire spread like tentacles through the stratosphere. The ground rumbled from the intense eruptions of outbound fire from the C-NAM. Winner moved quickly over the gravel toward the outer walls as LT Horgas trailed behind.

The general and his aide reached the thirty-foot cement wall that ringed the city. Spaced every few hundred yards along the wall were large watchtowers that looked out at the plain. Crew-served weapons pointed out from the enclosed watchtowers, swinging left and right in search of an approaching enemy.

Winner and Horgas hopped onto a platform grate which climbed upward along the face of the wall. Spade and Capt. Casey trotted up to the wall's base and looked up at the platform as it approached the top. Spade pushed a button that brought the empty platform back down to them.

They rode it up looking back at the jumbled skyline of Taji City. AAV-64s and AUV-60s were flying low in pairs beneath the heavy C-NAM fire, patrolling the outer wall from above.

Columns of smoke rose from at least three pods. A hangar along the airfield was engulfed in fire.

"They don't need a direct hit to burn this city down," Spade said. "Shrapnel from the explosions is raining down on us."

The platform climbed higher until reaching the top of the wall. The plain beyond the wall came into view. It was alight with a nuclear glow.

"Only two Craaldan companies are out there," Capt. Casey said. "But the whole planet is on fire."

The wall

Spade and Capt. Casey stepped off the platform and onto a narrow walkway atop the wall that ringed the city. To their left was the cityscape. To their right was a plain the stretched into a thick smoky haze that was aglow in a deep shade of orange.

Electric fire streaked over their heads and out over the plain. A constant deafening roar from explosions shook the wall to its foundations. The explosions flashed and boomed high in the sky, raining chunks of fiery metal down onto the planet.

Metal streaked down and peppered the plain. Debris was hitting the city at an increasing rate.

Winner walked hastily away from them down the narrow walkway. His silhouette grew feint in the thick orange haze.

Spade jogged after him.

As Spade neared, he saw Winner talking to Grimes. Winner was a head taller standing in his royal blue armor as Grimes, in his Heliac Ranger armor, looked up at him. Genie and LT Horgas stood next to them. Horgas was in Heliac armor. Genie was in her black formfitting combat suit and wore a cap with the visor pulled low over her eyes. Her weapon was held pointed down and to the side as she watched Winner and Grimes converse.

Spade trotted up to them.

"I need to talk to you, Jack," Spade said.

Winner lifted an armored hand to silence him.

"Your QRF is more critical than ever, Sgt. Grimes," Winner said. "You will have to move fast just like we trained. Faster. I want violence of action at any point along our line where they threaten to break though. Keep your ears open for my direction because they are going to hit us like a lightning storm and I need you to assault through whenever they get too close to the C-NAM."

"I hear you, General," Grimes said. "We will do the best we can with what we've got."

"I need you to do better than that," he said. "Darn it. Why did you have to pull that stunt and fly into their base camp and kill half your team? It was foolhardy and stupid."

Winner shook his head. He put his hands on his hips and looked out at the plain. "I need you, Grimes. And you, too, Genie. You two are the best we've got." He looked back at Grimes. "This city needs you."

"General Winner," Spade said.

Winner turned and faced Spade. Winner stood in his gleaming blue armor and looked through his blood red faceplate at Spade. The general's weapon was slung on his back.

Spade stood in his dented and discolored white and blue armor looking back through his black faceplate. He held his weapon with both hands, its muzzle pointed down and to the side.

Spade and Winner were just about equal in height.

"What is it, Specialist Spade?" Winner asked.

"General Monmath and the 29th Fleet will be reinforcing those heavy infantry companies out there," Spade said.

"So I've heard," Winner said.

"We've got to pull out of here," Spade said. "Issue the warning order. Get everyone aboard the Zephyrs and let's get off this rock before it's too late."

"Negative," Winner said.

"Are you asking the people of this city to commit suicide?" Spade asked.

"I've just about had enough of you, Spade. You have disobeyed direct order after direct order. You are fortunate that I am a patient man—a forgiving man. I am assigning you to the QRF platoon. You and Capt. Casey will defend the C-NAM. You now fall under Sergeant Grimes and you will obey his orders. Understood?"

Winner turned and placed his hand on Grimes' shoulder. "Don't let me down, Sergeant Grimes. Fight like the devil. We are all counting on you."

Winner pushed past Spade on the narrow walkway.

"You are going to let these people fight a meaningless battle before the arrival of a force of overwhelming superiority," Spade said. "Everyone who survives this fight is going to be butchered as soon as Monmath arrives. You are a Heliac Ranger. You know what he is capable of. There is no hope for victory. You have condemned all these people to violent deaths."

Winner stopped and turned and faced Spade. "What makes you believe General Monmath is coming here?"

"Mina was behind enemy lines," Spade said. "She heard their plans."

"She was sadistically tortured by a Craaldan military intelligence officer," Winner said. "That officer left her alive and allowed her to escape. Does that make sense to you, Specialist Spade? Now she is here providing us with information that might prompt us to retreat—to turn our backs on the enemy and run?"

Capt. Casey stood behind Spade looking over his shoulder at Winner.

Winner walked up to Spade and looked at him through his faceplate. "I know General Monmath and what he is capable of. You are a correct in that regard. Monmath is in the Marez System engaging three Diocon armies on four planets. This fight here is beneath him and the least of his concerns. Frankly, I am tired of your defeatism. No one here has time for losers. This is a time for soldiers, for heroes. You should be ashamed of yourself. You need to step up and start acting like a soldier, like a man."

Winner turned to Capt. Casey. "Don't get me wrong, Mina," he said. "I am thankful that you are alive."

The crew served weapon in the nearest watchtower coughed out rounds into the haze. A missile raced toward the tower, zooming low over the surface of the plain. It slammed into the tower and exploded. Chunks of cement erupted into the air.

Incoming heavy machine gun fire grazed the surface of the plain and impacted against a section of the wall beyond the flaming tower. The noise of the gunfire was tremendous, shaking the wall with extreme force.

C-NAM missiles shot over the city and exploded only a few hundred yards out over the plain. The missiles impacted against incoming rounds. The blasts from the impacts shook the top of the wall with the power of a rolling earthquake.

"They're getting close!" Winner said. He put both hands on the wall's ledge to hold on as he looked out at the plain.

Craaldan rounds were concentrating on a section of the wall, blasting it apart.

"I'm seeing movement," Winner said. "They are massing their fire on one section of the wall. Here they come!"

Several AAV-64s flew low over the wall and zoomed out over the plain. AUV-60s were hanging back in low orbits over this sector of the city. Heavy machine gun barrels scanned the scene from the sides of the utility aircraft. Fast moving AOV-58s scouted the city perimeter for movement.

The deafening noise of war intensified. The whole planet seemed to shake to its core. A low growl rumbled from across the plain as a roar like rolling thunder increased in volume and intensity.

Grimes looked out at the glowing plain. "The beast is ready to devour," he said.

"Get your team down there, Grimes," Winner said. "Don't let them through that section of wall."

"Roger that," Grimes said.

Winner stood up straight and swung his weapon around from his back. "Let's rock 'n' roll."

Urban warfare

"Follow me," Grimes said.

He and Genie jumped over the ledge and fast-roped down the face of the wall. Capt. Casey unspooled a cable from her utility belt, attached it to the ledge and rappelled after them. Spade did the same.

They ran along the base of the wall past the destroyed watchtower. Smoke billowed upward from magnesium fires where rounds had landed. The smoke wafted in the wind through the glowing orange haze.

The deafening roar from the C-NAM increased in volume. Streaks of flashing light ripped open the sky. The thick orange air seemed to pulsate with heat and light.

Their boots crunched on the gravel as they ran through alleyways and ducked through gaps between blast walls. Six-wheeled vehicles that were parked along the walls were burning after being struck by shrapnel. They sprinted between cement buildings and through half-collapsed hard-shell tents.

"Listen up, QRF," Grimes said as he ran. "Form a line on me on the far side of the blasted section of wall. Copy?"

Explosions roared over them and shrapnel rained down onto the city. Grimes ran fast through a complex of hard-shell tents. Genie, Spade and Capt. Casey chased after him, trying to keep up.

"Dragonmaster 6, do you copy?" Grimes asked.

"I copy, QRF," Ramone Bombero said.

"They are going to fight their way in through the blown section of wall," Grimes said. "Lay down a heavy base of fire as they approach your position. Blast them with all you've got. When I give the command, shift fire to your nine o'clock. QRF will flank them and assault through. Tracking?"

"Tracking," Bombero said.

"When we reach our limit of advance, unload on them," Grimes said.

"A word of advice, Sergeant Grimes," Bombero said. "Do not lollygag on the objective. We do not want to frag you with friendly fire, but we will defend ourselves if your flanking maneuver does not stop their advance."

"I hear you, Ramone," Grimes said. "We'll be moving fast."

Grimes met up with the rest of his team. His soldiers were lying in the prone in hastily dug trenches in front of a line of cement buildings. The destroyed section of the outer wall was about 50 yards to their front and right.

"Form the line," Grimes said. "Spread it out. Maintain your intervals just like we rehearsed."

When everyone was in place, Grimes walked down the trench and checked his men. Thirteen remained from his platoon of 40, not counting Spade, Capt. Casey, Genie and himself.

Grimes directed Spade and Capt. Casey to the center of the line near him and Genie. "When we assault through, stay in your lane," Grimes said. "Shoot anything in front of you. Don't stop running until we reach the limit of advance. Then hightail it to the rally point."

Spade and Capt. Casey got down in the trench and lay in the prone with their weapons facing forward.

The Craaldans were firing through the blasted section of wall from unseen positions out on the plain. Sporadic fire peppered the tents and buildings in their line of sight. Their yellow tracers zipped through the haze and bounced off rubble and rock.

"Hey, Joe," Capt. Casey said.

"Yeah," Grimes said. "Go ahead."

"How did General Winner know that General Monmath was engaged with three Diocon armies in the Marez System?" Capt. Casey asked.

"I don't know," Grimes said. "He knows a lot of things."

"I was in the Craaldan control center," Capt. Casey said. "General Monmath defeated those armies. That's why he's coming out here. We've become a nuisance to their empire so they sent him out here to finish us off once and for all."

"I hear you, Mina," Grimes said. "But right now I need you to forget about that. I need your head in the here and now when we assault through the objective."

"You believe me," Capt. Casey said. "Don't you, Joe?"

He was silent.

"Answer her, Grimes," Spade said.

"I believe you, Mina," Genie said.

The volume of fire picked up as Craaldan rounds zipped through the destroyed section of wall. The rounds tore through the wrecked structures beyond the gap.

The C-NAM was now concentrating its fire over the wall. Huge kinetic impacts exploded above the plain as the C-NAM's outgoing fire collided with incoming rounds.

Twelve AAV-64s zoomed over the wall, flying in pairs. They swarmed over a section of the plain. Their chain guns erupted and ripped across the plain in giant sweeping arcs of fire.

AUV-60s orbited above the city inside the wall's perimeter. Their guns swung back and forth on the sides of the aircraft.

Hundreds of missiles suddenly shot up from the plain, setting off the counter fire defenses on the AAV-64s. Flares shot out from the sides of the aircraft in brilliant streaks of arcing light.

But the countermeasures were ineffective. The Craaldan missiles hit their marks. All twelve AAV-64s vanished in brilliant explosions of expanding fire.

Anti-aircraft pulse cannons flashed to life out on the plain. The AUV-60s that were orbiting above the city burst open from the inside and fell to the surface, impacting on the city floor in violent crashes of metal and flame.

"There goes our air support," Grimes said.

The infantry battalion from Bombero's brigade unleashed a barrage of fire through the destroyed section of wall.

Out on the plain, a Craaldan heavy infantry platoon rose from the gravel and sprinted toward the gap in the wall. The big troopers ran at incredible speed in their black and yellow mechanized armor. Their big guns pointed forward. They ran in squads formed up in wedge formations. They skirted the fire from the human battalion that was screaming through the destroyed section of wall. Up in the watch towers, the crew-served weapons fired at the running Craaldans, but the troopers adeptly dodged the blasts and continued advancing at great speed.

Grimes monitored their advance on a video feed beamed into his helmet from a camera atop one of the watchtowers.

"They've unleashed their dogs of war," Grimes said. "They're coming in hard and fast."

The Craaldan platoon reached the wall and took cover behind it on both sides of the destroyed section.

"Stay sharp," Grimes said. "Wait for the command."

The human infantry battalion continued its high rate of fire, blasting at the rubble, which exploded into deadly shards of flying rock.

A Craaldan trooper darted out from behind the wall and fired a grenade from his weapon and then ducked for cover. The grenade arced over the rubble and bounced across the gravel toward Bombero's men.

"Grenade!"

The grenade exploded with a tremendous whump. A blinding flash was followed by a loud ring that filled the skulls of the human soldiers. The terrific force from the concussion flattened buildings and tents. Half of Bombero's infantry battalion was stunned by the blast and in a dazed state of blurred confusion. The rate of fire from the humans diminished to a few bursts and pops.

The Craaldans had their opening and stormed through the collapsed section of wall.

"Shift fire, shift fire, shift fire!" Grimes yelled.

The human battalion shifted fire to the west.

"Go! Go! Go!" Grimes commanded.

The soldiers in the QRF platoon climbed from their trench and sprinted in a line in front of the open section of wall.

Craaldan troopers hurtled over the rubble firing their weapons forward as they streamed into the city. The QRF platoon had them flanked and ran at them, firing at them and knocking them down at a full sprint.

Spade ran at a Craaldan trooper who was sprinting toward Bombero's position. Spade lined up the running Craaldan in his gun sight and fired his weapon at a full run. His round caught the Craaldan in the ribs. The big trooper went down and rolled forward under the force of his own his momentum.

Spade fired another round into the downed trooper as he sprinted past.

To his right, he saw an enemy trooper bayonet one of the QRF team members from a full sprint. Genie darted out of her lane and tackled the big Craaldan to the ground, kicking him in the faceplate with lightning quickness and then firing a round into his chest. She pulled the human soldier off the bayonet and slung him over her shoulder. She turned and fired her weapon with one hand at an advancing Craaldan, taking his head clean off.

Genie ran straight for the open section of wall, firing left and right, knocking down Craaldans as she ran with the wounded soldier on her shoulder. She ran through the rubble to the other side of the wall and fired from a squat, first to the left and then to the right. She then threw several grenades and turned and sprinted back over the rubble.

Bombero's troops commenced firing at the open section of wall. Genie ducked to avoid getting hit as she ran across the gravel to the rally point.

Cataclysm

Grimes was in a squat as his soldiers lay in the prone with their weapons pointed at the destroyed section of wall. Genie was on her knees working on the soldier she had carried on her shoulder.

"He's gone, Genie," Grimes said.

"He may be saved if we get him to a medical facility," Genie said.

"The medical facility has burned to the ground," Grimes said. He pulled Genie away from the corpse. "Rest in peace, PFC Coper," he said.

Grimes checked the rest of his platoon. Six were killed in the assault.

Ramone Bombero and his men began a counterattack. The big Megalan ran out in front of his troops and then waved them forward with a sweep of his huge arm. The soldiers bounded toward the wall firing their weapons.

A massive explosion in the western sector of the city shook the ground with a sudden, heaving force. The surface of the planet seemed to move like liquid in vibrating waves.

"That was a big one," Grimes said, steadying himself on the ground with his hand.

"Sergeant Grimes!" Winnner said over the radio net. "They've blown the wall on the western sector! The attack on your end was diversionary! Their main body is storming the city! They're going after the C-NAM and they've caught us flat-footed! I need you here now!"

"Let's go, QRF!" Grimes said. "Follow me!"

Grimes jumped to his feet and sprinted over the gravel past blast walls and collapsed buildings. Genie ran alongside him as the remains of the team chased after them. Spade and Capt. Casey tried to keep up.

"Mina," Grimes said as he ran along a blast wall. "I don't doubt you. I believed you when you said Monmath is coming for us."

"We need to get everyone to the Zephyrs before it's too late," Spade said.

"We can't turn our backs on them," Grimes said. "They will butcher us if we attempt to withdraw."

"I will give the order to retreat," Genie said. "We will need air support when we withdraw to the Zephyrs. Will you cover us, Captain Spade?"

"You know I will, Genie-baby," Spade said.

"Get to the Red Wrath," Grimes said. "We will cover the withdrawal from the ground. Hone in on my beacon and have old Red blast them to Kingdom Come. Go, Spade! Go!"

Spade and Capt. Casey broke away as the QRF team sprinted off.

Spade and Capt. Casey turned down a gravel road and ran toward the airfield. The city was now a smoldering expanse of rubble and wreckage. Fallen water towers had smashed through CHUs. A DFAC was in flames. The roofs and walls of the buildings along the roadway were caved in. Tents were pockmarked from fallen shrapnel.

The counter fire from the C-NAM had lessened. Streaks of light still arced over the city but the Craaldan artillery bombardment had decreased in intensity. Spade assumed it was because the Craaldans had breached the wall and were now inside the city.

Smoke and flame were rising from the western sector. The heat from the fires whipped up a powerful dust storm that lashed grainy blasts of hot air across the roadway. They ran on the road, jumping and scrambling over debris.

Three powerful explosions rocked the city from the western sector. The sound of weapons firing became constant and deafening. A firestorm was rising as the Craaldans mounted a ferocious attack on General Winner's lines.

"Incoming!" Spade yelled.

He grabbed Capt. Casey and pulled her down in the gravel and up against the side of a blast wall. Mortar rounds began to drop onto their sector of the city, impacting the city floor with tremendous, skull-splitting thumps. Gravel and dirt erupted in furious geysers. The metal siding from CHUs flipped through the air. Rock and cement rained down.

The powerful thumps grew closer. The ground shook with wrenching force. A blast wall in front of them toppled onto the road in a rush of gravel. The explosions walked toward them.

"Let's go!" Spade yelled.

He pulled Capt. Casey to her feet and they ran across the gravel roadway as shock waves from the detonating mortar rounds slammed them with bone-jarring power. Gravel pinged against their armor with painful stings.

They ducked into a half-collapsed cement building and found a stairwell that led underground. They ran down the steps into the darkness.

Spade turned on his infrared scanner. Six soldiers were hunkered down against the walls of the dark corridor. One soldier was on his back. His head was in his battle buddy's lap. His intestines were exposed beneath his shredded armor. His chest heaved.

Spade could tell by their size that this was a squad of Taji City men, led by a taller Taji City female.

The thumps from the mortar rounds walked closer to their position. The corridor shook violently with each detonation. Dust cascaded from the ceiling. Spade worried that the building might collapse and bury them.

Spade and Capt. Casey sat down in the dark with their backs against the wall, gripping their weapons.

Time seemed to slow as the thundering detonations grew louder and closer. Spade felt his heart pound under his chest and his breath quicken. Blood pulsed rapidly through his ears. The dark narrow corridor felt claustrophobic, like a tomb.

A soldier standing against the wall opposite them convulsed with fear after each impact from a mortar round. His back jerked spasmodically and his hands shook uncontrollably.

The mortar fire ceased. They sat in the stillness. Their ears rang loudly in the silence.

Capt. Casey kneeled over the wounded man whose head was held in his buddy's lap. She pulled a canister from her utility belt and sprayed a foam sealant on his wounds.

The squad leader of this little group was a tall Taji City female who was sitting motionless in a corner.

"You copy, squad leader?" Spade asked.

"Yes," she said. "Yes, sir."

"Get your men to Zephyr Crater. Get your wounded man on a Zephyr and then have your squad set up a defensive position on the main avenue of approach. We're pulling out so it's going to be a mad dash for the Zephyrs. Provide cover when everyone is boarding the ships. They are going to need it. Keep your head down and shoot at the pursuing Craaldans. Shoot to kill. Once everyone is aboard, we're blasting out of here. Roger?"

"Roger that."

Spade and Capt. Casey jumped to their feet and ran up the stairwell and back outside into the howling wind. The sky above the shattered cityscape was aglow in fiery orange.

They sprinted down the gravel road toward the airfield and came to a maintenance hangar and ducked inside.

The Red Wrath sat silently in the center of the empty hangar. The ship's mammoth engines were its most dominating feature. The big spaceship was black and red. It looked deadly, with shark's teeth painted under its nose. Stenciled under the cockpit was an image of Genie in the nude holding the ace of spades.

"Good to see you, old girl," Captain Casey said.

"It's times like these when she earns her pay," Spade said.

They entered the spacecraft through a hatch. Spade climbed up to the cockpit and sat in the pilot's chair. Capt. Casey sat next to him.

Spade typed at the control panel and the large door to the hangar slowly opened to the glowing atmosphere outside. The dusty air billowed inside in swirling clouds as the dust was sucked into the cavernous hangar.

Spade fired the engines. The Red Wrath lifted from the cement floor and shot forward out of the hangar. Old Red hovered and then picked up speed over the runway. Her big engines exploded to life in a deep-throated roar that shook the entire city with its power.

Spade pulled back on the stick and his ship went vertical and shot upward through the glowing haze.

Friction

Craaldan drones honed in on the Red Wrath as it climbed upward into space. Missiles from the surface streaked up in pursuit. Spade fired the engines to full power and pulled away from them.

The Red Wrath exited the atmosphere and entered into space. The Cextos sun was half eclipsed by the gray curve of Biop. Sunlight reflected off the shattered remains of the planet's moon, which was a string of cratered rocks that orbited the planet like an asteroid armada.

Spade circled his ship around and faced the pursuing drones and missiles head on. Capt. Casey fired flurries of targeted pulses from the Red Wrath's cannons, smashing the drones and missiles to bits.

"I'm reading Joe's beacon," Capt. Casey said. "They're being overrun, Jace."

"Find me some targets," Spade said.

"Roger that," Capt. Casey said.

Spade dove the Red Wrath into the planet's atmosphere. The ship was buffeted by the thick air. Hot fiery tentacles of air blasted over the forward screen as the Red Wrath ripped across the sky.

"Targets acquired," Capt. Casey said. "Bring her in as close as you can."

"Our sonic booms are going to flatten anything still standing down there," Spade said.

"There's not much city left," Capt. Casey said.

"Old Red is a space fighter," Spade said. "Strafing runs and close air support are not her thing, so we're going to have to make the first pass count."

"Their air defenses are tracking us," Capt. Casey said. "Pulse cannons firing on the surface! Surface-to-air missiles launching!"

Spade activated the Red Wrath's countermeasures. The ship's counter fire cannons intercepted the enemy pulse cannon fire with tremendous claps. The impacts erupted into exploding balls of lightning.

The ship skidded left and right and fired off streaming flares that arced outward in great glowing fingers of light. The surface-to-air missiles zigged and zagged and chased after the flares as the Red Wrath streaked downward toward the planet's surface.

"We're coming into range," Capt. Casey said.

Fiery heat blasted off the belly of the Red Wrath as the ship streaked through the glowing haze. Taji City came into view below on the rocky surface. The city was a smoking grid of wrecked structures enclosed by a high wall. Columns of smoke rose upward into the haze. The western sector of the city was engulfed in flames.

A formation of six black predatory drones raced upward to intercept the Red Wrath, but they came into range of the C-NAM, which fired flurries from its pulse cannons. The drones broke apart from the impacts and fell to the surface.

"This is going to be quick," Spade said.

"I'm picking up a lot of movement down there. They are right on top of Joe's position," Capt. Casey said. "Bring her in tight."

The Red Wrath came in fast and low. Capt. Casey had her targets displayed on the screen in front of her. She picked out what looked like platoon and squad leaders as well as troopers carrying the big CX-1049 Craaldan heavy weaponry. But most of the enemy was well concealed and many were too close to the human lines to engage.

Sonic booms shook the planet as the Red Wrath made its approach to the city. Capt. Casey fired the pulse cannons to devastating effect. In an instant, advancing Craaldan troopers were vaporized by the ship's guns.

The troopers turned their weapons on the ship that rocketed past with blistering speed.

"We're taking fire," Capt. Casey said.

Rounds ripped through the Red Wrath's skin. An onboard alarm squawked and flashed.

The ship streaked across the plain beyond the city's walls. Spade pulled back on the stick and went vertical.

"Hit them with the flash missiles," Spade said.

Capt. Casey fired a volley of missiles, which rocketed up and out and then downward before exploding into the Craaldan positions.

"Nice flying, Spade!" Grimes said over the net. His voiced crackled through the static and then faded.

Spade gunned the big engines and rocketed upward into space.

"We'll bring her around again," Spade said.

Down on the surface, Grimes looked up at the Red Wrath as its huge engines hurtled it upward through the hazy sky. "I love that old gal," he said.

"Don't make me jealous, Joe," Genie said.

"We've got the opening we need," Grimes said over the net. "Fall back to the Zephyrs!" he commanded.

"This is Warfighter 6," General Winner said. "That's a negative. Hold the line!"

Grimes was in the prone inside a collapsed building. The remaining members of his team were with him, pointing their weapons outward at the advancing Craaldan troopers who were moving quickly through the rubble and burned out structures. The human soldiers popped off shots at targets of opportunity.

"Hold the line," Winner repeated. "Colonel Ripper, move your reserve battalion into a flanking position on the proceeding grid coordinates. Do you read, Colonel Ripper?"

"Griffin 6 reads you loud and clear," Ripper said. "But there are not many of us left, General."

"Prepare to copy, Griffin 6. I am transmitting the grid coordinates," Winner said. "Get your men into position."

"Coordinates received," Ripper said. "Moving."

Grimes jumped up from his position behind a pile of rubble. He sprinted across the gravel until he reached Winner's command post, which was situated in the center of a large building that no longer had a roof. Grimes ran up to the tall man in blue armor.

"General, this is our chance to pull back to the Zephyrs," Grimes said. "Spade has bought us some breathing room."

"Negative," Winner said. "We stay and fight."

"The city is destroyed," Grimes said. "We can still bug out of here before Monmath arrives."

"Get back on the line, Sergeant," Winner said. "That's a direct order."

Grimes stood looking up into the general's blood red faceplate. The tall man in blue armor gripped his weapon and stepped closer to Grimes.

"We're going to win this battle, Sergeant. Victory is at hand. Now get back on the line."

Any victory would be a hollow one, Grimes thought. He contemplated stating his case for a withdrawal.

"I gave you a direct order," Winner said.

Grimes remained silent, peering up into the tall man's faceplate.

"Roger that," Grimes said. He turned and jogged back to his position.

Mortar rounds were dropping closer to their lines, shaking the ground with terrific thuds.

Grimes got down in the prone with his team.

"Genie, when Spade gives us an opening, I want you to jam Winner's commo. Can you do that?"

"Yes," she said.

"Then issue the order for everyone to bug out to the Zephyrs," Grimes said. "Third battalion from Ripper's brigade will cover the withdrawal. Copy?"

"Loud and clear," Genie said.

Grimes looked upward into the haze between columns of cement that once held a roof on this shattered building. "Here she comes," he said.

The Red Wrath streaked across the sky like a tracer round. It glowed brightly through the haze as white heat blasted off its belly. It passed over the city with blinding speed. Pulses ripped through the Craaldan positions, flattening buildings and cratering the ground with powerful cracks of light.

Deafening sonic booms rocked the city long after the Red Wrath had vanished over the plain. Brilliant fires appeared in the distant hazy sky as huge jets of flame shot downward from the Red Wrath's mammoth engines. The ship shot vertically into space as Craaldan missiles streaked upward after it.

Air power

"Why aren't they withdrawing to the Zephyrs?" Spade asked.

"They are still dug in," Capt. Casey said. "The Craaldans are resuming their attack."

"What are they thinking down there?" Spade asked.

"Our second pass wasn't as effective as the first," Capt. Casey said. "They saw us coming and took cover."

An alarm was sounding on the ship. Air was escaping through bullet holes.

"I'll plug the holes," Capt. Casey said.

"Later," Spade said. "We're going to make another pass. Let's drop something big on them this time."

"Incendiaries?" she asked.

"No. I've got a MAB-102 Crater Cutter in the cargo hold. I've used them for creating landing zones on rocky surfaces, but we'll use my last MAB as an antipersonnel weapon. It's got a 900-foot blast radius."

"It'll take out our own guys," Capt. Casey said.

"Not if we're exact. I'll give you the coordinates for the drop. I'll have to manually push it out of the drop door. You fly us down there and when you give me the signal, I'll shove it out the door."

Spade typed on the ship's computer. "OK, here's the altitude, speed and coordinates. When we hit this mark, give me a signal and I'll drop the bomb and we'll blast them."

"Are you sure about this?" she asked.

"No," he answered. "But I've always wanted to drop a Crater Cutter on a Craaldan. This is my chance."

Spade unhooked himself from his seat and floated upward in the zero gravity. He pulled himself out of the cockpit and down a transport tube to the cargo hold.

Capt. Casey steered the Red Wrath into the atmosphere. The ship shook forcefully in a turbulent descent. Superheated air blasted off its belly and shot across the forward screen.

"I'm picking up a lot of movement on the Craaldan lines," Capt. Casey said.

"Bring her in close," Spade said from the cargo hold. He dug through a compartment and pulled out footlockers, tool boxes and equipment cases, which floated upward in the hold as the ship dropped downward at tremendous speed. He found the Crater Cutter next to a water tank. It was a six-foot-long cylinder as thick as a coffin. He pulled it out of its storage compartment and over to the drop door.

"We'll be over the target zone in two mikes," Capt. Casey said.

"Copy," Spade said.

Spade shoved equipment back into the storage compartment and sealed it. He slipped into a harness and tethered himself to the deck. He put on his helmet and lifted the bomb, holding it sideways in the crook of his arms.

"I'm dropping the ramp," he said.

The ship jumped and jerked sideways.

"We're taking fire," Capt. Casey said.

"Keep her steady," Spade said. "Stay on target."

He pushed a button that opened the drop door. The air inside the cargo hold was sucked out of the door with a deafening roar. A hurricane of wind blasted Spade. He braced himself against the powerful flow, held down by his taut tether. He held onto the Crater Cutter with all his might.

The Red Wrath jerked sideways again as Capt. Casey evaded incoming small arms fire. Spade held the Crater Cutter tightly in his arms as the ship spun and twisted as it hurtled downward.

"Jace, a human battalion is within the calculated blast radius. It looks like they are positioning for a flanking maneuver."

"Recalculate," Spade said.

"We won't be able to score a direct hit on the Craaldan main body without wiping out our own guys," Capt. Casey said. "They're danger close."

"Recalculate," Spade said.

"Missiles inbound," she said. "The C-NAM is not engaging."

Capt. Casey yanked on the stick and the ship rolled. She fired off antimissile countermeasures.

"Grimes, can you hear me?" Spade said. "Do you read me? Grimes, respond if you copy?"

"I can hear you, Captain Spade," Genie said. Her voice crackled in the static. Gunfire and explosions could be heard in her transmission.

"We're coming in hot with a Crater Cutter," Spade said. "Beam us up some grid coordinates where you want us to drop it and we'll blast them."

"Roger." Genie beamed up coordinates to a point on their map.

"Got it," Capt. Casey said. "Recalculating."

"Tell everyone to get down, Genie, because we're dropping a big bomb danger close," Spade said.

"Understood, Captain Spade," Genie said.

"Pulse cannons firing!" Capt. Casey said. "Hold on, Jace!"

Capt. Casey yanked the stick. Spade gripped the bomb with all his strength as the Red Wrath spun around him. Intense g-forces seized his body and crushed his lungs. His neck strained against the forces. He could see from the open ramp the brilliant flares of the ship's countermeasures streaking outward through the haze. Explosions rocked the ship's hull with alarming power.

"Now, Jace!" Capt. Casey said. "Bombs away!"

Spade heaved the Crater Cutter down the ramp. It arced and fell as gravity pulled it downward. Capt. Casey pulled up on the stick and the Red Wrath rocketed vertically and shot out countermeasures that streaked from the hull in brilliant fingers of light.

A cyclone of air whipped at Spade's body as he watched the MAB cylinder through the open ramp. It detonated 50 feet above the surface. A massive shockwave flattened much of the city's western sector before a conflagration of fire burst and expanded at the speed of light. A fireball roiled upward above the blast zone.

Grimes lay in the rubble, stunned by the force of the shockwave. His head was ringing inside his helmet. The fireball rose above the western sector and he felt as though his body was cooking inside his armor from the heat. His helmet was pressed down into the gravel. The skeletal structure of the building he had been hiding in had been obliterated.

Grimes lifted his head and looked in front of him. The ground had been swept clean for nearly 1,000 yards. All that was out there was a flat, smoldering expanse of emptiness.

"Taji First Armored Infantry Division," a voice said over the radio net. It was Gen. Winner's voice. "Pull back to the Zephyrs. Load up and let's bug out of here. Third battalion, provide cover for the withdrawal. Do you copy, Griffin 6?"

"Loud and clear, General."

"I say again, pull back to the Zephyrs. Commanders, take charge of your units. Get them aboard those ships."

Human soldiers arose from the rubble and ran back through the city toward Zephyr Crater.

Grimes looked over at Genie. She was in the prone looking out over the barrel of her weapon with her finger on the trigger. She looked over at him and winked.

"Genie-baby," he said. "Your awesomeness arouses me."

An intense firefight broke out in front of third battalion's position. Craaldan troopers were moving across the open ground, surrounding the isolated human soldiers.

"The blast from the MAB-102 Crater Cutter was terrifying," Genie said. "But its impact on the Craaldan main body was negligible. They took cover before the detonation."

"Third battalion needs our help," Grimes said. "QRF, we're going to flank the Craaldan attack. By the numbers. Follow me."

Grimes jumped to his feet and charged through the rubble toward the firefight. Not counting Genie, five soldiers were all that was left of his QRF.

Zephyr flight

The Red Wrath circled at the edge of Biop's dusty gray atmosphere. The Cextos sun was a brilliant disk in space. The planet's shattered moon was a ring of rock in quiet orbit.

"They are loading onto the Zephyrs now," Capt. Casey said.

"It's about time," Spade said.

He pulled himself up the transport tube and into the cockpit. He floated over to his chair and strapped himself in.

"The Craaldans are harassing the withdrawal," Capt. Casey said as she monitored the screen in front of her. "They are giving chase and inflicting heavy casualties."

"They need us down there," Spade said. "We'll give them the incendiaries this time."

"Roger."

Spade steered the Red Wrath down into the atmosphere. The ship bounced in the turbulence.

"She's a tough girl, isn't she?" Capt. Casey said.

Spade looked over at her. "Yes," he said. "She sure is."

Down on the surface, humans ran in squads through the gutted city. Craaldan mortar and missile fire exploded around them. A metal storm of shrapnel ripped through the smoky air to deadly effect.

Grimes, Genie and the depleted QRF team had taken up a position on the flat roof of a cement building. They shot down at advancing Craaldans, providing cover for the human withdrawal.

"Do you copy, Ripper?" Grimes asked.

"At your two o'clock," Ripper said. "We're coming in hot. Keep us covered until we get behind the blast walls that line DFAC 4—what's left of DFAC 4. Once we're in fighting positions, you can leapfrog back."

"Roger that."

A few straggling humans ran down a gravel road below the QRF's position. Then the remains of Ripper's brigade swept past in a wave of fast-moving armored forms. They ran through the buildings, tents and rubble at a full sprint. A few soldiers stopped and turned and fired their weapons only to be cut down by Craaldan snipers.

The brigade was severely diminished—about 600 soldiers left from nearly 4,000.

Craaldan troopers sprinted after the humans with bayonets drawn, but Grimes and his QRF team unloaded on them, knocking down several and halting the pursuit.

"They've got a bead on us now!" Grimes said. "Let's move!"

The team sprinted and leaped off the backside of the building as mortar fire karumphed on the roof, collapsing it in a cloud of dust. Grimes and his five-man team fell back behind a berm. They took cover behind rocks and chunks of cement, lying in the prone with their weapons pointed at the enemy position.

"Here they come!" Grimes said.

The Craaldans were moving swiftly toward them, stealthily advancing through the shattered cityscape. Grimes and his team fired their weapons in an attempt to keep the Craaldans at bay.

"We're going to be overrun, Sergeant Grimes!" said one his soldiers. She was a Taji female named Private First Class Phoebis. "There are too many of them."

"Return fire, Private," Grimes said. "Make every shot count."

Private Phoebis fired her weapon at a Craaldan who was moving through the tattered skeleton of a clamshell tent. The Craaldan ducked and disappeared.

Movement was everywhere behind the dust and smoke. Grimes fired his weapon but couldn't get a clear shot off on any of the swift moving enemy troopers.

"They are getting close, Joe," Genie said. "We will be surrounded."

"Ripper, do you copy?" Grimes said. "We can't turn our backs on them without you covering us. Ripper, do you copy?"

Suddenly, pulse cannon blasts pulverized the cityscape in front of them. The Red Wrath silently zipped by overhead at blistering speed. Its fiery engines glowed blue and white as the ship disappeared into the distant haze. Incendiary bombs exploded in the Craaldan lines with tremendous thuds.

Then the sonic booms from the Red Wrath arrived with planet shaking force. The booms knocked down blast walls and collapsed shattered buildings. Grimes felt the sonic blasts reverberate in his bones.

A wall of magnesium fire shot upward between the human and Craaldan positions. A curtain of white burned blindingly bright.

"Now's our chance!" Grimes yelled over the net. "Pop smoke! Go! Go! Go!"

He jumped to his feet and raced down the gravel road with Genie and his team following behind. "Don't wait for an invitation, Ripper!" he said. "Get on the Zephyrs and let's get out of here!"

Mortar rounds were dropping around the ruins of DFAC 4. Geysers of gravel, metal paneling, cement chunks, and human bodies exploded around the blast walls. Ripper and the remains of his brigade jumped up from their hiding places and dashed down the gravel roads toward Zephyr Crater. They ran with their heads down as the mortars karumphed around them. They rushed down a gravel road in packs, running as fast as they could.

Gen. Winner stood in the center of the road in his royal blue armor. He wildly gesticulated for the fleeing soldiers to turn back, but they rushed past him in a torrent of armored bodies.

Winner stepped in front of Grimes and caught him in his arms. He held Grimes by the shoulders.

Grimes could see the general's mouth moving behind his blood red faceplate. His blue eyes were wild and bulging as he shouted angrily.

But his radio was jammed and the only person who could hear his words was himself. Grimes threw off the general's arms and ran down the gravel road with the rest of the retreating soldiers.

Winner pointed his weapon forward and made a solitary charge at the curtain of fire as the last of his retreating soldiers raced past him. Craaldan troopers leaped through the fire with bayonets drawn. Winner fired his weapon from his shoulder as he charged forward and attacked the advancing enemy.

A sea of humanity raced out of the city and across a flat expanse of ground. The humans were now a disorganized mob.

Grimes and Genie reached the edge of Zephyr Crater. The tarp that covered it had been removed. The three Zephyrs were on the crater floor with their main ramps down. Humans slid down the crater walls and ran toward the ramps in a crushing rush.

The big gray ships were nothing more than domes of metal atop squat fission engines. Through the smoke and dust, the Zephyrs looked like three immense iron bells on the crater floor.

"If the Craaldans reach the crater's edge, they will massacre us," Grimes said. "We're sitting ducks down there."

"Captain Spade, do you copy?" Genie said.

"Loud and clear, Genie-baby," Spade said.

"Please provide cover for the launch," Genie said.

"Roger that," he said. "Make sure those three Zephyrs synchronize their launches. If one pilot gets eager and launches early, the other Zephyrs will get nuked in the back blast. Once those fission engines ignite, there won't be anything left down there but a smoking radioactive hole."

"Roger, Captain Spade," Genie said.

A last wave of humans reached the crater's edge. The humans slid down the steep crater face and ran for the ships.

Craaldan troopers emerged from the city limits and ran across the flat expanse. Genie and Grimes fired off shots and the troopers ducked for cover and returned fire. Ripper and a few of his men fired off shots as enemy soldiers poured out of a smashed section of the city's outer wall.

"Here comes Red," Grimes said. "Get your soldiers to the Zephyrs, Ripper."

The Red Wrath fired its pulse cannons and dropped incendiary bombs which exploded and burned brightly on the flat expanse of ground.

A few human stragglers raced across the flat surface as Grimes, Genie, the QRF and Ripper's soldiers slid down the crater wall. They ran across the crater floor and then up the ramp into Zephyr One.

The dark ship was packed with armored bodies. The ramp began to shut as stragglers desperately jumped onto it and were pulled inside by their fellow soldiers.

The Red Wrath zoomed overhead and circled toward the flat expanse of ground between the city and Zephyr Crater.

"It looks like they are all aboard," Capt. Casey said.

Spade made a pass and Capt. Casey fired the pulse cannons.

"We better keep our distance," she said.

The Zephyr engines ignited in a brilliant flash of light. A huge shockwave bashed the Red Wrath's hull. In an instant, the Zephyrs' fission engines had ignited a powerful nuclear inferno. Zephyr One and Zephyr Two rocketed upward, propelled at whiplash speed atop the channeled atomic explosions. But Zephyr Three's engines did not ignite and the big ship vanished inside a fiery nuclear conflagration that spread outward in an instant from the crater and engulfed Taji City in a wave of fire.

Resumption of command

Spade floated through a dark, narrow transport tube, pulling himself along the handgrips in the zero gravity. He entered a dimly lit corridor. Lights set in the bulkheads glowed softly in the cramped confines of the passageway.

He came to a door and pressed the open button. The door slid open to a large conference room. Spade pulled himself inside.

"Room, attention!" Grimes said.

Everyone stood from their seats. Spade floated to the front of the room and landed with a click of his magnetic boots.

Supervisor Halex Page stood in the front row. Spade had made the tall, tawny haired Taji female the commander of about 3,000 human refugees. Standing next to her was Ramone Bombero who commanded a few thousand of what was left of his brigade. Malva Fung stood next to him as his second in command. Ripper stood next to her. He was the commander of the remains of his brigade and the other surviving humans who had managed to straggle aboard Zephyr Two.

Also in the room were Doxy and her cyborg companion, who were standing in the second row. Spade had assigned Doxy to be his logistics and supply officer. Vomica Nux stood next to her with Tanaka at her side. Vomica was Spade's intelligence officer. Standing at attention in the front of the room next to Spade was Grimes. Spade had made him his command sergeant major. Genie stood next to him. She was Spade's executive officer. Looking over at Spade from the front of the room was Capt. Casey. She was his deputy commanding officer.

A few other humans were in the back rows watching Spade in anticipation.

"As you were," Spade said.

The humans in the room sat in their chairs. Spade sat in his chair and swiveled around and faced his audience. They were in the main conference room on Zephyr One. Two Zephyrs had escaped from the Cextos System and were hurtling through space, propelled by their powerful fission engines.

Their journey through the void had begun with a sense of relief at surviving the Craaldan onslaught, but despair and despondency soon set in. The surviving humans were shell shocked and in mourning for those that were no more. The sense of loss was overwhelming and it affected everyone.

Spade, Capt. Casey, Grimes and Genie had organized the human refugees with the help of their commanders and staff. They had set to work upgrading the living quarters on both ships and rationing their supplies for a long voyage through the forbidding darkness of space.

"Doxy, give us the supply situational report," Spade said.

Doxy stood from her seat. Her stringy blonde hair was pulled back for the zero gravity. She ran her hand through her hair as she looked at the electronic notepad in her hands. It projected its display onto the large screen behind Spade. A graph appeared depicting food, water and oxygen supplies.

"As you can see, our oxygen supply has fallen below sustainable levels. Much of the breathable air on Zephyr One bled off into space due to faulty hull construction. We managed to repair the leaks, but not until 47 percent of our air supply was lost. Zephyr Two is in better shape with only 28 percent lost. However, we must replenish our oxygen supply within the next few Earth weeks or we will start losing people to suffocation. Our water supply is in better shape. It can last us six months now that our recycling process has been perfected. The food situation is good with a sufficient supply to last about twelve Earth years. But our oxygen situation is critical. Meglos is our last hope before our air runs out."

"Roger. Thank you, Doxy."

"Vomica, you're up," Spade said. "Give us your intel update."

Vomica stood from her chair. A galactic map appeared on the screen.

"General Monmath has departed the Cextos System and is now in pursuit," she said. "The 29th Fleet will overtake us in two weeks, seven hours and 32 minutes, according to my calculations. Our current trajectory will put us in orbit around Meglos in two weeks, six hours and 53 minutes."

"Is there any way we can increase our speed and get their sooner?" Spade asked. "Ramone?"

"Negative, Captain Spade," Bombero said. "We are at max power."

"Governor Zegra is not going to be happy when we show up at her planet with the 29th Fleet on our tail," Spade said.

"Captain Spade," Vomica said. "I have received Governor Zegra's reply to your transmission."

"You did?" he asked. "When?"

"I received her transmission while you were on your way to conference room," Vomica said.

"Let's hear what the governor has to say," Spade said.

Vomica pressed some buttons on her handheld display and Governor Zegra's face appeared up on the screen. She was a striking woman, with an attractive, but strong Megalan face. Her lips were full and red. Her deep blue eyes looked over a pair of glowing green Paltran lenses that were perched on her nose. Her reddish black hair was pulled back in a bun. She was wearing some sort of chrome colored armor, but the screen shot ended just below her neck.

"It's been a long time, Jace," Zegra said. "I've missed you, you sexy man, you. We will have to spend some quality time together when you arrive at Capital City, if you're not still obsessing over Tetrailani cyborgs.

"Much has changed since our last encounter. I am Governor Zegra no longer. It's General Zegra now. I have assumed command of the Meglos Planetary Guard. We have been training long and hard to defend our planet from the Craaldan

Empire. I know it sounds crazy, but that is what we are going to do. We are prepared to defend our homes.

"Before we received your transmission, we were aware of General Monmath's intentions toward us. We knew of the destruction of Paltros.

"Joe, are you there, too? I still haven't forgiven you for what you did to me the last time you visited Meglos. But that doesn't mean you are not welcome in my suite. I look forward to seeing you again. I could use a good man like you. You are welcome here, but I'm warning you, if your crazy cyborg lays a hand on me, it's over between us. Actually, if you can keep that robot under control, she may be a valuable asset to us here.

"I must warn you, Jace, you won't be able to just show up here, supply your ships and leave. From the information you have sent me, I see you have Heliac Rangers with you, and quite a few Megalans, too. Your motley mix of humanity has gained valuable combat experience that will be useful to us. I have decided to attach your people to the Planetary Guard. You will be my reserve brigade charged with the defense of the city should the Craaldans breach our walls.

"I am happy you are coming, Jace. We need you here. This is a historic time in the galaxy. On Meglos, humanity will make its last stand."

The transmission cut out.

"If Zegra thinks she's got a chance against General Monmath, she's crazy," Capt. Casey said.

"What was the armor she was wearing?" Spade asked. "I've never seen anything like it."

"It is Tetrailani construction," Genie said. "It appears the Tetrailani have expanded into military manufactures."

"Mech armor," Capt. Casey said, "brought to you by the galaxy's leading manufacturer of sex bots."

"Governor Zegra has never been one to back down," Bombero said. "But we must convince her to abandon this folly. She has no idea what she is up against."

"I think she knows," Grimes said. "I expected her to want to stay and fight, but I didn't think she would actually lead the defense. It's not like her. She usually delegates." Grimes contemplated for a moment. "What I found interesting about her message was her demeanor. Zegra doesn't know the first thing about military matters, but what I saw up there was a woman with complete confidence in her ability to command an army. Maybe she has an ace up her sleeve."

"Great," Capt. Casey said. "Here we go again."

Chrome 6

Zephyr One and Zephyr Two approached the giant, yellow planet of Meglos. The gray, bell-shaped Zephyrs skirted an asteroid belt and then passed close to the planet's outermost moon—a large pockmarked rock called Spo, which was one of five moons that orbited Meglos.

Spade, Grimes and Genie sat at a table on the Zephyr One observation deck. A crowd of humans had gathered on the deck to watch the final approach to the planet.

The humans stood or sat at tables. They looked out into space through a wide observation window that was three decks in height.

Outside, two brilliant disks of sunlight merged and then separated as they circled each other in a close and fiery orbit. They were called Altiva Cantos—a binary star that was the center of this solar system.

"There is Vanaria," Grimes said.

The ships passed close to the misshapen Vanarian moon.

"I hate that place," Genie said.

Grimes gazed out the window at yellow Meglos. "I can already feel its gravity weighing down on me," he said.

Ramone Bombero floated over and sat in a chair. "You two shouldn't speak ill of my home world," he said. "You are hurting my feelings."

"I'm sorry, Ramone," Genie said. "Governor Zegra and I have never seen eye to eye. She has made my visits here unpleasant."

"I wish these were peaceful times," Ramone said. "Then I would make your visit to Meglos an enjoyable one. Regardless, the thought of feeling the pull of her gravity pleases me."

Spade watched Capt. Casey across the observation deck. She sat at a table by the window, engaged in what appeared to be deep conversation with Mingus.

"If you'll excuse me," Spade said. He pushed off and floated across the deck, landing next to Capt. Casey's table with a click of his magnetic boots.

"May I?" Spade asked, motioning to an empty chair.

"Be my guest," Mingus said.

Spade sat at their table. "Just thought I'd check in on two of my favorite ladies," he said. "I'm not interrupting, am I?"

"Mingus was telling me her thoughts on life and death," Capt. Casey said.

"On death, mostly," Mingus said.

"Enlighten me," Spade said.

Capt. Casey put her hand on top of Spade's. "You don't need to hear it, Jace," she said. "You're not the dying type."

"Neither are you," he said.

"There is only one thing you need to know about death," Mingus said.

"What's that?" Spade asked.

"It sucks."

Genie signaled from across the deck, motioning for Spade to return the bridge.

"We better get going," Capt. Casey said. "We're almost there and we shouldn't keep Governor Zegra waiting."

"General Zegra," Mingus corrected.

They floated up from their chairs and pulled themselves to the transport tubes and up to the bridge, which was at the apex of Zephyr One's bell-shaped dome.

A cacophony of static and radio transmissions filled the bridge. Crew members busily talked to their counterparts down on the surface.

Vomica Nux was on the bridge standing next to Tanaka. They were monitoring the communications with the surface.

"General Zegra is not wasting any time," Vomica said to Spade and Capt. Casey. "As soon as we establish orbit, she is going to shuttle us down to the surface. Hopefully, the last of us will make it inside their nuclear umbrella before General Monmath arrives."

"What are their air defenses down there?" Spade asked.

"They have a sophisticated nuclear umbrella that should force the Craaldans to keep their distance," Tanaka said.

"Where'd they get it?" Spade asked.

"The Tetrailani," Tanaka said.

"We've got five ships inbound," a Paltran man said from his communications station.

"Roger," Spade said.

Megalan transport ships rounded the yellow sphere of Meglos and approached the Zephyrs. The technicians on the bridge guided the ships in.

Three ships docked with Zephyr One and two with Zephyr Two.

"Let's greet our big friends," Spade said.

Down in the docking bay, the humans of Zephyr One were lined up to board the Megalan transport ships. The three ships barely fit inside the bay. One had scraped up against the docking bay wall before it had come to a stop.

A ramp to one of the ships dropped and a squad of huge Megalan soldiers floated out into the bay.

The soldiers wore chrome colored armor that gleamed in the artificial light. They floated over to Spade, who was standing on the docking bay floor with Grimes behind him.

The Megalan soldiers landed on the floor in front of him. The squad leader saluted smartly and Spade saluted back. The soldiers removed their chrome helmets.

The squad leader had a blonde crew cut, an angular Megalan face and a square jaw. He stood nearly nine-feet tall in his armor. "Sir," he said in a deep baritone voice. "We need to board your people immediately."

"Roger," Spade said. "They are ready to go."

"Load 'em up!" Grimes bellowed.

The humans began to file onto the Megalan ships.

"Hey, sergeant," said Grimes, who was standing behind Spade. "What's this armor you all are wearing?"

"The latest and greatest, Sergeant Grimes," the big man said. He slung his weapon around for Grimes to inspect. "Check this out. T-949. This bad boy will tear a Craaldan up."

Grimes looked over the silver rifle. "Armor piercing rounds?" he asked.

The big man nodded. "Explosive tipped. Fire and forget."

"You got any extra of those?" Grimes asked.

"Negative, sarge," he answered. "You're going to have to fight with what you've got."

The squad leader put his finger to his ear and lowered his chin. "Chrome 6, this is Saber 7. The refugees are boarding the transports. I have eyes on Captain Spade."

"Chrome 6 copies, Saber 7," Zegra's voice said over his radio. "Can you hear me, Jace?"

"I hear you, darling," Spade said.

"We're cutting this close," Zegra said. "The 29th Fleet is nearing the asteroid belt and will be in striking distance momentarily. Any tarrying and those transports will be blown to bits before they hit the ground."

"Roger that, Zegra," Spade said. "We're on our way."

"Get them boarded on the double, Saber 7," she said.

"Understood," the big Megalan said.

"Chrome 6 out."

An alarm squawked and a red flashing light filled the docking bay. "They are getting close," Grimes said.

"Grimes, head down to the surface with the ships," Spade said. "We'll cover the descent in the Red Wrath and meet up with you once the Zephyrs are cleared."

"Roger," Grimes said.

Spade pushed across the bay as the lines of humans filed onto the Megalan transport ships. Capt. Casey followed him. They pulled themselves through transport tubes as the alarm squawked and red lights flashed.

Spade twisted open a hatch and entered the Red Wrath, which was attached to the side of Zephyr One. Spade and Capt. Casey pulled themselves up to the cockpit. Mingus sat in one of the cockpit chairs in front of a display panel. Vomica and Tanaka were in seats on the far wall. Spade sat in the pilot's chair and Capt. Casey sat next to him.

"The 29th Fleet is about to round Vanaria," Tanaka said. "This is going to get ugly."

Spade detached the Red Wrath from Zephyr One. He steered past Zephyr Two just as one of the Megalan transport ships pulled out of its docking bay. The bullet-shaped transport rocketed for the yellow atmosphere of Meglos.

Surprisals

The Red Wrath circled the two Zephyrs that orbited at the edge of the yellow Meglos atmosphere. A transport ship rocketed out of Zephyr One and raced toward the planet.

"That's two," Capt. Casey said. "Three transports left."

"Where are our Craaldan friends, Tanaka?" Spade asked.

"The Craaldan fleet is about to clear Vanaria," Tanaka said.

A transport ship shot out of Zephyr Two.

"Zephyr Two is cleared," Capt. Casey said. "Two transports still in Zephyr One."

A vast armada of Craaldan ships rounded the misshapen moon of Vanaria. The endless line of cruisers, destroyers, troop transports, gunships, weapons barges and interceptors stretched around the moon and was seemingly limitless in scope.

"A mass of interceptor drones is swarming out of the Craaldan fleet!" Tanaka said. "Thousands of them headed our way!"

"I see them," Capt. Casey said.

"Missiles launching from their destroyers!" Vomica said.

Another transport rocketed out of Zephyr One.

"One left," Capt. Casey said.

"Come on, guys," Spade said. "Hurry it up."

"Whoa!" Tanaka said. "Are you seeing this?"

Tanaka pulled up a video feed on the cockpit's central screen. Silver flash missiles zoomed up from the surface of Vanaria and zig-zagged madly to avoid the intense counter fire from Craaldan gunships. Laser cannons on the Craaldan cruisers and destroyers joined in and blasted away at the silver missiles, which zipped in every direction to evade the fires.

A few of the missiles exploded in nuclear bursts. Brilliant bubbles of radioactive light expanded and ripped apart several of the ships at the leading edge of the Craaldan fleet. Huge shockwaves rocked the ships down the line.

The fleet broke up and its ships dispersed in haste as more missiles shot up from the surface of the moon.

"Somebody just blasted the daylights out of them!" Tanaka said.

"What are those missiles?" Mingus asked. "They didn't have technology like that when I left Meglos."

"General Zegra has acquired sophisticated weaponry from the Tetrailani," Tanaka said. "This could be a game changer."

"My fingers are crossed," Vomica said.

"Missiles inbound," Spade said.

"Tracking," Capt. Casey said.

Spade gunned the Red Wrath's engines. He set his interceptor on a steep angle of pursuit.

"We've got to hit them before their warheads detonate," Spade said.

"The last transport still hasn't pulled out of Zephyr One's docking bay," Mingus said.

"What are they doing in there?" Spade asked.

"Just a little closer, Jace," Capt. Casey said. "I need a lock."

"Sergeant Grimes, do you copy?" Mingus said into the radio.

"We've got mechanical problems," Grimes said over the radio. "Our last transport lodged into a bulkhead as we were trying to pull out of here. We're going to need a few minutes to dislodge ourselves."

"Make it quick, Grimes!" Spade barked.

Capt. Casey fired the Red Wrath's pulse cannons and scored direct hits on three inbound missiles.

"Drones inbound at our three o'clock!" Vomica said.

Laser cannons on several of the drones fired furiously.

"Hold on!" Spade said. He jerked on the stick and fired the engines.

The Red Wrath turned tightly and spun away from the black, predatory drones. Dozens of them honed in on Zephyr Two, firing their cannons into it. The big Zephyr ripped apart in fiery detonations.

"Captain Spade, a Craaldan Five Cruiser is making a run at us," Vomica said. "We can outrun their drones but a cruiser is another story. Those Fives have some big guns. I suggest we get inside the air defense umbrella."

"I'm going to try to lead the cruiser away from Zephyr One to buy Grimes more time," Spade said.

"That cruiser is getting close, Captain Spade," Vomica said, worriedly.

Spade gunned the Red Wrath's engines and blasted past a squadron of drones. Capt. Casey fired a pulse cannon broadside into the swarm and then launched a salvo of flash missiles.

The big gun on the nose of the approaching Craaldan 5 Cruiser fired a massive burst.

Spade turned tightly and the burst grazed the Red Wrath and threw it into a spin.

"That was close!" Spade said.

"They've got our number!" Mingus said.

"Come on, Red," Spade said.

Spade recovered from the spin, but the Red Wrath had lost ground. The cruiser was gaining on them. Its main cannon acquired a lock. The Red Wrath's cockpit filled with squawks and flashing red lights.

"They've got us in their sights!" Tanaka yelled. "This is it!" He grabbed Vomica's hand and held it tightly. He looked at her over his glowing green lenses with wide eyes. "I have never loved anyone the way I love you!" he yelled. "I love you, Vomica Nux!"

The Craaldan 5 Cruiser loomed behind them. Suddenly, the dark ship vanished in a flash of blinding light.

Spade checked the sensors. The cruiser had disintegrated into a cloud of fiery space wreckage.

"What just happened?" Capt. Casey asked.

"The cruiser just exploded," Mingus said. "Somebody blasted it."

"We're still alive?" Tanaka asked.

Vomica turned to Tanaka who was still holding her hand. "Did you just say you love me?"

Tanaka smiled sheepishly.

"Hey, Vomica," Spade said. "The last time this happened, he said he loved me."

A blue raptor-like ship zoomed past their forward screen.

"The Blue Falcon!" Mingus said.

"Do you copy, Spade?" Gen. Winner said over the radio.

"Loud and clear," Spade said.

"More cruisers are coming in fast," Winner said. His blue ship rocketed vertically in front of the Red Wrath. Its mighty engines spewed nuclear fire. "You provide cover for the last transport and I will hold off the cruisers."

"Understood," Spade said.

The Blue Falcon turned sharply and rocketed away.

Spade punched it for Zephyr One.

"Grimes, what's your status?" Spade asked.

"We've got the obstruction cleared," Grimes said. "We're pulling out of the docking bay."

Drones descended on Zephyr One like frenzied killer bees. The black drones blasted with their cannons at the Zephyr's thick hull.

The final transport ship shot out of the docking bay and raced toward the edge of the planet's yellow atmosphere. Several drones changed course in pursuit.

Spade zoomed at the drones from behind. Capt. Casey blasted at them with the pulse cannons.

Behind the Red Wrath, Zephyr One exploded into smithereens.

"I've got at least a hundred drones on our tail, Spade!" Tanaka said.

Silver missiles streaked upward out of the yellow atmosphere and zoomed past them. The missiles detonated at the edge of space, releasing shock waves that struck the Red Wrath with terrific force. The ship spun violently as nuclear fireballs expanded behind it. The Red Wrath hurtled downward into the atmosphere in a chaotic and blistering descent.

Center of gravity

White heat blasted off the hull of the Red Wrath as it hurtled downward through the yellow Meglos atmosphere. Spade wrestled with the stick as the cockpit spun violently around him.

"I'm going to hurl!" Mingus said.

Spade gained control and recovered from the spin. He smoothed the descent through the thick atmosphere.

"Don't hurl, Mingus," Spade said. "I just had her washed."

Mingus held her hand over her mouth and dry heaved as Capt. Casey watched her with concern.

"Drones on our six," Vomica said.

"Tracking," Capt. Casey said.

Fiery fingers of heat blasted over the forward screen. Spade gunned the engines.

Blue pulses flashed from the planet's surface. The yellow air was illuminated by columns of light that pulsed around the Red Wrath. The pulses demolished the pursuing drones in crushing kinetic explosions.

"We are inside their aerial defense system," Tanaka said.

"No more drones," Capt. Casey said.

Down on the surface, the rounded peaks of the Megalan Mountains came into view through the gaseous orange and yellow air. Massive elongated domes of smooth, bleached rock rose dramatically from the orange-tinted terrain.

"I first made love atop that peak there," Mingus said. "I will never forget that mountain. Mount Fornos. It was a romantic setting for an orgy."

"Wow, too much information, Mingus," Capt. Casey said.

The Red Wrath zoomed high above an expansive plain interspersed with mesas and gullies. Immense orange skyscrapers came into view on the horizon of the plain. The Megalan metropolis of Capital City was the planet's principal population center. It was made up of towering buildings that rose upward into the yellow haze. The thickness of the buildings gave them a squat appearance.

Tanaka wheezed and appeared uncomfortable. His large head was pressed against his seat back.

"You OK, Tanaka?" Spade asked.

"Yes, I'm fine," he said, testily.

"I'm feeling the gravity, too," Spade said.

"Isn't it wonderful?" Mingus asked.

High walls came into view at the city limits. In front of the walls, columns of soldiers were lined up in formations of thousands. Masses of armored soldiers thousands deep stretched along the wall from one end of the city to the other.

"A lot has changed since I left," Mingus said.

"That's at least three field armies down there," Spade said.

"The soldiers are wearing Tetrailani mech armor," Tanaka said. His thin neck was unable to lift his head, which was pinned against his seat. He breathed heavily.

"Are you OK, buddy?" Spade asked.

"Yes," Tanaka answered. He closed his eyes.

Spade circled above the city and passed over the Government Center, which was a rounded dome surrounded by massive skyscrapers. Spade descended his scorched ship between buildings. He set down on a rocky clearing between the enormous bases of two skyscrapers.

"We'll join up with Grimes," Spade said. "Suit up and we'll head out."

"Captain Spade," Vomica said. "Tanaka doesn't look so good."

Tanaka's eyes had rolled back in his head. He appeared almost compressed onto his seat. The gravity level on Meglos was three times that of Earth, and nearly seven times higher than on Tanaka's home world of Paltros.

"Get him into his prosthetics," Spade said to Vomica. "He'll be OK, but he's going to need first aid. Stay here with him, but keep in touch over the radio. Roger?"

"Roger that," she said.

Spade, Capt. Casey and Mingus suited up in their Heliac armor and put on their helmets. They grabbed their M-929 weapons systems and entered the decompression chamber before stepping out into the thick yellow atmosphere. They trotted between skyscrapers toward the Government Center.

"Man," Capt. Casey said. "My boots feel like they're made out of lead, and my head feels like a giant pumpkin. How do you guys live in this gravity?"

"Don't complain, Mina," Mingus said. "It will do wonders for your figure."

Spade found an outer door to the Government Center and opened it. They stepped into a decompression chamber, which flushed out the noxious yellow air.

They removed their helmets and walked down a hallway that was crisscrossed with metal support beams. They stepped out into an expansive rotunda. Massive, squat columns held up the arched ceiling. Webs of metal struts lined the walls. The Megalan architectural style was rough and sturdy, although they had progressively added a few ornate flourishes and comforts to their constructions over the generations since their initial settlement of this planet.

A few Megalan soldiers in chrome colored armor walked across the polished rotunda floor. Smaller humans in Heliac armor trotted behind them.

"Grimes, do you copy?" Spade asked.

"Roger," Grimes said. "What is your location?"

"We're at the Government Center in the rotunda."

"We're on the observation platform," Grimes said. "Take the main elevator up."

"Copy."

Spade, Capt. Casey and Mingus stepped into a large elevator and rode it up to the top of one of the towering skyscrapers that ringed the rotunda. They stepped out onto the observation platform, which was a carpeted lounge dominated by a large window. A few Megalans in chrome armor sat at communication stations. Others looked out the window through the yellow air at the plain beyond the city's walls.

Grimes stood at the window with Genie. He waved Spade over. Grimes was engaged in a three-way radio conversation with Ramone Bombero and Ripper.

"I hear you. I hear you. I'll do what I can. Grimes out."

"How goes it?" Spade asked.

"The Paltrans are not adjusting well to the Meglos gravity," Grimes said. "Neither are the Escalonians and some of our space drifters. Our Rangers are ready to rock and so are the Megalans. Surprisingly, the Bioppians are adjusting just fine. Those little guys are turning out to be some of our best soldiers."

"What's the battle plan?" Spade asked.

"General Zegra has tasked us to provide support for the defense of the city if the Craaldans break through her lines. Our main priority is keeping them from destroying the city's aerial defense system. If they can break through the wall and destroy it, they will bombard us from space and it's all over."

"What's the situation out on the plain?" Spade asked.

"The Craaldans have begun their landings," Grimes said. "Their transports are setting down just outside our nuclear umbrella. They've landed a heavy infantry division and a battle tank brigade with more transports on the way. It looks like their order of battle is tankers supported by heavy infantry in a frontal assault on Zegra's lines. They will probe for a weak point and then attempt to break through and drive straight for the walls to breach them and enter the city."

"Can the Megalans hold them?" Spade asked.

"Nobody has ever held them," Grimes said. "General Monmath has never lost a battle that I am aware of."

"Zegra should have made a run for it when she had the chance," Spade said.

"She had the choice to run or stay and fight," Grimes said. "She knew that if she ran, she would be hunted down in the darkness of space. She made her decision to stay here and fight."

"General Zegra has never been one to run from conflict," Genie said.

"She was right about one thing," Capt. Casey said. "This is where humanity makes its last stand."

Tip of the spear

The masses of Megalan soldiers began to move out onto the plain and away from the city's wall. The soldiers' silver armor gleamed through the yellow atmosphere in the light of twin suns.

"The Craaldan battle tanks are on the move," Grimes said.

Grimes held a pair of electronic binoculars to his eyes as he stood in his polished blue and white Heliac armor in front of the large window. Genie was at his side watching over his shoulder with her arms around his waist. She was in her form-fitting combat suit with her weapon slung at her side. She had three single-shot anti-tank weapons tubes strapped to her back.

"Infantry battalions are supporting the battle tank companies," Grimes said. "They are coming in fast and orderly. Three divisions are spearheading the attack due west. They just crossed under the aerial defenses."

A barrage of missiles launched upward from inside the city walls. The missiles streaked over the Megalan lines and toward the advancing Craaldans.

Craaldan aerial defense laser cannons unloaded on the Megalan missiles, effectively destroying them in cracking bursts of metal above the plain.

"The Meglos Planetary Guard, First Army, Second Division, Second Infantry Brigade is going to meet the attack head on," Grimes said. "First and Third brigades are performing a pincer movement."

Enormous clouds of orange dust billowed upward on the plain as the huge black Craaldan battle tanks roared toward the Megalan lines. The big main guns on the tanks fired. Megalan soldiers flipped through the air in the shell blasts.

"Take cover, for goodness sakes," Capt. Casey said.

The Megalan soldiers from the Second Infantry Brigade charged at the advancing tanks, which crushed into them. Craaldan and Megalan infantry clashed between the tanks.

"The anti-tank crews aren't effectively employing their weapons," Grimes said. "General Zegra needs some Rangers down there."

Explosions, smoke and dust out on the plain masked the battle. The Megalan soldiers from Third Brigade charged into the melee from the north.

Air bursts in the sky to the west of the city sprayed shrapnel into the towering skyscrapers.

"Their tanks are getting close enough to shell the city," Grimes said. "Any closer and our aerial defenses will become ineffective."

The aerial defense system was shooting down the incoming tank rounds but the impacts showered the city with deadly shards of molten metal.

A tank round slipped through the aerial defenses and exploded in the midsection of a skyscraper. The massive building shuddered from the powerful blast and then leaned as the strong Megalan gravity pulled the structure down. The top half toppled over into its neighbors in an incredible ground-shaking crash. The top of another skyscraper took a direct hit. Its top floors burst open in a giant explosive bloom of smoke and flame.

"It's getting dicey up here," Spade said. "The shrapnel is getting thick and we're standing in front of a glass window."

Grimes pointed toward the plain where a company of battle tanks had broken through the Megalan defenses. "That is not good," he said.

The tanks emerged from a cloud of smoke and dust and raced toward the city walls, firing their big guns. Rounds exploded into buildings. Another huge skyscraper broke in half at the midsection and crashed downward onto its neighbors, engulfing the city in giant plumes of roiling dust.

The tanks raced toward the city, firing their guns at the wall and blasting it apart.

"They've got an unobstructed approach," Grimes said. "Bombero. Get your engineers to the west gate. We've got twelve battle tanks coming in fast. No infantry supporting."

"Roger that," Bombero said.

"Ripper, get your anti-tank crews out there. Double time."

"On it," Ripper said.

"They are going to get creamed, Joe," Capt. Casey said.

Grimes put on his helmet and unslung his weapon from his back. "The last time I took on Craaldan battle tanks was on Jing," he said. "It didn't turn out well and I would advise against doing it again. But what choice do we have?"

They stood in front of him in silence.

"I am open to suggestions."

He got no answer.

"Get your helmets on," he said. "Lock and load. Stay close. Stay tactical. Roger?"

The battle tanks fired their big guns into the city as they raced relentlessly forward. The tanks were less than a mile from the wall.

A roar of engines shook the planet and rumbled across the sky above the plain. They watched from the window as the Blue Falcon dropped out of the yellow atmosphere and swooped down on the advancing tank company. The raptor-like spaceship spewed nuclear fire as it shot down low and then pulled up vertically. Missiles shot off its sides and streaked downward. The missiles scored 12 direct hits that obliterated the advancing battle tanks in explosions of metal and dirt.

Craaldan missiles and laser cannons honed in on the blue spaceship, but its pulse cannon counter fire effectively neutralized the threat. The Blue Falcon disappeared high in the atmosphere as the planet shook under the roar of its mighty engines.

"Wow," Mingus said. "That was awesome."

A tank round burst in front of the observation window and shrapnel smashed the glass with a shattering crash. Yellow air flooded into the lounge.

The Megalans in the lounge headed for the stairwells and elevators.

"Let's get to the ground level," Grimes said. "Follow me."

"Lead the way," Spade said.

They rushed into a large elevator that dropped in a rapid descent.

"Ripper," Grimes said into his radio. "I want your best anti-tankers to report to General Zegra. The Megalans are going to need some Ranger support. Hooah?"

"Hooah!"

"What's your status, Ramone?"

"We are constructing defensive works where the wall was compromised."

"Roger that. Out."

Grimes, Genie, Spade, Capt. Casey and Mingus exited the elevator and ran across the polished rotunda floor. The rotunda shook from blasts outside.

"Where are we going, squad leader?" Spade asked.

"My friends, you are now attached to Sergeant Grimes' ad-hoc QRF team," Grimes said. "Keep your eyes on me. We'll be moving fast. We go where we're needed."

Grimes led his team outside into the swirling yellow air. Shrapnel, glass and chunks of concrete rained down as shells impacted against the city's skyscrapers. The sky seemed to rip open behind the tank shells that were pummeling into the sides of buildings. Grimes led his small team between buildings and across a paved surface as waves of roiling dust from collapsed skyscrapers swept over them.

"I've got bad news, Grimes!" Ripper said over the radio. "That first attack was a feint. The main armor attack is coming in from the south. Three armor battalions inbound. The battle tanks are thick on the ground and they're coming in hard!"

The Blue Falcon's powerful engines rumbled across the sky. The blue ship roared over the city and then pulled into a tight turn before blasting away toward the south.

Fire team

Grimes and his team took up a position in a residential tower that had been cut in half by Craaldan tank shells. The building's top half had broken off and crashed into the surrounding structures. The team was in what was now the wrecked, roofless top floor of the building.

Grimes, Genie, Spade, Capt. Casey and Mingus were in the prone with their weapons pointed outward. From their vantage point, they could see a ferocious battle underway out on the plain. Masses of Megalan troops had blunted the Craaldan advance at great cost. The Megalans were now dug in and their anti-tank crews were playing a fast-moving chess match with the Craaldan tanks and heavy infantry squads. The fighting now was at close quarters.

The noise from the battle was a constant and thunderous cacophony. Megalans in their gleaming silver armor and Craaldans in their black mech armor exchanged fire at close range. Craaldans with bayonets drawn charged fiercely from behind the battle tanks whenever they managed to isolate pockets of Megalan troops.

A roar of engines rumbled above the plain. The Blue Falcon swooped down over the battlefield and unleashed barrages of missiles and pulse cannon fire at the Craaldan positions. The blue spaceship roared upward into the yellow atmosphere, releasing planet-shaking sonic booms.

"With all the dust and smoke out there, I can't tell who's got the upper hand," Spade said.

"The Megalans have the numbers but the Craaldan tactics are superior," Grimes said. "The Craaldans are using coordinated small unit attacks to isolate Megalan troops along the line, and then rush them and overwhelm them. They are probing for weak points."

"It looks like they found one," Capt. Casey said. She pointed. "Their tanks are converging and massing right there."

Thirty battle tanks overwhelmed a dug-in Megalan platoon. The tanks smashed right over a Megalan trench while Craaldan heavy infantry jumped into it slashing with their bayonets. The Megalan soldiers ran from the trench and fled, only to be cut down from behind by fire from Craaldan tanks and infantry.

The Craaldan tanks broke through and raced across the plain toward the city wall. Tanks and Craaldan infantry converged and poured through the opening and raced behind the Megalan lines toward the city, while absorbing heavy fire on their flanks.

The big guns on the tanks fired and the city wall exploded into cement shards. A horde of infantry followed behind the tanks as the Megalan lines appeared to collapse outward from the breakthrough point.

"Grimes," Ripper said. "Draw them in on your position and then fall back. Once they are inside the walls, lead them down the main boulevard. We will ambush them once they enter the plaza above the city mall."

"Roger," Grimes said. "Our priority is to protect the aerial defenses at all costs. If they take down the defense system, we are done for. Grimes out."

The incoming fire was now intense. Rounds shattered into buildings. The impacts threw up powerful explosions of glass, cement and flame.

The lead battle tanks plowed over the destroyed wall and entered the city. The big, black armored vehicles slowed as their tracks crunched over rubble.

Grimes stood from his hiding place and fired his weapon at the lead tank. His rounds bounced off the thick hull of the machine. Its turret swung around and pointed upward at their position.

Genie stood holding the tube of an anti-tank weapon on her shoulder. She fired and the rocket whizzed from the tube. The fiery back blast from the tube scorched the wrecked floor of the building behind her. The rocket scored a direct hit on the tank, blowing the turret right off. Genie tossed the spent tube to the floor and ducked down.

Another tank fired its gun. The round impacted the side of their building with a tremendous explosion.

"Follow me!" Grimes said.

Grimes rappelled down the backside of the shattered building as his small team followed. Once at ground level, he directed them with hand signals to positions in the wreckage.

A flood of Craaldan tanks and infantry stormed into the city through the destroyed section of wall.

Genie stepped out from her hiding place and took aim with her second anti-tank tube. She fired and scored a direct hit. The round pierced the armor of a tank and then exploded, blasting the big battle tank open from the inside. Genie leaped and rolled for cover.

"Fire!" Grimes said. "Give 'em all you've got!"

His team fired their weapons and knocked down a few Craaldan troopers. Their Craaldan comrades returned fire. The enemy rounds exploded into the sides of the surrounding buildings, throwing off rock and glass and metal in violent bursts.

"Follow me!" Grimes yelled.

He raced down the boulevard. Spade, Capt. Casey and Mingus raced after him. Genie stood in the rubble and tossed several grenades and then sprinted after them.

Craaldan tanks fired their big guns. The shells exploded with tremendous force, collapsing whole sections of the skyscrapers that lined the cement expanse. Grimes ran out into a rubble-covered plaza and then darted into the demolished lobby of a building. His team followed closely behind.

Craaldan tanks and infantry advanced down the boulevard. Six tanks and a heavy infantry battalion charged between half-collapsed, skeletonized buildings. The tanks entered the plaza with infantry troopers following behind.

Ripper's brigade had taken up positions in the buildings around the plaza. Anti-tank crews fired their weapons and scored direct hits on the lead and rear battle tanks below. The anti-tank rounds pierced the armor and exploded inside the metal vehicles, splitting them open in fiery blasts. Ripper's Rangers fired down on the Craaldan troopers, knocking them down in a rain of fire.

The Craaldans attempted to retreat back down the boulevard but the Rangers were awaiting and ambushed them and cut them to shreds.

"Three Craaldan brigades are breaching the walls from the south," Bombero said over the radio net. His voiced crackled in the static behind the staccato roar of explosions and gunfire. "We are outnumbered. We are pulling back to the city center."

To the north and the west, thousands of Megalan soldiers rushed into the city to meet the Craaldan assault.

Buildings were collapsing throughout the city. Huge tsunamis of dust rolled down the urban canyons between the skyscrapers. Visibility dropped to near zero.

Grimes was hunched down behind a collapsed stairwell in the lobby of what was once a residential tower. He could see the four members of his team on the rolling map on the display in his helmet. They were lying in the rubble in the lobby.

"All right, guys," he said. "Assemble on me."

Spade, Capt. Casey, Mingus and Genie climbed over rubble piles and trotted through the smoke and dust to Grimes' position. Grimes was squatted down as his team assembled around him. Gunfire raged outside.

Big Mingus stood in front of him in her ill-fitting armor. Spade, tall and lanky, stood cradling his weapon. Capt. Casey squatted down in front of Grimes. Genie squatted down as well, watching him with her iridescent eyes under the visor of her cap.

"Are you guys feeling this gravity?" Grimes asked.

"I am," Capt. Casey said. "It's weighing me down."

"Lightweights," Mingus said.

"OK, listen up," Grimes said. "Ripper is falling back. This building is about to collapse, and the Craaldans are going to overrun this sector. We're going to move fast across the plaza and try to get behind the Megalan lines. No more running in a cluster. We're going to fall back to the city center in a modified fire team wedge." Grimes used a piece of a metal rod to trace on the dusty floor an illustration of their positions in the formation. "I'm on point. Mingus, you are my automatic rifleman on my left. Genie, you're my grenadier on my right. Mina, you're my rifleman on my right behind Genie. Spade, you're center. I want you to maintain our formation integrity and watch our intervals. Ten meters. Spade, you and Mina are responsible for rear security. Communicate. We're going to move fast. Everybody copy?"

"Copy that," they said.

"Stay together," Grimes said. "Stay sharp, stay tactical and we'll get through this."

"Do you really think we'll get through this, Joe?" Capt. Casey asked.

Grimes looked at her through his faceplate, and then looked at each of his friends. He looked up at Spade. "What do you think? Are we going to get through this?"

"We always do."

Grimes stood. "OK. Follow me." He raced out of the lobby onto the plaza with his team in pursuit.

Violence of action

A torrent of fire ripped up the pavement and the walls around them as they ran. Huge plumes of dust and smoke roiled between the buildings. Dust clouds surged onto the plaza with explosive force.

Grimes skirted the edge of the plaza and sprinted toward the domed Government Center with his team on his tail. A Craaldan squad took chase. Spade and Capt. Casey fired on the run at the pursuing Craaldans.

"Give 'em your grenades, Genie!" Spade yelled.

Genie tossed a grenade back as she ran. "Frag out," she said. The grenade exploded with a clap.

"Frag out," she said again.

The Government Center appeared through the smoke in front of them. The domed structure was surrounded by wrecked buildings that were engulfed in rising black smoke and flame. A section of one of the Government Center's walls had collapsed. The rotunda inside was now open to the outside air.

Grimes scrambled up the rubble of the collapsed wall and ran down onto the rotunda's polished floor.

Huge Megalan soldiers in chrome armor stepped out from behind massive columns that held up the high domed ceiling. The Megalans held their weapons at the ready.

"Hold your fire, hold your fire!" Grimes said over the radio net. His teammates were behind him with their weapons at the ready.

"Is that you, Joe?" Zegra asked.

"The one and only," Grimes said.

Gen. Zegra stepped out from a hiding place at the far end of the rotunda and waved him over. Grimes and his team trotted across the floor to her as the big Megalan soldiers returned to their concealed positions.

"Well, aren't you a merry band of heroes?" Zegra said.

The giant woman towered over them in her gleaming chrome armor. Four stars were lined up down the center of her chest. Hundreds of her soldiers were spread out around the rotunda, hiding behind the columns and up on the balconies and down the hallways.

A large, armored Megalan ran up to her keeping his head down. "We've drawn them into the city," the armored Megalan said. "We've got them outnumbered and surrounded."

"Thank you, General Rathbone," she said. "When their main body reaches the city center, lay down a heavy base of fire. When your maneuver element is in position, lift fire and have them assault through with extreme violence of action."

"Roger that," Gen. Rathbone said. He snapped a salute and trotted away down the hallway with three armored Megalans running after him.

"General Monmath has entered Capital City," Zegra said. "I dared him to meet me here. Let's see if he's got the guts."

A few blocks away, thousands of Craaldan troopers streamed onto the plaza from the main boulevard. A torrent of fire rained down on them from Megalan soldiers in fighting positions at the plaza's opposite end. Craaldan battle tanks emerged from the boulevard and unloaded on the Megalan positions as the infantry charged forward.

At the back of the rotunda, Gen. Zegra and her battle staff monitored the developments from a makeshift command post.

"We are being overrun, General," a deep Megalan voice said over the radio net. "They are cutting us to pieces. There are too many of them."

"Fall back to the Government Center, Colonel Bowitzer," Zegra said. "Do you copy, Colonel Bowitzer? Fall back."

The radio crackled with static.

"Colonel Bowitzer?"

A Megalan soldier next to her was squatted down over a portable communications panel. "He's gone, General."

"Prepare for their assault," Zegra said. "Get the shock troops here on the double. We're in for some close-quarters combat when the Craaldan troopers breach the rotunda wall. If General Monmath shows up, I want the shock troops to take him down."

Grimes directed his small team into fighting positions at the far end of the rotunda. "Every shot counts," he said. "One shot, one kill. Here they come."

A wave of Craaldan soldiers stormed over the rubble and into the rotunda. The Megalan soldiers inside unleashed a firestorm of rounds onto them. Several of the lead Craaldans went down but more flooded over the collapsed wall in a fast-moving stampede of armored forms. The big Craaldan soldiers in their black mech armor rushed at the Megalans with their weapons blazing. Some had slung their weapons on their backs and had their bayonets extended from their fists.

The Craaldans and the Megalans slammed into each other in a violent hand-to-hand head-on clash. Craaldans pierced the Megalan armor with stabbing bayonets. Huge Megalans bashed with their rifle butts at the yellow Craaldan faceplates.

Rounds exploded off the columns and balconies. Sections of the ceiling collapsed atop the tumult. Craaldans stormed through the collapsed wall while Megalan shock troops streamed out of the hallways onto the rotunda floor and crushed into their alien enemy.

The noise was deafening. The clamor, dust and smoke created a riotous confusion. The battle spiraled into bloody anarchy.

Grimes, Genie, Spade, Capt. Casey and Mingus were in prone positions peeking around columns and down the sides of a hallway that opened onto the rotunda. They calmly picked out targets of opportunity, firing their weapons and knocking down Craaldans whenever they had clear shots.

A soldier in blue armor appeared in the hallway behind Spade. It was Winner. He squatted down looking out at the chaotic melee through his blood red faceplate. He looked over at Spade.

Spade nodded at him. Winner pointed out across the rotunda floor.

Through the smoke and dust and above the furious fight, a monstrous armored figure appeared atop the rubble of the collapsed wall. The giant black form stood at least 15 feet tall. He cradled with both hands a massive Craaldan gun that had a long thick barrel. The colossal Craaldan looked down through a gleaming yellow faceplate at the battle raging below him.

Gen. Zegra ran up to Spade and Winner with her head down. "It's Monmath!" she said.

Gen. Monmath lowered his big weapon and fired. Molten metal exploded out of the huge barrel with a thunderous roar. The inside of the rotunda lit up with maniacal flashes of light.

Monmath's rounds whipped around columns and down hallways and up into the balconies. The guided rounds exploded into Megalan soldiers and blew them to bits. Their armor split open and their guts sprayed into the air and onto the walls and floor.

Monmath ceased firing and the rotunda fell silent. A few Megalan soldiers popped off rounds which sparked and ricocheted off Monmath's black armor. Monmath fired a short burst and the rounds hit their marks, ceasing the Megalan fire.

Behind him, the wrecked city skyline burned in the thick smoky air. The giant Craaldan general let his big weapon fall to his side.

Black metallic wings unfolded from his back. He stood to his full height and spread his metal wings. The city skyline burned in an inferno behind him. Buildings collapsed. Columns of black smoke rose high into the glowing atmosphere. Monmath seemed the vision of an enormous bird of prey, or an angel of death, as he looked down on the smoldering and mutilated bodies spread in mounds across the rotunda floor.

Megalan shock troops rushed out of the hallways and charged across the floor toward him. The Megalans fired their weapons at the giant general. Their rounds bounced harmlessly off his thick armor.

Monmath raised his arms with his fists pointed outward. Long bayonets zinged out of the tops of his clenched fists. The Megalans rushed at him, but Monmath cut them down with scythe-like swings of his long blades. He turned his giant body to the left and to the right and his bladed wings sliced through his Megalan attackers in sickening butchery.

The Megalan charge fizzled and failed. The giant general stood on the rubble unchallenged, surveying the carnage around him, scanning the balconies and the hallways.

"He can't be stopped," Zegra said. "I'm done for. We're all done for."

Genie stepped out from behind a column and took aim with her last anti-tank tube. She held it up on her shoulder and fired. The rocket whooshed from the tube, ejecting a powerful back blast. The fast-moving rocket zipped over the rotunda floor toward the general's chest.

Monmath folded in the tips of his wings and adeptly turned his huge body to the side. The rocket grazed his chest and then corkscrewed away into the smoky sky.

Monmath lifted his weapon and fired at Genie. The rounds exploded around her as she flipped and cartwheeled across the floor. She darted left and right and kicked off a column and then combat rolled down a hallway, disappearing into a doorway as Monmath's huge rounds ripped the rotunda apart.

Monmath dropped the barrel of his smoking weapon and took a step forward, searching the smoky building for movement.

Gen. Zegra looked up at the massive general who stood atop the rubble. He was surrounded by massacred Megalans.

"After all our preparation and effort, this is the moment I feared," she said.

Winner stood from his crouch. He slung his weapon onto his back. "This is the moment I've been waiting for," he said. "I was born for this moment."

Winner charged forward across the rotunda, leaping over bodies as he sprinted toward the general. Winner raised his arms and bayonets zinged from his fists.

Gen. Monmath stood atop the rubble with his metallic wings fully extended. He slung his gun and re-popped his long bayonets, which pointed downward from the ends of his huge arms.

Winner leaned forward as he ran and then sprung into the air with lighting speed. The general slashed at the human in gleaming blue armor, but missed. Both heels of Winner's boots landed square on the expansive chest of the giant general. Winner punched his bayonets into the general's chest, sinking them in just below the collarbone. The general's arms grasped at the human on his chest. His metallic wings flailed at the air and against the walls, which crumbled around him.

Gen. Monmath fell backward behind the rubble with Winner still atop him.

Gen. Zegra directed more of her shock troops into the rotunda, waving them forward. The big Megalans streamed inside and cut down the remaining Craaldan soldiers, who were in disarray after witnessing the fall of their invincible general.

Inhuman

Spade walked out onto the rotunda floor. The bodies were thick on the ground. He stepped over them and climbed to the top of the rubble pile.

In front of the Government Center, Winner stood on the chest of the giant armored Craaldan general. He held up Monmath's severed head.

The city was an inferno. Smoke billowed thickly from buildings that were ablaze. Winner pulled Monmath's head out of its helmet. The general's yellow eyes were rolled back. His gray face was set in a ghastly countenance.

Winner hopped down from the general's chest holding the giant severed head under his arm. He leaned down and picked up a long piece of rebar from the rubble. He stuck the steel bar firmly into the ground and then jammed Monmath's head atop it, mounting it on the tip as if on a pike.

Winner climbed up the rubble toward Spade. He clasped Spade by the shoulders.

"This is a great day," Winner said.

Grimes stood on the rubble behind Spade.

"I am glad to see you both alive," Winner said. "No hard feelings, Spade."

"No," Spade said. "None."

Winner slapped Grimes on the shoulder and gripped his hand. "Today is a great day for humanity. You are a hero for the ages, Sergeant Grimes."

"No," Grimes said. "You are, sir."

Grimes gave a weary salute. Winner stepped back and saluted smartly and then climbed down the rubble into the rotunda.

Winner walked over the bodies with his bayonet drawn. A badly wounded Craaldan was moving in the mass of flayed armored corpses. Winner put his boot on the back of the Craaldan's helmet. He pierced his bayonet into the Craaldan's back.

He stepped over the bodies, searching for other surviving Craaldans. He stuck another with his bayonet.

"Have you ever seen a Ranger move that fast?" Spade asked.

"I've never seen any human move that fast," Grimes said.

Spade climbed down the rubble pile and onto the rotunda floor. He spotted Capt. Casey. She was on her knees in front of a Craaldan body.

Spade stepped over bodies and walked toward her. She was looking down at a wounded Craaldan who had been shot several times. His yellow faceplate was cracked. The Craaldan writhed slowly on the slippery floor, unable to get up.

Winner walked over and stepped forward to stab the writhing Craaldan in the chest with his bayonet.

"No!" Capt. Casey said. She stood and got between Winner and the Craaldan, holding up her hands.

Winner stood silently for a moment and then moved off to slip his blade into another Craaldan.

Capt. Casey kneeled down at the Craaldan's side. "It's Major Zeth," she said. She looked up at Spade. "Do you remember him?"

"How could I forget?" Spade said. "He stabbed me in the gut."

Capt. Casey removed a first aid kit from her utility belt. She sprayed foam from a canister to plug the bullet holes in Zeth's armor, and then sealed his cracked faceplate.

"Vomica," Spade said into his radio. "Do you copy, Vomica?"

"I read you, Captain Spade," Vomica said.

"How's Red?" he asked.

"Things got a little sketchy over here, but the Red Wrath is in one piece," Vomica said.

"How's Tanaka?" Spade asked. "Is he still feeling compressed?"

"I am fine, Spade," Tanaka said.

Spade watched as Winner stepped over bodies, sticking Craaldans with his blade. Genie stood at the opening to a hallway. Her form-fitting combat suit had been ripped to shreds. What was left of it clung to her body in tatters. Her perfect figure was silhouetted in the smoky, fading light. Grimes stepped over bodies and walked to her.

"While you were out, I thought we were going to be overrun and killed so I made calls to the Blue Falcon for air support," Tanaka said.

"Did Winner save your life, too?" Spade asked.

"Affirmative," Tanaka said. "When he answered my call, I established a link with his ship and gained access to the Blue Falcon's main computer."

"You hacked the Blue Falcon?" Spade asked.

"Affirmative," Tanaka said. "I was only trying to assist his strafing runs by feeding target data to the ship's mainframe computer. But you know me. Curiosity got the best of me and I snuck a peek at his files, and I couldn't believe what I found. Winner keeps files on all of us. He keeps files and recordings of everything he does."

"Yeah, so?"

"Jack Winner is not who he says he is," Tanaka said.

Spade watched as Winner walked out of the rotunda. He disappeared down a hallway. Spade stepped over bodies and walked after him.

"I am going to show you a video," Tanaka said.

As Spade walked toward the hallway, a video played on the display inside his helmet. It depicted a rusted, cylindrical water tower in Taji City on a dusty, gray day. The wind howled and clouds of dust whipped through the air. A long bodied man in Bioppian outerwear climbed a metal ladder on the side of the water tower. Down below and standing on a gravel pile was Winner in his royal blue armor. The man on the ladder stopped halfway up and looked down. Winner pointed upward and the man continued his climb. Winner pulled a pistol from a holster on his leg and took aim. He fired a shot and hit the man in the back. The man fell from the ladder and landed hard on his back on the gravel. Winner walked over and kicked the body. The video cut out.

"That was Dr. Ebos," Tanaka said.

Spade saw Winner disappear down the end of a dark corridor. Spade trotted after him.

"Winner killed Viz?" Spade asked. Disbelief and confusion filled his mind.

"I am going to show you another video," Tanaka said.

Winner appeared on the display standing in Mayor Lourdes Magna's office. Lourdes was seated at her desk wearing her sleeveless white top, cut low at the chest. Her skin was golden brown. Her black hair was pulled back and her long tight braid fell over her shoulder. Winner stood behind her, rubbing the back of her neck. She was enjoying it, slowly rolling her head from side to side with her eyes closed as he massaged the tension from her muscles. Winner leaned down and calmly brought his arm around her neck and placed the crook of his elbow on her throat. He reached around and grasped his own bicep. With his other hand, he slowly pulled back on Magna's forehead and quietly sank in a chokehold. He pulled his hand over the top of her hair and then pushed down slowly on the back of her head. He brought his elbows together and squeezed. Lourdes Magna's eyes opened wide when she suddenly realized she was being choked. Winner applied more pressure and her eyes bulged with fear. She grabbed his forearm but he sunk in the choke forcefully and pushed forward on the back of her head with increasing pressure. Her mouth opened wide in an attempt to inhale but her windpipe was completely blocked. She struggled for a moment and then her eyes rolled back and she went limp. Winner held the choke for a good while and then eased her off her chair and laid her flat on the floor of her office.

"He strangled her," Tanaka said. "Then he tossed her off the roof."

"No," Spade said. "She jumped. I saw the video."

"The video he showed you was fake," Tanaka said. "I could make a more convincing one in about 20 minutes."

Spade ran down the hallway and then out a door. He pushed through a wrecked decompression chamber and ran outside. Buildings were engulfed in flames. The flat expanses between the burning structures were strewn with debris and smoldering armored bodies.

Winner ducked behind a building and disappeared. Spade ran after him.

"Mayor Magna had tasked Dr. Ebos to collect a DNA sample from Winner," Tanaka said. "She had grown suspicious of him. Winner killed Dr. Ebos before he could show Mayor Magna his findings. Then Winner killed her."

"It can't be true," Spade said.

"I've been searching through his files and I am learning much about this Jack Winner character," Tanaka said. "He was born from a biotank on a Diocon factory ship two years ago. He emerged from the tank as a fully mature adult. They used your DNA to create him. The DNA was stolen from skin grafts taken from you when you were tortured on Goff. Jack Winner's genetic makeup is 80 percent you. The other 20 percent is from a man named Verman Jod. Apparently, Jod was a casino and brothel owner on Gallos."

"It can't be," Spade said.

"Jack Winner is a genetically altered humanoid with a cybernated nervous system," Tanaka said. "They wired up his brain shortly after he was born. His neurons are meshed with computer chips that give him memory and direction. He is not a Heliac Ranger, but all Heliac Ranger training and all their skills have been downloaded directly into his brain and into his nervous system."

Spade ran around the corner of a half-collapsed building and spotted the Blue Falcon parked in an open area between low-roofed warehouses. The ship's ramp was down. Winner walked up it.

Spade ran toward the blue spaceship as the ramp began to close. He jumped up onto the ramp as it clamped shut.

Ambassador Vihris

The darkened interior of the Blue Falcon seemed familiar. It was almost a replica of Spade's own ship. Spade stepped silently through the narrow transport tubes with his helmet on and his rifle held at the ready.

He peeked around a bulkhead into the galley. Winner stood in the galley with his back to him. Winner's blue armor was on but his helmet was removed.

"You are amazing, Captain Jack," a giddy voice said. "Remarkably so. Quite amazing indeed!"

Spade could not see the source of the voice.

"Thank you, Ambassador Vihris," Winner said, humbly. "I am honored by the compliment." Winner's tall armored form completely blocked from view his partner in conversation. "Coming from you, such a compliment means a lot to me."

"This entire turn of events has been extraordinary," the voice said. "Our mission has succeeded beyond my wildest expectations. My only desire was for you to lure General Monmath away from the Marez System long enough for the Diocon 1104th Army to retake it. But for the humans to defeat the Craaldan 29th Expeditionary Fleet and kill General Monmath— Why, it is a momentous victory for backward peoples everywhere. It is an unprecedented development!"

"The path is now clear for the 1104th to reclaim this sector without resistance," Winner said.

"Of course, you are correct. Our advances against the Craaldan are proceeding faster than I had anticipated, not just here, but all across the galaxy. The collapse of the Craaldan Empire is accelerating as we speak. I must say that I remain flabbergasted by this human victory, however."

"The battle for Meglos could have gone either way," Winner said. "The new Tetrailani armor and weaponry acquired by the Megalans leveled the playing field."

"Yes. The Tetrailani must be destroyed. Meglos must be destroyed."

"I have planted a nuke in the center of Capital City," Winner said. "As soon as the Blue Falcon reaches orbit, I will detonate the nuke and the human species will be no more."

"Excellent, Captain Jack. Excellent, indeed!"

Spade stepped out from behind the bulkhead and pointed his weapon. "What is this?" Spade asked.

Winner spun around and a bayonet zinged from his fist.

Spade took aim with his weapon.

A cloaked little Noctish humanoid was seated in a chair behind Winner. The diminutive alien had a somewhat human appearance, but was only about four feet tall and had fuzzy ears, and whiskers that twitched beneath a pointy nose. Its tiny pink Noctish eyes were wide with fright at the sight of Spade in Heliac armor pointing his weapon.

"Oh dear!" the Noctish said, clasping his hands to his chest.

Winner stood still at the center of the galley with his bayonet pointed downward at his side. "What's the plan, Spade?" he asked.

"All your heroism was deceit and trickery," Spade said. "All this war and all this death was for a lie. It was just a game for you."

"A game played with fools," Winner said. "Admirable fools at times. But fools nonetheless."

A decision left Spade's brain to direct his finger to squeeze the trigger, but before the impulse reached his fingertip, Winner sprung forward and sliced the weapon from Spade's hand.

Winner cracked his elbow into Spade's faceplate and knocked him back against the bulkhead. Spade was stunned, but managed to spin off the wall. He got into a fighting stance in the center of the galley and faced off against Winner. Winner slashed at him with his bayonet. Spade ducked beneath the blade, narrowly avoiding the mighty swing.

Winner tackled Spade to the deck and raised his blade high and stabbed it forcefully at Spade's chest. Spade shrimped his body to the side and deflected the blade with the palm of his armored hand. The bayonet pierced the deck and plunged into the metal.

Spade reached for the holster at his thigh and pulled out his pistol. Winner was atop him trying to free his blade from the floor.

Spade fired the pistol with a pop. The armonium round pierced Winner's chest and exploded out his back, spraying guts onto the ceiling of the galley.

Winner collapsed on top of Spade with a groan. Spade heaved him off and stood up, aiming the pistol down at Winner, who looked up at him from his back with a grimace.

"You got me, Spade," Winner said. "Shot me clean through." Winner lifted his head and looked at the puncture hole in the chest of his blue armor. "I'm bleeding out. I'm going to expire in a moment." He looked up at Spade. "I'm bleeding out quick now. The walls are closing in. A doctor with skills can revive me. Transport my corpse to a medical facility. Will you do that for me, Spade?"

"Negative," Spade said. "You're going to the crematorium."

A dark red puddle of blood pooled on the galley floor around Winner's armored form. Winner's face turned white and his eyes went dead. His head fell limp on the floor and his arms fell to his sides.

The little Noctish stood with his back pressed against the edge of the Blue Falcon's control panel. His pink eyes were wide as he stared up at Spade who was holding his pistol.

"Oh, dear me!" the Noctish exclaimed.

Spade raised his pistol and took aim at the little alien.

"I know the whereabouts of Dr. Zander," the Noctish blurted. "Yes, Captain Spade. I know his exact whereabouts. Please don't kill me. Please, Captain Spade."

"His whereabouts?"

"Yes, Captain Spade. I can take you to him. I can, indeed. Please don't kill me."

"Where is he?"

"Dr. Zander is in the Malafax System. But you will never find him without me. I promise you that. I do."

Spade holstered his pistol. He grabbed the little Noctish by the scruff of the neck and pinned him to the floor. He pulled a cord from his belt and hog-tied him by the wrists and ankles.

He lifted the little alien and searched the Blue Falcon until he found a sack. He stuffed the Noctish inside it and slung it over his back.

Spade lowered the ramp and stepped outside the ship. The yellow air of Meglos was thick with black smoke. The city was aflame. Nearly every structure was destroyed.

Spade stood in front of the Blue Falcon holding the Noctish in the sack on his back. He looked up at the fires and the destruction. His faceplate was cracked and his helmet was badly dented.

Big Mingus trotted up to him through the smoke in her ill-fitting armor.

"Jace, General Winner is not who he says he is. He's some kind of Diocon agent. He can't be trusted."

"He's dead."

"Oh. Nevermind."

"Where's Mina?"

Spade followed Mingus down the rubble strewn boulevards as the buildings burned and collapsed around them. He followed Mingus into a transport station and then through a maze of corridors that were crisscrossed with steel beams and carved stone support structures. They entered an enormous airy atrium that was now serving as a casualty collection point. Megalan medics treated wounded soldiers who were lying in the thousands across the atrium floor.

Spade removed his helmet as he followed Mingus across the floor. She stopped and stood seemingly overwhelmed by the suffering she saw around her. Spade walked past her to Capt.

Casey who was seated on the floor. Maj. Zeth was lying in front of her with his head in her lap. Zeth was stripped of his black mech armor. His granite-colored torso was wrapped in gauze and bandages. The rock hard muscles beneath his skin twitched up and down the length of his body. His faded yellow eyes looked up dimly at Spade. Zeth was in great pain.

"He's dying," Capt. Casey said.

Spade looked down at them. He still had a bandage wrapped around his head. It was soiled. His face was black and blue and peppered with cuts. The long gash on his forehead above his right eye was scabbed over, as was another gash across his left cheek.

"I know where Dr. Zander is," Spade said. "Come on. Let's go find him."

"No, Jace," Capt. Casey said. She cradled Zeth's head, looking down at the suffering Craaldan. Her short black hair was slicked back with grime and sweat. The white skin of her face was smeared with soot. Under the dirt, her cheeks were a rosy red.

"It's real this time," Spade said. "I've got a tangible lead. A fix. Not like before. Come with me, Mina."

She gazed down at the chiseled face of the dying Craaldan in her arms.

"Mina?"

"Go to him," she said without looking up.

Spade opened a segment on his armor and reached into a pocket in his flight suit. He pulled out a cigar and put it in his mouth and lit it. He puffed on the cigar for a moment.

"You sure?" he asked.

She looked up at him. The lit cigar was stuck in the corner of his mouth. The sack holding the Noctish was still slung over his shoulder.

"Go find him," she said.

Hail and farewell

Mingus hauled the last of the provisions they could muster onto the Red Wrath. Even with all the destruction around them, they had scrounged up enough fuel, food and water for a voyage to the Inner Galaxy and back.

Fires throughout the city flickered and glowed in the darkness of the Meglos night. The Red Wrath was banged up and its hull was scorched. The shark's teeth and image of Genie stenciled on the nose were barely visible under the scorch marks. Spade walked up the ramp into his ship. He had no intention of staying in Capital City for a moment longer than necessary.

The fight still raged in isolated pockets around the city, but it was a mopping up operation now. The Craaldan attack had been decisively defeated. With the death of Gen. Monmath, the remaining Craaldan troopers fought without cohesion. The well-organized Megalans and their Heliac Ranger allies were surrounding and cutting off Craaldan survivors, methodically eradicating them with deadly efficiency. It was only a matter of hours before the last surviving Craaldan on Meglos became a smoldering corpse.

Zegra had handed off leadership of the Meglos Planetary Guard to Gen. Rathbone. She wasted no time in turning her focus toward the future. Her city was destroyed. Megalan civilization had just suffered a cataclysmic setback. It would take decades to restore what had been lost. Gov. Zegra took charge with a newfound purpose.

Spade sensed the exhilaration in the big woman when he saw her walking the corridors giving direction to her staff. She had met the Craaldan threat head on and had survived. Her day of reckoning was behind her. She was now determined to rebuild a newer and stronger civilization atop the ashes of the old. Spade knew the twin suns of a new dawn were rising for Gov. Zegra and for the humans of Meglos.

Inside the Red Wrath, Tanaka and Vomica were in the galley seated at a table playing a game of chess. Tanaka's glowing green lenses examined the chess pieces. His long fingers lifted a knight with the aid of the mechanical prosthetics that encased his arms and legs and wrapped around his long torso.

Vomica's elbows were on the table. She held her chin in one hand as her sultry green eyes alternated between studying the chessboard and looking up at Tanaka's face. She was a skinny space drifter, her spiky hair tinted purple on top, fading to green on the sides and then yellow and red at the tips where it fell over her shoulders and onto each side of her chest. The purple tint of her multicolored hair shone in the light of the galley.

Tanaka looked up through his glowing lenses at Spade who walked up to them. "Attention on the deck," Tanaka said, wryly.

"Attention?" Vomica asked. "Attention for what?"

"For a Vomis nematode."

Spade stood over the table and looked down at the chessboard. His face was still bruised and cut, but he had cleaned up and looked rested. "Who's winning?" he asked.

"He wins, I win," Vomica answered.

"But the balance of power is shifting to my favor," Tanaka said.

"He thinks I'm a puzzle to be solved," Vomica said. "A code to be cracked."

"Are you two ready to get off this rock?" Spade asked.

"The gravity of our situation impels me to answer in the affirmative," Tanaka said.

"Let me translate," Vomica said. "That means yes, in Tanakanese."

"That is a dialect that took me years to master," Spade said. "But you are quick and talented, Vomica. This could be Red's best crew yet."

"Now, if only we could find a new captain," Tanaka said.

Spade made his way up to the cockpit and sat in the pilot's chair. Mingus sat down next to him. Vomica and Tanaka entered and sat in the chairs behind them.

"Systems check," Spade said.

Mingus ran through the diagnostics. "All systems go," she said.

"Prepare for takeoff," Spade said.

"Wow," Mingus said. "A thrill just ran up my leg. Is it weird to feel excited right now?"

"Yes," Tanaka said. "It is."

"It's really weird," Vomica said.

Spade fired up the engines and the Red Wrath blasted upward from the smoldering ruins of what was once Capital City. The ship rocketed up through the yellow Meglos atmosphere and into space.

Mingus' long black ponytail floated up and writhed around the cockpit in the zero gravity.

"Goodbye, Meglos," Mingus said.

"What a weight off my shoulders," Tanaka said. "Hey, where are we headed, anyway, Spade?"

Spade pulled his cigar out of a pocket and stuck the stub in his mouth. He lit it and puffed on it, blowing smoke rings at the forward screen. His crew watched him with anticipation.

Spade looked out into the cold blackness of space. Hulks of shattered Craaldan destroyers drifted in orbit above yellow Meglos. An abandoned troop transport was slowly pulled toward the edge of the Meglos atmosphere. A scorched, skeletal segment of Zephyr One rotated in slow silence at the edge of space. The twin suns of Altiva Cantos glowed brightly in the blackness beyond the edge of the yellow planet.

"Wake up, Spade," Tanaka said. "Our heading?"

"Right. Our heading." Spade gunned the Red Wrath's mammoth engines. The ship exploded forward with engines ablaze.

The Red Wrath passed close over the misshapen moon of Vanaria. Spade thought about the Noctish he had stuffed in a sack and stashed in the cargo hold. He resolved to keep a watchful eye on the little alien.

"This Dr. Zander guy," Vomica said. "What's his deal?"

"He's the smartest man in the galaxy," Mingus said.

"Smarter than Tanaka?" Vomica asked.

"Oh, way smarter," Mingus said.

"Is that true, Tanaka?" Vomica asked.

"He is pretty smart," Tanaka said.

"I've always been attracted to smart men," Mingus said.

"You're attracted to any man with a pulse," Tanaka said. "You'd have had your way with me if I wasn't taken."

"You wouldn't survive me," Mingus said.

Vomica looked over at Spade. "Are you OK, Captain Spade?" she asked. "You seem distracted."

"He's thinking about Mina," Mingus said.

"I sure wish Mina was with us," Vomica said. "All I have to say is that we better be going somewhere cool where they understand good music. I'm tired of backwater planets."

"Jace, will you tell us already?" Mingus asked. "Where are you taking us?"

"Tanaka, set our heading for the Malafax System," Spade said.

"Malafax?" Vomica asked. "Oh, brother. What have I gotten myself into?"

"After all we've been through, how bad could it be?" Mingus asked.

"With Spade as our captain," Tanaka said, "expect the worst."

The Red Wrath streaked over the pockmarked moon of Spo and then past the system's asteroid belt. Spade took a puff on his cigar and looked over at his friends. He smiled and stuck the cigar in the corner of his mouth. He looked forward and gunned Red's engines to full power.

"To Malafax," he said.

The End

THE RED WRATH: Galaxy Of Heroes III
Available July 2016

Made in the USA
Charleston, SC
17 August 2016